THE LAST HOTEL

A Novel in Suites

THE LAST HOTEL

A Novel in Suites

SONIA PILCER

 Heliotrope Books

New York

This is a work of fiction. Names, characters, places, and incidents either are products of the author's imagination, or are used fictitiously. Any resemblance to actual events or persons, living or dead, is coincidental.

Cover design by Judy Tipton-Katzman

Designed and typeset by Naomi Rosenblatt and Judy Tipton-Katzman

This book is dedicated to

the memory of my father

Benjamin Pilcer

ALSO BY SONIA PILCER

Teen Angel
Maiden Rites
Little Darlings
I-Land
The Holocaust Kid

"New York is a diamond iceberg floating in river water."
—Truman Capote

"What a bad-ass city!
Que pasa New York?
Que pasa New York?"
—John Lennon

LAST HOTEL

53 West 72nd Street

Endicott 2-4860

Hotel Manager: Saul Ehrlich

CURRENT RESIDENTS

Suite 21	Ron Tannenbaum
Suite 22	Leonard Katz
Suite 27	N. Reardon
Suite 31	Gittel Szabó
Suite 32	Faye Meyer
Suite 36	Pincus Shreiber
Suite 42	Rachel Weinstein
Suite 45	Monica Parker
Suite 49	Esther Fein
Suite 52	Amber Adams
Suite 55	Hana Wolf
Suite 62	Fred Janov
Suite 63	Peter Mahoney
Suite 64	Duc Christian

Superintendent: Henry Thompson

L st Hotel

Someone stole a letter. Passersby wondered. Was the missing letter an A? LAST HOTEL? O? LOST HOTEL? Or a U? But why would anyone steal a chrome letter from the hotel awning? Because it was there. Because it could be destroyed. Because no one cared about New York City, circa 1979.

Manhattan was broke, and a general air of lawlessness governed, if you didn't live in select neighborhoods. Graffiti snaked the subway in ghetto nightmares. Dog turds, garbage on the street. Plastic bags floated in the sky like bloated ghosts. Metal gates klunking heavily over store windows. Abandoned buildings, nailed wooden boards painted with fake flower boxes.

It was a place to escape from, not visit. Certainly not bring a car. Whole neighborhoods were abandoned. A stroll through Central Park, especially after 5, you took your life in your hands. Riverside Park was positively murderous.

Nedick's, 69-cents stores, Max's Kansas City, CBGB's, Cheetah, the Tunnel, and the Limelight. Housed in an Episcopal Church on 20th Street, a young man was murdered as hundreds hustled to Donna Summer's "Love to love you, baby..." You had to have a strong stomach to live in the city.

Let's call it the Last Hotel: a small residential hotel on the corner of 72nd and Columbus Avenue, when such places still existed. When hotels were, in fact, a respectable way of life. Clean and affordable. For single women, especially, who liked to have a concierge-type downstairs, without the sorority of the Barbizon Hotel, which forbade gentlemen visitors. Men liked it mainly for the longer term. Like renting an apartment, but they could pay weekly. No lease. No commitment.

Understand, residential hotels were not SROs, those scary, transient Single Room Occupancies that housed foul-scented dens of iniquity and worse. No, these hotels were faded movie queens who still possessed good bones and solid brass fixtures from the gilded splendor of a New York that was once piss elegant.

Inside, you could still see remnants of its glory days. An absurdly grand lobby of marble walls with ornate moldings and sconces, white and black tiled floor, full-length smoked mirrors, and a glorious, non-working chandelier. A long turquoise vinyl couch, a mahogany coffee table, and a plastic rubber tree plant were chained to metal loops drilled into the floor.

Stories circulated about the hotel's mythic speakeasy past of illegal booze, gambling, jazz, and rooms rented by the hour. There were nights when ghosts twirled past bewildered tenants. Sex juices rose in loud gurgles from the radiators! Many swore the vibrations of those licentious days still lived in the walls and inspired its current inhabitants.

A mere six floors, the Last Hotel was surrounded by tall, elegant hotels and doorman apartment buildings, limousines parked outside.

Women in minks walked snooty little dogs past heaps of garbage mounting each day as the Sanitation Workers' strike continued. The Athena, a Greek diner, occupied a ground floor storefront, floating in a sea of black plastic bags. Scents from the kitchen wafted into the lobby—sizzling garlic, onion, eggplant, feta cheese, and souvlaki.

The Dakota was at the end of the block at Central Park West. Celebrities lived in palatial twenty-room apartments. John Lennon and Yoko Ono occupied the penthouse. It was not uncommon to see them stroll into Central Park, arm in arm. Lauren Bacall shopped at the corner bodega, which sold fetish dolls, votive candles, and love potions in the back. Nearby, an elderly man huddled inside a cardboard refrigerator box as a chill wind blew off the Hudson River.

The Last Hotel attracted the thrifty, the broke and broken, surviving spouses, divorcées and émigrés. It was a hotel of dreams and lusty dreamers. Most lived alone. Saul insisted. "Too small for two people. You'll kill each other."

The place had a crummy charm—for those who disliked pretension and could handle funk. All the surfaces bore a coat of antique dust and the occasional cockroach. Yet the residents shared rent pride. The smug satisfaction of having found a bargain in the toughest city in the world. Lincoln Center, built a decade earlier, was six blocks south. The New Yorker and Thalia theaters were nearby, not to mention The Embassy, which was just down the street. You could see an Ingmar Bergman double feature anytime and alternate Szechuan Chinese and Cuban Chinese restaurants.

Living in the Last Hotel, one became part of random, raucous humanity, separated by cracked plaster walls. The lobby was the family room. The elevator offered daily rites of passage. The suites were paved with golden stories. Or rather, fragments of stories, curious particles of people's private lives. What one could glean from a chance encounter in the lobby, a ride up or down the elevator, a trek to the laundry room in the basement. Puzzle pieces that glittered like Manhattan schist, enticing one to stay.

Suite 32

Once a week, Henry slipped rent envelopes under residents' doors. Saul collected on Fridays. Faye approached his ancient office, a cubicle with black cubbyholes for mail, a cracked pegboard with keys, and an extinct switchboard.

He was studying his ledger with everyone's names and room numbers. Finally, he looked up.

Faye Meyer paid him forty-five dollars. He stared at her check, peering in the light as if he hadn't received the identical amount for two years.

"Okay." He put a mark next to her name in the large ledger.

"Thanks."

"Don't mention it." He grumbled something in Polish or Yiddish to himself.

Though Saul could be a petty, parsimonious pain in the ass, everyone respected, even protected him. It was hard not to stare at the blue number tattoo on his left arm when his sleeve was rolled up. There was a letter, which looked like a *B*, a hyphen, five or six numbers. Faye tried to make out the exact numerals but feared he'd notice her staring.

With his glossy, thick hair, black tight curls streaked with silver, his strong physique, Saul must have been something as a young man. But thinking about his youth, she realized how he had spent it—in some German camp in Poland where they branded him like livestock.

Reardon, the Irish bartender on the second floor, stepped to the side of the elevator as Faye entered. A strikingly handsome man with sculptured features, he had white skin like a baby's that had never seen the light. A regular vampire with white hair, very black brows, deep-set black eyes. Black turtleneck. Once, he'd been an actor. Rumor had it that he'd had a role in a Fellini film.

They nodded at each other. He was polite enough but never made a moment's eye contact. Oh well. Faye reminded herself that she was a member of the Invisible Women's Club. As he walked out of the elevator, he nodded at her again.

Faye liked living at the Last Hotel. The random roll of the dice every time you stepped in the elevator. If you were going to live alone, as she did since Putzface walked out on her, this wasn't bad. All the people to watch, to imagine their lives. And it was a crosstown bus to Hunter College, where she taught. Often she walked across Central Park in the morning. People said she was crazy to go by herself, but she loved the park and stepped briskly.

Now Faye sat down on her couch and took off her shoes. Then sighed. The end of another week. She'd only had a few classes. She had to read her graduate student's thesis proposal. And her Colette article was overdue.

She walked into her tiny kitchenette. Opened her small fridge, took out a package of sirloin wrapped in butcher paper. Laying it flat on a wooden block, she contemplated the red meat. She could never be a vegetarian. She began to hammer the meat with her fists.

If only I had someone. He doesn't have to be terrific or even great. But weekends sometimes seemed so long. She'd go for B+, B, maybe even B-. She said this to herself not with self-pity. She'd had her share of lovers. And she really didn't mind being rid of Shmuckeroo.

Gathering her ingredients, she now wondered how she would build him. Her Fantasy Man. Of flesh and sinew, of course. Broad shoulders. She liked that. Strong arms. Dark, curly hair, but not too much. Asswipe had black hair on his back. Now the truth could be told. She despised it! Graceful in body and speech.

Faye massaged kosher salt into the meat, imagining she was on a beach, spreading oil on her lover's back. The salt felt like sand. Peeling the onions, she wept real tears, which she laughed at as she wiped them with her sleeve. Pathetic. Peeling potatoes. Carrots. Blending them all in her mother's black iron pot as more tears trickled down her cheeks.

Faye swirled her onions slowly in oil until they were thick and golden, floating in their own juices, oil sizzling. How she loved the smells. And how it reminded her of her mother, who she'd lost one year ago.

Once, she'd read an article in a women's magazine. "Are You Just Like

Your Mother?" Well, she had her pot. It was like a few hours with Sadie Goldstein, who spent all of Friday preparing for the Sabbath. Brisket was her specialty. She too rubbed kosher salt into the beef, kneading it into the folds, until her fingers were raw, the salt pinching her skin.

As Faye stirred the iron pot, steam rose to her face, curling her hair. Double, double toil and trouble. She added the sliced steak pieces and turned the flame down. Wiping her forehead with the back of her hand, she caught her reflection in the small window.

She had a strong face—a prominent nose that might overwhelm but for her jutting cleft chin. Red hair dyed to the limit of respectability, definitely a hussy shade, created a nice frisson with her Ph.D. Once Faye had been sought after, mooned over, whistled at, loved, and then not. Now she was an aging siren. Would anyone hear her song? Would she ever be loved and desired again?

"The Invisible Women's Club," she reminded herself. Her sexuality was obscure to men of all ages, except those close to the grave, who wanted a caretaker. How could she accept it though? *To not want someone to see you? To look at your face, meet your eye?* Yet women of the club were hardly invisible to each other. They scrutinized each other's hair and makeup, every lost or gained pound, not to mention, any work done. "Darling, your wrinkles disappeared!"

"I had a good night's sleep."

No, Faye hadn't done anything, nor did she intend to. She'd worked for every line on her face. Get surgery so one part of her would look young while the rest sagged?

At that moment, the telephone rang. Faye didn't move. Five rings, her outgoing message, then she heard her editor Judi's voice. "The deadline is past. Where is it? Faye, I won't be pleased if it's not on my desk on Monday."

She was supposed to deliver an article: "Women Transitioning: Colette as Role Model." Publish or perish. Well, not really. She already had tenure. But she had to finish the last part.

Faye had a doctorate from City College, specializing in French Twentieth-Century Literature. She'd lived in Paris for a year, fallen for a French painter, Claude. A year at the Sorbonne. Lots of wine, lots of sex. And a thesis: "Master or Muse: The Subjugation of Colette's Art," which she had turned into a monograph.

Most of her article was written. Just needed a final read-through and a strong ending. Her mother's brisket would keep her company. She set the timer for an hour and a half.

Faye walked over to her wooden desk and opened a notebook. She found the quote from Colette that she'd been thinking about.

"You have to get old. Don't cry, don't clasp your hands in prayer, don't rebel; you have to get old. Repeat the words to yourself, not as a howl of despair but as the boarding call to a necessary departure."

Colette faced the same daunting struggle. To put a so-called good face on it. Yet in 1921, before turning fifty, she had a facelift. Then she became entrepreneurial, created a beauty institute where she dispensed her 'secret recipes,' and conducted makeovers in a white lab coat! Never underestimate a woman's vanity. Faye raised her cheeks with her fingers.

Walking into her small bathroom, she turned on the hot water for a bath. Just hot, hot water. It was a good, old-fashioned tub with claws. This was one of her Friday rituals. To cleanse herself of the week. Her own mikvah before the Sabbath, though definitely of a secular nature. She threw in desert bath salts and sprinkled lilac essence, plus a little baby oil to soften the rough spots.

As she melted into the water, she felt a tweak in her bijou. Her lovely jewel. She still lived! Jewel had the word *Jew* in it. What Jonathan, when he loved her, called the Little Man in the Canoe. Faye raised her legs and pointed her toes. Studying Martha Graham technique had preserved her stomach muscles, given her strong, muscular legs. She exhaled and raised her pelvic floor. Squeezed. Oh, those Kegels! "Not *kugels!*" she said aloud, then giggled mischievously. Perhaps like so many other things, sex was wasted on the young. Would anyone ever see her again? More seriously, would she ever make love again with someone else? She massaged the anti-aging crème into the pores of her face.

Wrapping herself in a towel, she wandered back into her kitchenette. Raised the lid of the iron pot. Beef effluvia filled the room. She dipped a wooden spoon, blew, then tasted. It still needed time. She added half a cup of wine and a pat of butter for greater succulence. Cholesterol, be damned!

Jonathan had been a great appreciator of her brisket. Though a self-hating Jew, like so many of the lefties they knew from City College, he made an exception for Jewish food. Good Jewish food and deli, of course. She'd married him when he was finishing graduate school. She worked for a French publishing company for a year. He taught linguistics and Foucault deconstructionism at City College. They had two grown children. After Elissa, their second daughter, graduated college, he spent several weeks of his sabbatical writing a novel at an artists' colony in Virginia. He couldn't publish the novel. He returned to teaching. He started fucking his linguistics intern. Some linguistics they must have performed right in her own bed, as she discovered them that Wednesday afternoon when her shrink rescheduled her appointment.

The narrative piqued her colleagues in the lunch cafeteria at Hunter.

"A woman is incomplete until she is married," said Betty Alecson, Applied Sciences, married to a reborn Scientologist. "Then she's finished. You're lucky to be free of Jon."

"True, true," agreed Selena Grosbard, an abandoned Byron scholar, whose husband ran off with a graduate student. "When a woman steals your husband, the best revenge is to let her keep him." Her pause very pregnant. "Don't worry. She'll find out."

"You have two choices in life," added Alice Valens, a never-married Chaucerian. "You can stay single and be miserable, or get married and wish you were dead."

They were her Greek chorus. Like so many women, feminists like her, they often sounded like they despised men. She didn't. Her father, Isaac, was not an educated man, but had a gentle, compassionate nature, though he worked hard on the docks at Sheepshead Bay. Yes, Jonathan was a putz. No doubt about that. She slipped into blue jeans and a denim shirt.

That's when she heard the sound. Turning around, Faye saw something curious. Slowly, her window rose by itself, and a fully formed, rather tall hooded figure crawled in through the fire escape. She would have screamed, if she hadn't sat on her bed in pure open-mouthed amazement.

Was this her Fantasy Man? Had her imagination created a golem? She didn't believe in supernatural kinds of stuff, but she sat as if paralyzed. Whatever it was, was cloaked in darkness, but there was an aura of light surrounding it. She couldn't see a face, but a ruby stone shone from a long, delicate finger.

"Who are you?" Faye asked the apparition.

"Who do you think I am?"

"My projection. That's what my analyst would say. That I am transferring my need for love in my life, for a man—"

"Oh, shush, you! Think of me as a fairy godmother," she said, pulling down her hood. "I'm just here to give you a good turn."

"How come?"

"Because we had a lottery, and I drew you."

"What kind of lottery?"

"You wouldn't understand. It's a complex equation of *mitzvot, tzedakah,* and because you need it."

"Excuse me, I don't understand, but I do have to check my brisket," she said. "I'll be right back."

The apparition followed Faye into her kitchenette, watching as she stirred the beef, onions sizzling in her black iron pot. "How did you prepare it?" she inquired.

"A steak, I used sirloin this time, oh, I don't know, a little tomato paste, onions, carrots, potatoes. Salt and pepper. I throw in red wine."

"And garlic?"

"No, my mother didn't use garlic in her brisket."

"You should. Whole cloves that you sear—"

"What are you? The Cooking Dybbuk?"

Faye looked but couldn't make out a form. Who cared. She was really enjoying this, whatever it was. Maybe she was just losing her mind. "So what can you do for me? Are you like a genie who offers wishes?"

She laughed.

"What's funny?"

"That a woman like you goes to bed alone every night."

"Huh?"

"We know your husband was a worthless piece of garbage."

"So?"

"You shouldn't give up. You're still young."

"I'm over fifty."

"I'm not impressed. I'm over several hundred. Go find a lover."

"There's no one around."

"I see a man. A man of fine character."

"Oh. Who is that?"

"Think close to home."

"The hotel? There's no one. Saul is married. Lenny, never. Ugh. Reardon doesn't talk, and besides he's not interested."

"Nu?"

"Pincus?"

"Pincus."

"He's an old man."

"Pincus," she said solemnly. "There's more than meets the eye."

"How do you know?"

"I was married to him in one of my lifetimes. He doesn't eat well anymore."

"Pincus?" she asked the apparition.

"There's more than meets the eye," she repeated. Then disappeared.

Faye walked over to the window with the fire escape. It was shut. She tried to raise the window, but decades of paint prevented its budging. Had she imagined the whole thing? Was it a hallucination? Maybe something in the brisket. She sighed. Could Pincus be her Fantasy Man?

That's when her eyes fell on the silver candlesticks, placed high on a shelf above her table. They had belonged to her mother. She took them down, blowing dust off their surface. She had the impulse to light candles. What the hell. Faye was not a believer. She was, in fact, a devout disbeliever. And yet. The Sabbath bride was on her way. Faye lit the first candle, then the second. She closed her eyes, hands cupped over her face, and said a soft prayer.

Lobby

Saul Ehrlich sat with the *New York Times* spread out on the table in the lobby, eagle-eyeing stock listings. He kept a school notebook in which he kept track of his stocks.

When residents greeted him on their way to work, Saul grunted, "What?" not looking up from his newspaper. Then he stood up, followed them out through the glass vestibule, and leaned in the doorway.

"Have a good day, Saul."

"What's so good about it?" he answered, then grumbled to himself. "Americans. They're like children."

Saul had a whole category of things that in his mind he called American Stupidity. This included smile buttons, baseball games with grown men running around in circles, and Coca-Cola. And there was the jungle out there. The city was an insane place. Filth and graffiti everywhere. Garbage on the street. Abandoned buildings. A man had held him up at knifepoint and taken his wallet with the only photograph he had of his father.

He felt safe here. The hotel had two stairwells—one in the front of the building on 72nd Street, the other in the back, facing 73rd Street. Many a visitor slinked up the back stairs, trying to avoid meeting a rival. He remembered when Anthony Quinn kept a girlfriend at the hotel. He always walked up the back steps and gave Saul an autographed photo of himself as Zorba the Greek.

As he returned to his seat, he noticed the tall Samoan man, Duc Christian, Suite 64—he checked his list—slink past him. The young man, well over six and a half feet, stumbled toward the elevator. As he pressed the button, he leaned unsteadily against the door. "Long night," he mumbled.

He had told Saul that he worked at a place called Studio 54.

Rachel Weinstein, Suite 42, hobbled out of the elevator in her high heels. Her perfume nearly overpowered him. The silly woman flashed a sexy smile, batting fake eyelashes at him.

"The bathroom faucet is still leaking," she told Saul.

"Henry didn't fix it yet?"

"I don't think so. I'll be out for a few minutes," she said, walking out.

Saul tapped his foot impatiently. "Henry! Where is he? I haven't seen him all morning." He stood up. "Henry!" he screamed into the stairwell. His voice echoed. "HENRY! Where are you?"

Saul pressed the elevator button with the heel of his hand. "He's never around when you need him," he mumbled. "Probably up to no good."

When the elevator door opened, he stomped out. "Henry! Where are you? HENRY!" He walked through the basement.

A wrapped-up hose hung on the brick wall, which was painted a sickly green. Saul passed the elevator machine room. The motor rumbled as the drive whirred. Next door, the boiler room had a large sign: *NO ADMITTANCE*. When he opened the door momentarily, the furnace belched loudly, a flame rising in its belly. He slammed the door shut.

These were the guts of the hotel. Huge pipes and ducts hung from the ceiling. Clusters of wires twisted along the walls, leading to fuse boxes with rows of control switches. Noisy fluorescent lights buzzed. In the trash area, newspapers and magazines were stacked in one corner, the garbage in black bags nearby. What a stink! Saul held his nose. He opened the door to the storage room, crowded with residents' bicycles, lamps, and old pieces of furniture. He'd have to clear out all this junk one of these days, before the next inspection.

As a boy, the cellar in his family's house terrified him. Wooden barrels of potatoes and onions stored under the stairs grew fingers that reached out to choke him. He coughed from the dust. When he turned on the lights, he often surprised rats at a feast. All around him, the stench and slime of decomposing life.

Saul pressed the doorbell of Henry's apartment for several seconds, then turned the knob. "Henry!"

He had a good life. Henry lived rent-free and got a decent salary. Residents gave him tips, too. Still, he was never around when you needed him. "Are you in there? HENRY!" he screamed.

A dark-skinned, matronly woman with a huge bosom rushed to the door, wiping her hands on her apron. "Please, Mr. E.! You'll awake the dead!"

"Where is he?" Saul demanded.

"You get a stroke if you keep this up," Bessie scolded. She was a nurse's aide at Roosevelt Hospital.

Saul peered into their apartment. The oil paint in the kitchen shone from grease. No matter how much Bessie cleaned, fumes from the basement coated the walls. Saul could see into the living room, the old couch and chairs, the spindly standing lamp that he'd given them. That's when he noticed a framed photograph of their sons.

Saul knew Henry's boys. When they were younger, they used to operate the manual elevator. That was before the partners insisted Saul replace the elevator with a new automatic one. Two years ago, Henry Jr. had died in a shoot-out in the subway station at 155th Street. The middle son, Nathan, stole from the building. Saul had to throw him out. The youngest, Harrison, went to high school but was already up to no good.

"If you must know," Bessie told him, "he's sitting on the toilet."

"For how long?"

"For as long as he needs, Mr. E.," Bessie said. "My husband works for you, but he's not your slave."

"Well, tell him I'm waiting for him."

"He knows," she said. "Everyone in the hotel knows already."

"Hrmph," Saul grumbled, crossing his arms. "Tell him to check the board."

Closing the door behind him, Saul pressed the elevator button. Just then, Henry's door opened. He rushed out, adjusting his belt. "Sorry, Mr. E.," he said.

"You got stomach problems?" Saul asked.

"No, I'm fine."

"What's the matter?" Saul asked. If Henry wasn't smiling, his dark face filled with shiny, white teeth, something was wrong.

"Nathan," Henry said grimly.

"That good-for-nothing junkie," Saul said.

"He's my son." Henry shrugged. "What can I say?"

"What did he do this time?"

"He took the TV while I was out," Henry said, shaking his head. "He tried to do that last week, but I gave him a twenty-dollar bill when Bessie wasn't looking."

"*Gevalt*!" Saul said. "I told you to call the police. They'll take care of him."

"I can't, Saul," Henry said. "He's the only one I have left."

"Don't worry. I'll ask Fred from Suite 62 to get you a small black and white," he said. "He finds everything on the street."

"Thanks, Mr. E.," Henry said.

"You got to do something about your son," Saul said. "Talk to that social worker again."

Henry had worked for Saul for over twenty years. Saul remembered when each of his sons was born. He loved Henry and trusted him more than almost any other living being. He paid for his family's health insurance and Henry's life insurance, but he couldn't protect him from his own sons.

"I know," Henry said sadly.

They were almost the same age, sixty-two. One, a Polish Jew, who stood over six feet, his hair still dark and glossy. The other, a gentle, gray-haired black man from Georgia, who could fix anything. Both had problems with their children. Saul's daughter didn't talk to him unless she needed something.

"Have you seen Leah?" Saul asked.

"Not since the last time I told you about," Henry said.

Two months ago, Saul had installed her in the hotel since she had nowhere else to live, having been thrown out by her last "friend." Since that time, he had tried to talk to her, but she walked away. She pretended not to be there when he stopped by.

"I don't see her, Mr. E. She must keep strange hours."

He shrugged. "Children. They make you love them when they're little so they can break your heart when they grow up."

"I could knock on her door."

"Never mind. Enough talk. Get to work!" Saul started yelling. "Suite 42 has water leaking from her faucet." He pointed to the board.

There in black and white: *BATHROOM FAUCET, SUITE 42* was chalked in Saul's jagged handwriting on the blackboard. "That's Mrs. Weinstein. The one, you know—"

"I'll just get my tools, Mr. E."

"And don't spend too much time there either."

"Sure, Mr. E.," he said. "Don't you worry about a thing."

Entering the elevator, Saul muttered, "He tells me not to worry. If I don't worry, who should?"

As he walked out, Amber was waiting for the elevator. She smiled her Rita Hayworth smile. "Hi, Saulie."

He nodded to her. Amber Adams, Suite 52. A regular American beauty with long legs and golden red hair like silk.

"Who's the new guy?" she asked. "Very tall, long black hair?"

"Oh, that's Duc. He's from Samoa."

"Somalia?"

"No, Samoa. South Pacific Ocean."

"Bali Hai…" She sang out the opening. "He's gorgeous!"

"Suite 64. Next door to that *meshugenah*, Fred."

"You're a sweetheart!" she called out to him as she ran out the door, heels clacking.

Truth be told, Saul loved every moment of being manager of the Last Hotel. He had escaped the bondage of a textile factory in Leonia, New Jersey, and then managing dangerous dives without bullet-proof glass in Harlem, for the relative ease of a clean-shirt job where he mostly sat on his *tuches*.

His father had worked at the Grand Hotel on Piotrovska, the fanciest boulevard in Lodz. Saul had watched as he registered guests in his careful, tiny script. He carried luggage, opened doors, delivered room service, and received tips.

Saul loved to sit in the lobby. People in and out all day, leaving suitcases covered with stickers from foreign countries. When he touched them, it was as if he could feel the air from the exotic places. Barcelona, Prague, Paris. That was before his father was fired. And the trouble began. And it got worse. And worse… His sisters forced at gunpoint to walk into the Baltic Sea. His baby brother suffocated. He hastily shut the door. Firmly.

Now he sat at his desk like none of it ever happened. It was a fairy tale from Europe. How could Saul have imagined that he might one day sit in the lobby of a hotel on 72nd Street and Columbus Avenue that he partly owned. Well, ten percent plus five percent for management.

There were thirty-five apartments in the hotel. Suites, they were called. Each one had a brass plate on the door with its number. They'd always been called suites.

Most residential hotels in the neighborhood had fancy names. The Regency. The Oliver Cromwell. The Franconia. The "Think Yiddish, Dress British" school. A few men who knew one another from Poland, some having survived the same ghettos and concentration camps, many who came on the same boat to America, scraped their savings—maybe ten thousand dollars each—and since the West Side was considered a war zone, picked up these dollhouses for a dime.

He had wanted to name it Hotel Lodz, after his beloved city. The other partners were against it.

"How can you even think of it? Your neighbors collaborated with the Germans!" Heniek had demanded.

"I like the sound of Hotel Lodz," Saul said.

"Americans can't even pronounce it," Janusz said. "Have you ever heard how they say swastikas?"

He shook his head.

"Swat-stickers."

"Sounds too *greener*, frankly," Bolek added in his fake British accent.

"*Vot?*"

"Like we just got off the boat and can't speak *Yinglish.*"

"We did just get off the boat, Bolek. We were on the same boat, in case you don't remember." Saul raised his voice. "Out of respect."

"What's to respect? They turned us over to the Germans and stole our apartments."

"I still can't get my father's stocks out of the Polish bank vaults," Janusz added.

"You know how many generations my family lived in Lodz?" Saul said. "My grandfather started our dry goods store from nothing. My father worked at the Grand Hotel on Piotrovska."

"And didn't they kill him and take the store?" Heniek asked.

Victor Last, with forty percent, had been silent until then. "Okay, we'll call it the Last Hotel. After my father, may he rest in peace."

As the elevator door was about to shut, Henry rushed in, carrying his metal toolbox.

"That's Mrs. Weinstein in Suite 42," Saul barked, pressing the elevator button. The elevator door opened at the first floor. Saul stomped out. Henry continued to the fourth floor.

At six o'clock, Saul locked his safe and his office and left for the day. Nothing kept him an extra minute away from his Luba. They were newlyweds! The word amused Saul. They had only been married two years.

Saul found the Sofa Club gathering in the lobby.

"Gold is selling at a hundred and thirty-seven dollars an ounce," Lenny said. "If you have the dough, you should buy some."

"When I listen to a loudmouth like you, I'll have to get my head examined," Saul answered.

"Just what I read in the paper."

"Don't you have a home to go to?" Saul admonished. "*Shlemiels.*" He hid a grin in his cheek.

Sofa Club

Most hotels and boarding houses have a certain place where the habitués hang out, the professional tongue-waggers. Theirs was the turquoise vinyl couch near the elevator, chained to the wall so no one stole it. An overflowing pedestal ashtray stood nearby. That's where the Sofa Club met most evenings after Saul left.

"So what's the news?"

Lenny Katz took his designated seat on the couch, sucking on a chewed, unlit stogie, the daily racing form in his hand. His second home was the OTB parlor on 72nd Street. He drove his own cab, mostly to the airports.

"Lousy," Lenny grumbled.

Pete Mahoney, already seated, nodded. He spent his days outdoors, operating a cherry-picker machine. A Red Sox cap slung low, he exuded a robust health like a fat baby as he sipped from a Budweiser in a paper bag.

Pincus Shreiber joined soon afterward. His black leather briefcase overflowed with books and papers. He still had his hair though not much of it.

"Nu?" Pincus said, sitting down on the vinyl couch.

"The world is going to hell in a handbag," Lenny said.

"Yeah, that's for sure."

"Did you see Jimmy Carter? It's pathetic. His hands are tied. He can't do nothing. And the Iranians are having a great old time burning our flags."

Lenny's voice rose. "Fifty-two American citizens. Hostages. And Raghead is screaming about Great Satan."

"That's why Reagan's my man," Pete said. "He wouldn't take this kind of crap."

"Reagan is an idiot!" Lenny said. "All he does is smile. What, me worry? I can't stand looking at his mug."

"He wasn't even a good actor," added Pincus.

Gittel, a Hungarian woman with bright, thinning paprika hair and an unpronounceable last name, brought a metal thermos of tea with lemon and paper cups. Her bony hand caught the new resident, a young woman, Hana, as she walked to the elevator, trying to avoid the Sofa Club.

"Don't vorry, *tzatzkeleh*," Gittel said as she tried to pass her. "*Teppel gefint zich zaya shtertzel.*"

"Huh?" uttered the frizzy-haired, full-figured young woman.

"She don't understand Yiddish," Lenny said.

"Every pot finds its lid," Pincus translated. "It's a Yiddish expression."

"You want an expression," Lenny began, "how about '*Itliches petzl gefint zok zein lechl*'? My father used to say that."

"*Meshuggeh!*" Pincus said sharply. "What kind of nonsense—"

"It means," Lenny translated, "every little pecker finds its own little hole."

Pete looked up drunkenly. "Where are we? Delancy Street? Too much kosher pastrami around here."

"What's it to you?"

"They're always talking about eye contact," Pete said. "You know why men don't make eye contact? Because breasts don't have eyes." He laughed and took another slug.

"Haven't you ever heard of women's lib?" Lenny said.

"I've had enough women's lip to last me a lifetime."

Lenny dropped his voice. "I heard someone wants to buy the hotel."

"This place?" Pincus asked.

"You must be kidding."

"We should talk to Saul."

"Yeah, you try," Lenny said.

"Talking to Saul is like talking to a volcano," Pete said. "You never know when he'll erupt."

At that moment, Esther Fein entered the lobby, carrying a bag of groceries from Pioneer. She studied the motley group on the couch. "Hi, Pincus," she said, her pretty blue eyes smiling behind rhinestone-initialed glasses. "Hello, Leonard."

Lenny, pacing back and forth, read his racing form aloud. "Hey Pete, whadaya think of Disco Kelly? Favored five to one."

"Excuse me," Esther said, trying to pass him, leaning away from his cigar.

He looked up at her. "Well, if it isn't Queen Esther. Can I help you?" He took her bags.

As he bent down to place the bags in front of the elevator, she peered at the seam of his sleeve, which was splitting, the lining dropping out from his jacket. She couldn't help herself. Bachelors, what do they know? Esther reached for his jacket, checked the lining with him in it.

"It's falling apart," she said.

He shrugged. "So don't look at it."

"I'll fix it for you," she offered.

"You would?"

"Give it to me," she said, helping him out of his jacket. "Do you have other things too?"

"My good pants are split in the *tuches*."

"So bring them over." She looked down modestly. "Suite 49."

"When?"

"Whenever."

"I'm free as an eagle."

"Tonight at seven?"

"Ya got it."

"Don't eat anything before," she added.

Lenny strutted peacock proud. "Strangers in de night…" He hummed to himself as he joined his cronies. "Da, da, da, da, da, da…"

Gittel stood up. "De insides," she said, pointing to her chest, "is de same." She ran her wrinkled hand over her wrinkled body. "Just dis change. De outside."

As they waited for the elevator, Esther turned the jacket inside out to look at the lining. She tsk-tsked, shaking her head. "They're totally helpless without us."

Hana shrugged.

"What are you, a writer?" Esther asked.

"Do I look like one?"

Esther pointed to her Channel 13 canvas bag, filled with blue manuscript boxes.

"I'm an editorial assistant at a publisher," Hana said.

"Very impressive..." she murmured.

Hana was part of the corps of English majors who, having graduated with honors, sat in cubicles, brought authors coffee, and logged manuscripts from the slush pile. After six months, she rose to reading the scripts and writing reports, which sent her to weekly chiropractor appointments not covered by insurance. She earned a heaping seventy-five hundred per annum pre-taxes.

"So are you a writer or not?" Esther demanded.

"I'm trying to be."

"Why don't you write about the people at the hotel?"

"Maybe I am."

When the elevator arrived, a woman with spiky dyed black hair walked briskly past them. She wore dark glasses and a wrinkled black trench. You couldn't tell her age or ethnicity. She stared down at her huge black clodhopper boots.

When the woman was barely out of earshot, Esther whispered, "Do you know who she is?"

Hana shook her head. People always seemed to want to talk about her.

"She lives in the penthouse. Very unfriendly," Esther said. "I tried to introduce myself, but she wouldn't even look up."

"Maybe she doesn't speak English."

"And she mainly comes out at night," continued Miss Marple. "I bet she's a hooker or a drug dealer."

"Or under a witness protection program."

"She has a tattoo," Esther added. "I saw it once."

Hana looked up. She had heard that the elevator had once been manually operated. Now it was automatic and had one of those slanted mirrors in the corner, which showed the mugger/rapist after it was already too late. Or you could check your hair. Just as the elevator door slid shut, Monica Parker of *Forgive Us Our Passions*, stepped behind Esther and Hana.

She nodded to Esther but gave Hana an unfriendly snub. She lived in the suite below Hana and had made it clear she wasn't into Miles Davis by poking a broom against her ceiling. She was tall, thin, and leggy. A total *goyishe* cupcake. The kind that drove Jewish guys nuts.

Monica carried a large black bag. All of a sudden, a yelp issued from it. Then another. She reached into the bag and whispered, "Shhh, Bogie."

Monica looked around anxiously.

So she had a dog! Animals weren't allowed in the hotel. A little Pekingese face stuck out of her bag.

The door was about to shut when an intense-looking man rushed in. With thick black hair, caterpillar eyebrows, darting eyeballs, black mustache, he resembled Peter Sellers. Dr. Tannenbaum. Resident headshrinker. He saw patients in his suite on the second floor. Monica gave him a smoldering glance.

As he went through his pockets for his keys, something fell to the floor. It was a small ceramic elephant. A hash pipe! He hastily pocketed it. The Shrunken Head of the Last Hotel! Monica saw it, offering a knowing smile.

The elevator stopped at two. The door opened. Dr. T. seemed deep in thought and didn't move, though it was his floor. The door shut. Next was the fourth floor. Esther got off the elevator. Monica didn't. That was her floor. The elevator climbed haltingly until it reached five. Hana stepped out. Monica and Dr. T. turned to each other as the doors closed.

The scent of Parfum de Joy filled the fifth floor. Amber must have passed through. How often does one get to live next door to an honest-to-God queen? Hana knew because she had confided in her. And still she could only think of her as her girlfriend, though somewhere in the far reaches of her brain, she knew Amber had a penis. She was pre-op and took Hana for her first manicure and pedicure. Wasn't the city a great place?

As she walked down the hallway, approaching her door, another scent hit the olfactories. A very different, delicious one. Beef brisket simmering in its juices, the smell of fried onions wafted up through the vents.

Suite 55

The first time she saw the brass plate on the wooden door, Hana Wolf had the sensation of having dreamed it. Or seen it on a TV show. Mary Tyler Moore. Okay, Rhoda. Her very own place in the city. The rent was forty dollars a week. No deposit, no lease. Even she could afford it on her slave wages as an editorial assistant at Coward and McCann.

Her studio was a corner suite on the fifth floor. Sweet it wasn't, but she loved every cramped inch of it. A kitchenette the size of a tiny bathroom, with a mini fridge and a double hot plate. The bathroom was a closet. But who cared? She lived in Manhattan. Not one of the boroughs, especially Queens, and not New Jersey.

Like Dorothy Parker, she could live and write in a hotel room. The Last Hotel would be her Algonquin. Besides, it sounded so glamorously, dangerously existential. *The Last Exit to Brooklyn. Last Year in Marienbad.* The perfect place for a writer, which was what she called herself, even if she was mostly unpublished.

A month earlier, Hana had moved out on Eliot Gold, D.D.S. They had lived in an apartment in Forest Hills, where he had his office. She was not ready to settle down. Or settle. She was hungry for experience. It didn't matter much whether it was good or bad, and often it was very bad. A writer needed that. What didn't kill you made you strong. But she'd die trying. The best revenge was writing well.

"You stupid girl! What do you think is out there for you?" her mother, Bella, demanded. "A dentist makes money, and believe me, that makes life better. Much better."

As if her father, Stashek Wolf, managing editor of *Cookie Times*, a baking-industry trade journal, had showered her with diamonds. "Kill me," she said,

"I want better for you."

Hana had headed for the city of eight million.

Q65A bus to the subway. F train at Continental Avenue, changing to the D train at Seventh Avenue to Columbus Circle, where she picked up the uptown IRT to 72nd Street and Broadway. Carrying her *New York Times* real estate section like a beacon, listings circled in red, she had spent hours traipsing up and down the streets of the Upper West Side and hadn't found a single affordable studio. She didn't want a roommate. She was at 72nd Street and Columbus Avenue, about to give up hope, when she saw the awning:

L st Hotel

The second letter was missing. A wicked smile crossed her face. *LUST HOTEL.*

Something was happening in the lobby as Hana entered. One of those dramas she had heard the city occasionally offered free of charge. She stood in the doorway, privileged to be in the audience.

"Go to your brother's, Spiros," the older man insisted. "He'll take you in. Stay with him until you get some money." He spoke with a strong European accent.

"I told you, Saul. I'm taking the owner to court. He fired me so his nephew could get my job. It's *nebotism*. That's what it is."

"*Nebech*. Too bad. Whatever it is, you have to get another job. There's always work for a waiter."

The younger man raised himself to his full height, maybe five feet five inches with lifts. "Saul, I'm a professional waiter," he said. "I've been with the Athena since it opened six years ago. They can't throw me away like *garbage*." He paced back and forth. "They owe me my back pay. Then I can give you everything I owe."

"That's vot you told me last month!" Saul shouted. "It's almost two months. I still don't have a broken nickel from you."

Spiros was inspired. "Saul, I'll give you my air conditioner! My air conditioner is still on warranty. It's a Kenmore."

"Stop *hondling* me!" Saul blew up, his voice booming. "I don't need your *farshtinkener* air conditioner!" He crossed his arms. "*Vy* do you do this to me?

I like you, Spiros," he cried. "You're a decent man. A clean tenant." He shook his head. "But I can't carry you no more."

Several residents had stopped to watch. A greasy-haired guy, racing form in his hand, stood jawing an unlit cigar. He was joined by a dignified older gentleman, who carried a briefcase overflowing with papers.

Spiros turned around, discovering the onlookers.

"Please, Saul," he begged, clasping his hands. His voice rose plaintively. "As soon as the case is settled, I'll have the money. Look, I have a court date." He showed him a piece of paper.

"I can't do it." Saul turned away, shaking his head. "Okay? Go! Now, already. I've had enough."

Shoulders heavy, Spiros walked toward the elevator.

"I CAN'T DO NOTHING!" Saul yelled. "I'm just the manager. I have partners. I don't own this place."

As Spiros was about to enter the elevator, he turned toward his neighbors. First, the women. His dark, long-lashed eyes implored theirs. Spiros looked around. No one spoke. What could a person say? Life was tough. He entered the elevator.

In the corner, Hana overheard three older women. "Oh, you know that? They tell you the intimate details of their relationship?"

"One knows these things."

"I've seen you flirt with Spiros."

"She'll flirt with a board if it has a hump."

"That little *pisher*? I wouldn't let him smell my underwear."

"Just what he's dying to do."

"I hate to spoil your pleasure, but the show is over!" Saul yelled over their voices. "Would you all go back to your apartments, please? I've had enough for one day."

That's when he noticed Hana. "What do you want?"

"Do you have a vacancy?" she asked, a little afraid of him.

"A vacancy?" He laughed for some reason.

Before she could answer, he demanded: "What's your name?"

"Hana Wolf."

"Wolf," he repeated, though it sounded like *Volf.* "Where are your parents from?"

"Brooklyn," she said.

"Americans," he said dismissively. "Well, you never know what will happen in this place. When Spiros leaves, it's possible."

At the time, she'd had no idea of the extent of her good fortune. Names languished on long waiting lists for a suite at the Last Hotel, and she was able to move in the following Monday.

For once in her life, she had been in the right place at the right time, after being in so many wrong places at the right time and right places at the wrong time. This was a confirmation. She had walked away from security to the terror of her own life and entered the world of the Last Hotel.

Bella the Gorilla called as soon as the phone was installed in her room. "So how big is it?"

"A studio with its own bathroom."

"Thank God for that." She paused. "How many locks do you have on your door?"

"Two. And a police bolt."

"You should buy a can of Mace and always carry it in your handbag whenever you're walking outside."

"It's not such a dangerous neighborhood."

So what if addicts shot up on city benches at Needle Park on Broadway, right outside the 72nd Street IRT station. "Weed, weed," a boy with dreadlocks whispered to passersby. Sometimes he recited his own poetry.

"I read the newspaper. There are murders, rapes, right on your street. Whoever heard of a woman living in a hotel? You could be living in the lap of luxury."

"Mom, don't start again."

She was right, of course. Pickpockets and handbag snatchers were not uncommon in the neighborhood. Hana had learned to walk with her wallet in her pocket, hand firmly grasping it, other hand holding her keys just in case she needed a weapon.

"I'll never understand why you didn't marry Elliot," Bella lamented. "And why don't I have grandchildren? All my friends' daughters…" She went on as Hana softly hung up the phone. She wasn't even thirty but already a spinster in her mother's eyes.

Hana had painted the room a pale, dreamy blue to offset the green shag carpeting. Henry, the super, removed the daybed. She bought a double mattress, which she laid on the floor, covering it with an Indian spread and Moroccan silk pillows. Henry hung a rice-paper shade from Azuma over the bare bulb. In the closet, on an upper shelf, Spiros' shoe lifts remained lined up like Dorothy's slippers, as if awaiting his return.

She found a seven-foot wooden door at the hardware store. Henry helped her prop it on two black file cabinets, placed several feet apart, in front of the only window. If she leaned over her new desk, she could see a toenail slice of the Hudson.

Suite 36

As Pincus entered his room, the orange glow of the setting sun lit up the white walls. He heaved a long sigh of relief. Dropped his heavy briefcase on his bed. Lying down next to it, he stared up at the ceiling, whose cracks he'd memorized like a map of the world. He'd made it to another Shabbes.

For most of his life, Pincus had lived in Washington Heights with the other Jews, originally from Germany and Austria. A walk down Fort Washington Avenue, all you heard was broken English and Yiddish. Kissinger had grown up around the corner.

When his father, Max, had sent him to Yiddish school, no one had suspected that it would become his passion. His longing for a lost people he never knew, a lost self, perhaps, a very nearly extinct culture. He spent most of his waking moments reading old and some new Yiddish texts. He translated several books a year, while he kept his job at the *Jewish Daily Forward*, where he'd worked since 1958.

Then the *yekkers* started to leave Washington Heights because of *die nishgutnicks*. *Shvartzehs*, Puerto Ricans, Dominicans entered. Pincus wouldn't move. This was their neighborhood too. He had grown up among immigrants on the Lower East Side. He enjoyed the vitality of Broadway. It was just one subway to work: the IND, which he picked up on 168th Street to the 28th Street stop and a brisk walk across town.

But after Sylvie died, the apartment grew too large. Too many rooms, too much dust. Every corner, especially the kitchen, which he avoided, reminded him of their life together. He had to move.

Originally, he had found the Last Hotel in the Yellow Pages, taken by its name. Over the phone, he spoke to the manager in Yiddish.

"We have only a small studio apartment. Suite 36."

"Thirty-six!" Pincus gasped.

Eighteen was the numerical value of *chai*, the Hebrew word for life, for luck. According to Gematria, thirty-six was double chai. "*L'chaim.*" May it be so. It was *beshert*. Written in the stars.

"Thirty dollars a week for a studio."

"Oh, yes. That's fine."

"Come today," Saul commanded. "With a check."

The sun had set. It was good that Pincus had prepared his table earlier, two white candles in the silver candlesticks Sylvie had found at an antique store in the West End. Two crystal glasses and a bottle of red wine, the challah wrapped in a cloth embroidered by Sylvie.

He lit the candles, covering his eyes. After reciting the blessing, he stood, eyes still covered.

He remembered his mother, Helah, lighting candles in their home. Covering her eyes, she prayed, then walked over to his father, who had washed up, his wet hair combed back. "*Gut Shabbes*, Max." She kissed him on the lips. Then he went around the table, laying his hands first on his sister Ella's head, then on Pincus' head, blessing them both. Max sat down at the head of the table like a czar, though he had worked through the night in their store and would open it again tomorrow at sunset. But on Shabbes, he recited the prayer for grain from the earth, salting the challah, breaking pieces off and passing them around.

He opened his eyes. "*Shabbat shalom!*" He turned to Sylvie. "*Mine ziskeit.*"

Taking a large magnifying glass from a shelf, Pincus laid it over his prayer book. So difficult to read. If he couldn't read, how could he live? The doctor had convinced him to have the cataract operation on his good eye. "You'll see how much your vision will improve," he had said. Sure. Now his good eye was worse than his bad eye. He could hardly read the *New York Times*. A *shandeh*! Scandal. Pincus squinted through his page-sized magnifying glass at *Yedid Nefesh*. The love song between God and one's soul. He sang the Hebrew psalm with a robust voice, so unlike his normal near-whisper.

"You who love my soul, sweet source of tenderness, take my inner nature and shape it to your will...Let your sweet love delight me with its thrill. Because no other dainty will my hunger still."

He looked up at Sylvie again. It was a good likeness. The painter had caught her shiny brown hair, intelligent brown eyes, her smile, which was warm and generous. She was not a beauty, thank God. What a *neshomeh* Sylvie had, a sweet soul like no other. She laughed at his jokes, no matter how many times he told them. That's true love. How he missed her. Every day of his life.

He lit the *Yahrzeit* candle on April 22nd, the day the cancer finally took Sylvie after a year of suffering. But he never stopped thinking of her, talking to her. He sighed again. Oh, Sylvie. Why had his Maker seen fit to take his love from him?

People said to him, "Go out. For God's sake, live a little!"

Saul brought it up to him. "Pincus, isn't your *shivah* over yet?"

Even Sylvie urged him. "Pinkeleh, find yourself a woman," she told him. "You'll get crazy if you don't. You won't eat. And who's going to take care of you if you get sick, God forbid. Not me. Enough is enough. Stop with your *krechts*. I don't want sainthood."

I need a woman like a *loch in kop*. A hole in the head. He poured wine into their two glasses. Raising one glass, he recited the blessing for the fruit of the vine. "Mine Sylvie." He sighed, clinking the other glass.

After a few minutes, he walked into his kitchenette. He turned on his hot plate. Reaching for a can of beef stew from the cupboard, he poured the contents into an aluminum saucepan and placed it on the hot plate. Then he emptied his briefcase on the bed. Five Yiddish titles poured out. He picked one up. A Peretz book. He began to leaf through the pages. Very interesting. Several minutes passed. *Oy vey!* Pincus rushed to check that his pot didn't burn the hotel down.

Suite 45

Monica Parker, née Manyi Pacz, emigrated from Hungary with her brave, tight-lipped mother, Olga, in 1957. Now she was known to millions as arch villainess Emerald Lee. Often, she wished her life was like her character's, whom she would probably play until the grave unless they wrote her out, whichever came first.

The hotel was only six blocks from the studio at ABC. It was a good address. She used to live at the Barbizon when she first came to New York. A hotel for ladies. You weren't even supposed to bring a man to your room. And then Enrico began to stalk her. She figured he'd never find her uptown. Besides, the hotel was across the street from Charivari, where she could shop her fantasies. Last week, she had bought rabbit-fur-lined mules for her freshly pedicured feet. And Off-Broadway, a boutique managed by a former showgirl, whose fashions looked like they came from Cher's closet.

She ran her fingers through her blue-black tresses, fluffing the curls with her fingers. Monica had definite big hair. You couldn't buy that kind of thickness. That's why Proctor and Gamble loved her. On a subliminal level, her hair inspired millions of viewers to buy extra-body conditioner.

Monica freshened up, patting her face with a moist sponge, massaging rose-beige foundation into the pores of her skin. She stared into her Hollywood mirror. The five bright lights never lied. They were honest but not kind. Her wrinkles, lifelines, as some called them, were visible in this light. Tragic cracks in her mask. Good God! A stray hair under her chin. She hastily tweezed.

She moved away from the mirror, fixing the outline of her lips. A perfect heart. None of that "pleating" older women had around their lips. *Yet.* She added just a dab of gloss for shine, then turned off the light switch in the bathroom.

The shades were drawn, the light dim but for the glow of scented candles.

It was almost religious. If the sisters could see her now.

She'd gone to St. Olaf's Daughters, where the sisters carried paddles, which they used if they caught a girl using the Lord's name in vain. Jesus Christ! They had to wear scratchy wool skirts with stiff white shirts and blue ties. She shuddered as she thought of Sister Agnes, who had a special hatred for her and liked to slap the back of her knees with a ruler.

A squeak sounded from the corner of the room, then a soft bark. "Where are you, Bogie!" she called. She turned on the light and found the creature nestled in her fur coat. "Come here, you!" She smothered the animal in her arms. "You, you, you, Bogie face!"

She decided to slip into something comfortable. Sexy but not whorish. Just a wee bit transparent. No. She shook her head. She couldn't decide, then pulled out her coral satin kimono with the golden dragon and shimmied into it. The satin felt amazing. She strolled over to the gold-leaf full-length mirror, bought for a song (and a dance for the owner, a gay boy, who recognized her) in an antique shop on Columbus Avenue. Three hundred was a steal. Her mirror image stared at her.

A dream came back to Monica from several nights earlier. She was looking at herself in the mirror when suddenly she fell into the mirror. She found herself floating in space like Alice, through infinite glass images of herself. She tried to escape but couldn't. She was trapped in Mirror World, surrounded by reflections of her face, her smile, her hair times a zillion. She couldn't move. All she could do was to stare at her own image. Now she shrank back from the mirror.

Sitting down in an upholstered chair of burgundy velvet, she lit a clove cigarette, inhaling the sweet smoke, exultantly exhaling. How she loved the taste, the overpowering scent, the whirl of smoke around her. Her eyes wandered back to her image in the mirror across the room.

People said that she resembled Vivien Leigh. Her pale, white, never-exposed-to-the-sun skin, her dark shoulder-length hair, red lips and cheeks.

Now her hair was dyed. She wore too much makeup and lipstick. She had an image of herself as Gloria Swanson walking down the staircase in *Sunset Boulevard*. She understood the meaning. Sunset. The sun was setting fast. Soon it would be dark. Soon she would be old and alone.

Just then the telephone rang. Monica picked up the black phone receiver. "Hello?"

"I just finished working." It was a male voice. "What are you doing?"

"Who is this?" Monica asked.

"Don't you know?" The timbre was deep.

"Tell me or I'll hang up."

"Everyone is always in such a rush."

She took a wild guess. "Dr. Tannenbaum from the second floor?"

"You got it."

"You waited to call."

"Let's just say I had some unfinished business."

"Did you finish your unfinished business?"

"Finished," he replied.

They both laughed.

"I saw your face that day."

"Huh?"

"You don't remember. We were in the elevator and something fell out of my pocket."

"The pipe!" Monica cried out. "Shaped like an elephant."

"I'd appreciate if you wouldn't publicize it."

"I was impressed."

"What are you doing now?"

"I'm studying my lines for Monday."

"Could you take a break?"

"Not tonight."

"Another time then."

"I'm not sure."

"Well, let me know," he offered. "We could have a drink at my place."

"I don't really think I should."

"We could share the elephant."

"What's your suite number?" she asked.

"Twenty-one."

"Just in case."

Suite 42

"Holla, Superman," said Gittel, as she got on the elevator at the first floor. Her arms were filled with grocery bags from Pioneer. Henry helped her put them down, then pushed number three for her. He was going up to four. Suite 42. Leaky faucet. Ms. Rachel's suite. Bathroom. Like Mr. E. told him to do. The Hungarian lady got off at three. Henry stepped out on the next floor.

He knocked on the door of Suite 42. Waited a moment. Then rang the doorbell. Once. Twice. He leaned against the door, his ear pressed against the metal. Finally, when no one stirred, he used the master key.

Without casting a glance, Henry walked straight into the bathroom. Water dripped from the faucet. He tried to turn it all the way, but a trickle of water continued to run. One more try. Guess not. "I'm gonna have to take this sucker apart," he said aloud. Henry took the wrench from his tool box.

As he walked past the bedroom, out of the corner of his eye, he saw a brilliant plumage of color. Wrench in hand, he followed his eyes and entered Ms. Rachel's bedroom.

First there was the scent. He followed his nose and sniffed fresh lilacs in a crystal vase on the table. Thought of his grandmother's garden in Sweet Briar, where he had spent his boyhood summers.

He looked around. There were a million things. And things that held things. A royal blue ostrich boa was flung over the vanity. Five white heads with wigs of different styles and colors. A golden hand-held mirror. China figurines. Cups holding brushes of many sizes. Little jars of makeup. Powders and sequins. Necklaces, earrings.

Peeking into her closet, which was open, he spied glittery movie star gowns, hundreds of shoes. And turning to face her bed, he saw that it was covered with red satin sheets!

"Sheeet!" He laughed aloud. "White people." He shook his head. When he was alone, he liked to talk to himself. One of the perks of the job.

He'd seen everything at the hotel. Like that Dr. T. on the second floor who covered his ceiling with mirrors, then almost flooded the place with his water bed. Miss Amber had klieg lights, a full-length mirror with a camera mounted on a tripod. What was she taking pictures of? He smiled to himself. "I could write a book."

He sat down on a purple velvet armchair, leaning back comfortably. A midnight blue ostrich boa floated over him. He wrapped it around himself. "So that's what luxury feels like…" He sighed. As he looked down, he saw a pile of paperback books at his feet. Most had pictures of women with their blouses torn and fiery titles like *Her Beloved Lust* and *By Love Possessed*. He was about to pick one up when Henry heard a sound. He looked up. Rachel was standing in the doorway.

He stood up hastily, dropping the boa. "Ms. Rachel, I was, uh, fixing your faucet in the, uh, bathroom sink," he answered.

He walked stealthily away from the chair.

"Want to try it out?" he called a few minutes later.

She seemed to be studying him.

"The faucet."

Henry followed behind Rachel, unable to avoid noticing the lovely rhythmic sway of her ample hips and ass. She sure was a good looker.

He shook his head. He was too old and too sick for this kind of nonsense. And yet the fire wasn't done yet—there were still a few red embers. He chuckled to himself, then thought of Bessie, whom he'd met in Lynchburg and had married over thirty years ago. She was a smart woman with big motherly thighs.

Curiosity got the better of him. He opened his mouth. "Do you wear those wigs?" He pointed to several white heads covered with different colors and styles of hair.

"I have," she answered.

"The Angela Davis?"

"I thought it was *Mod Squad*."

He cracked up, flashing his enormously likeable smile with its many imperfect teeth.

"I once wore it to a Halloween party with Harvey. That was my last husband. He came as Abbie Hoffman, not a stretch 'cause he had that kind of hair. Harvey. I miss him. I really do."

"How long ago did he die?"

"A couple years ago. But I still think about him. You know, I heard that when people die, they sometimes come back to visit you. That hasn't happened with Harvey. I keep hoping he'll come. You think he's mad at me?" she asked a bewildered Henry. "I don't know why though. Except maybe he's not happy that I've had lovers."

"Don't worry. I'll ask Bessie, if you like. She talks to dead people all the time."

Rachel smiled. "You're a good man, Henry."

"Did you turn it on?" he asked.

She looked confused.

"It turns on and off now," he said, bending over to twist the chrome cap. "The faucet. It turns off now."

"Turn on, turn off, thanks Henry." She leaned over. "Do you mind?"

He smiled his toothy smile, so full of goodwill.

Rachel planted a kiss on his cheek, then reached into her designer bag to give him a twenty. He sure didn't mind that.

$\mathcal{S}uite$ 22

"Da, da, da, da, da..." a booming voice bellowed from a tiny bathroom on the second floor of the Last Hotel. Lenny stepped out of the shower. As he wrapped a green Atlantic City towel around his waist, he gave the little man a cursory nudge. Still there, nose up in the air. Lenny gargled with Listerine.

He had spent the day driving, mostly to JFK. Lenny Katz wasn't just any cabdriver. He owned the gold medallion on the hood of his car, free and clear. He had paid ten big smackers, but now it was worth twenty-five. He nodded to himself with satisfaction.

A large guy, Lenny was over six feet, two hundred and thirty pounds of manliness. He had large hands, large belly, size-thirteen feet. He lathered his five o' clock shadow the old-fashioned way with his soap cup and shaving brush. Lenny had a heavy beard. If he wanted to be smooth at night, he had to shave a second time. Must be his Cossack blood. As the razor sailed through white foam, carving a wide path across his cheek, Lenny did his best Sinatra. "Strangers in the night, exchanging glances, wondering in the night, what were the chances...."

What were his chances with Queen Esther? He had always thought she was a snob with her Metropolitan Opera tickets and classes at the Whitney Museum. And he knew he wasn't exactly Mr. Suave, pronounced *swave* where he came from. Yet she had not only offered to fix the lining of his jacket, but Esther said she'd mend the split in his good pants. Then to his total shock, she added, "Don't eat anything before you come over."

God, she must really want me! He smiled fondly at his reflection.

Filling the sink basin with hot steaming water, he splashed his face till he cried out, "Yes!" Then he started whacking his face with cold water from the tap. Slapping hard to get the blood going. Good for circulation. Now he patted Aqua Velva aftershave on his face and neck. "Yes!" he groaned. Sure, it stung like hell, but he enjoyed the masculine smell and feel of it. His skin, a bright ham pink, tingled.

Peering closely in the mirror, he noticed a few errant nose hairs. He trimmed them with round nub scissors, then snipped several hairs from his ears. What a hairy ape he was. Those Cossack genes. Lenny was convinced that his Russian grandmother had been raped by Cossacks, though he had no evidence other than his hirsuteness. He knew some big words.

It wasn't like he thought he was anyone's dreamboat. He'd never make *The Dating Game*, but Lenny had a few charms. He pressed a tube of Brylcreem into his hands, rubbed them together, then worked it through his hair. Luckily, he hadn't lost his hair like his brother the accountant, Max. Lenny's hair was thick and dark. He sculpted the front into a pompadour with one spit curl falling over his forehead. Just like Tom Jones. "It's not unusual…" he sang out as he stroked Extra Strength Right Guard under his pits, then sprayed Brut for good measure.

"Cool it," he said aloud.

Although Lenny liked women, they invaded your life if you gave them just an inch. They took everything. He was a bachelor, and that's the way he wanted it. Looking around his room, he saw clothes he'd worn over the last few weeks draped over the single chair, hanging from doorknobs, countless socks on the floor in the midst of empty Chinese food cartons and a large pizza box, not to mention a few empty cans. A woman would go nuts living with him.

He liked to live alone. No one to tell him what to do. That's why he liked living in the hotel. You get all your privacy. Once he was married. Couldn't take it. Never again. "When Jews say never again, I say, yeah. I'll never get married again." He had made this remark to anyone who would listen, for over twenty years.

He plunged an arm blindly into the dark over-crowded closet, pulling out an orange cotton shirt. He sniffed the pits. Clean. His good bowling shirt with the name of his team *WESTSIDE LANES* printed on the back.

He found his split pants on the chair next to his black pants. He smelled them. They could use a wash. Oh well. It wasn't like Esther would sniff his pants, but who knew? What were the chances? Maybe he'd get lucky. "Da, da, da, da, da…"

He stuck his keys and wallet into his back pocket. Then he pulled out a Budweiser six-pack from his tiny fridge.

Suite 36

What was that? Pincus stopped and listened. There was a soft knock on his door! Who could it be? He placed his magnifying glass and prayer book down on the table. Another knock! "A minute," he called.

Who would come at such a time? He looked down at himself, tucked his shirt in his pants, put on his jacket, then opened the door.

"*Gut Shabbes.*" A voice with a feminine lilt greeted him.

He opened the door slowly. The woman looked vaguely familiar. Who was this?

"Don't look at me like you don't know me," she said. "I'm your neighbor. Faye Meyer in Suite 32."

"Oh, yes. Near the elevator."

"Is this a one-bedroom?" she asked.

"No, a studio." He stood still as a statue.

"What do you pay, if you don't mind my asking?"

"Thirty dollars a week," he answered.

"Mine has an 'alcove,' whatever that is. Where you can your hide your bed, I suppose." She laughed. "I pay forty-five. How long have you been here?"

Pincus thought about it. "Eight years."

"Oh," Faye said. "I've only been here two years."

He stepped back. "What can I do for you?"

"You can wish me a good Shabbes," she said. "Actually,"—she handed him a black covered pot—"here."

"What's this?"

"Can I come in?" she asked.

"Why not?" he answered, adding a little joke. "Unless you're a golem."

Faye entered like a fire engine, or was it the color of her hair? Her silver bracelets made a ringing sound as she walked around the room.

"Very nice," she said.

She stopped in front of the painting, which filled the wall above his couch.

"That's Sylvie," he said as if he were introducing her.

As she took it in, especially the ruby ring, Pincus studied Faye. Her red hair fell in long waves around her face. Tight-fitting black slacks showed off her hips, which were ample.

"I made a brisket with carrots and potatoes, but there's too much for one person. I thought you might like to share some with me." Faye raised the lid of the black pot.

Pincus stared into the pot.

"So have a 'lek un a shmek' as my grandmother Lyla used to say. A smell and a taste."

"Gut." Pincus sniffed. "Very good."

"Come," she said, taking his hand. Then she looked down at the table and noticed the two glasses.

"What's this?"

"That's Sylvie's glass."

"Sylvie?"

"My wife."

"I don't understand." Faye was flustered, thinking of her visitation. "I thought that—"

"We were married for twenty-two years. She was fifty-four years old when she died."

"Oh, how terrible! I had no idea." Faye gasped. "How long ago was it?"

"Eleven years," Pincus answered matter-of-factly.

"Oh." Faye paused. "You talk like it just happened. Like you're still in mourning."

"I never stop missing her," he admitted sorrowfully.

Faye stood up. "I'm sorry."

"No," said Pincus. "It's all right."

"I should go. I just thought maybe we could have a little time without all the others, especially that Lenny with the big mouth. I can't stand his cigars! To see if we could get along." She wanted to tell him about the vision she had of Sylvie but was afraid he'd think she was crazy.

Pincus mumbled something inaudibly.

"I was thinking it could be nice," she continued wistfully. "We're neighbors. We could help each other. But I see I made a mistake."

She reached for her pot of brisket.

Pincus held on to it.

"If you give me a bowl," she said, "I can leave you some of the brisket."

"To be honest, after such a long time, I don't know how to talk vit a voman," he declared awkwardly. "I recognize your effort—"

"Oh, do I get an E for effort?"

"Why do you say that?"

"It's just an expression."

Pincus put the black pot down on the table. Then he removed Sylvie's glass and brought it to the sink. He found another wine glass and gave it to Faye. "May I?"

He poured wine into her glass. "Let's say the blessing."

Together they recited the prayer, finishing off with "*borey pre hagafen.*" Bless the fruit of the vine. Then they clinked glasses and drank the wine.

"Manischewitz." Faye winced.

"What else?"

"Let me heat this up," she said, standing up. "You don't mind?"

She removed the pot of canned stew, then set her black pot in its place, turning the burner low so it could simmer slowly. The flame slithered as they regarded each other frankly.

Not bad for an *alte kocker*, thought Faye. He had a good head of silver hair, thick and curly. Probably at least ten years older than her, maybe fifteen. But age was a number, like hers, and didn't have to be a prison cell.

She stared at the painting of Sylvie and that ring. As a work of art, it wasn't much. Oh, but to be loved like that!

It was as if Pincus was slowly awakening from a deep sleep. In the dream, he was blind to the world. He had walked the streets of Manhattan with his eyes on his shoes, looking up only to check the traffic light. *Gottenyu!* A woman stood before him. A mature, full-bodied voman. Faye was like a Henry Moore statue with huge *brosts*, a soft stomach, ach, a knish. Vagina. *Oy vey!* Pincus shut his eyes tightly. He was undressing his neighbor.

"I better check the brisket." Faye sidled away from Pincus, swinging her *zoftik* hips. She raised the lid, and a cloud of heavenly smells descended. Pincus sighed, remembering the smell of his mother's kitchen.

The brisket was a masterpiece. Soft, sumptuous pieces of beef in a thick gravy, sauce-soaked potatoes, onions, and carrots. Such a thing! The meat soft as butter. You didn't even need a knife! Pincus had never liked other briskets than Sylvie's, but Faye's forced him to reconsider.

"I'd love to have a drink," Faye said after they finished dinner. "What do you have besides the Manischewitz?"

Unworldly until this very moment, Pincus had nothing else.

"Just a minute," Faye announced, standing up. "I'll get something from my apartment."

A look of desperation crossed Pincus' face. "Don't worry. I'll be right back." She grabbed her keys and ran out.

At the table, Pincus sat unmoving as if afraid that if he stirred, it would all end. He was stupefied by his *mazel*. Luck. Astounded by his own stupidity, his self-denial, and martyrdom. He couldn't get the vision of Faye's *brosts* out of his mind. He'd forgotten what it was to desire.

Faye returned with a bottle of Absolut, another with a brown liqueur, and a container of half-and-half. "Kahlua," she said, pointing to the bottle like a schoolteacher. "Pincus, have you ever had a White Russian?"

"I don't really drink," he said.

"It's like coffee au lait."

"I used to be a Bolshevik," he joked. "Now I'm a Czarist!"

What a sweet taste the White Russian had. Pincus drank two glasses and found himself beaming. To be talking with a voman again! He felt a boyish glee as he heard about that *shmendrik* husband of hers. "I've been divorced a long time," she said. Faye had a daughter in Denver. Pincus' daughter lived in London, where Sylvie's people were from.

"Faye, are you a *faigeleh*?" Pincus asked. "The little bird that flies out in the field. There's a beautiful Yiddish song, 'Faigeleh.'"

"Actually I am. It's what my grandmother called me."

"Faigeleh…" He pronounced the word with tenderness.

"Pinkeleh," she answered.

"That's what Sylvie calls me," he said.

"I'm sorry." Faye pulled away. "There I go again, saying the wrong thing."

"No, no!" Pincus said, stroking her smoky hair like the forest. A person could get lost there. "I like that you called me Pinkeleh."

They looked at each other, then he turned away bashfully. Vot did a mensch say who had been with one voman, Sylvie, and then for eleven years, *gornisht*. Nothing. He was a young boy masquerading as an old Jewish man. He took Faye's hand. "So you know a little *malmaloshen*? Our mother tongue. Yiddish?"

"A *bissel*. Just a few words from my *zeyde*. But I love the sound. It always makes me laugh."

"I'll teach you," he said.

"You're a teacher?" she asked.

"I'm a translator, actually. But since my cataract operation, I don't see so well. I translate Yiddish."

"I teach French literature at Hunter," she told him.

"My boss' daughter goes there," he added.

"My *zeyde* used to read 'A Bintel Brief' so he could tell us everyone's business."

He rolled his eyes. "I edited and rewrote most of the letters. You vouldn't believe vot some people write. I can't even tell you." He blushed, his cheeks turning bright pink.

"You should see how some of my students write."

They laughed at the same time, ending up in each other's arms. He kissed her softly on the lips. *Baruch Hashem!* He still remembered! She kissed him. They embraced for several minutes. Faye gently pulled away.

"Did I do something wrong?" he asked.

"No, no. It's just that…" She hesitated, then smiled. "Would you like to see my apartment?"

He looked disoriented. "What?"

"It's maybe a little more comfortable." She dropped her eyes shyly.

Slowly, stealthily, they opened Pincus' door, turning to look in each direction to make sure none of the neighbors saw them. They snuck from his place to hers, tiptoeing like teenagers out after their curfews. Down the long hallway, a suspenseful distance of five doors. Hastily, she dug out her keys and unlocked her door. When it closed behind them, both exhaled gasps of relief and exhaustion.

Pincus smiled at the sight of Faye's flickering Shabbes flames.

"I like to light the candles," she said, "though I'm not really religious."

"Come." Pincus took her arm in a courtly old-world manner. They sat down on her couch, holding hands. He kissed her.

"Pinkeleh," she said softly.

"Faigeleh."

"You have such nice hair," she said, touching his silver locks. "A widow's peak."

The lights from the candles glowed softly. Pincus took Faye into his arms, kissing her in a way he had forgotten about for twenty years. Her lips were luscious to him, like her brisket. He fell upon her with twenty years of passion in his embrace.

Faye drew back.

"What's wrong?"

"We should wait, get to know each other a little more…"

He drew back. "You're right. Yes."

"You're not supposed to say that," she teased. "But that's probably good."

"It's better that vay," he said breathlessly.

"Let's dream about each other," Faye whispered in his ear.

"Yes, yes, I will," Pincus said, slowly backing out of her living room. He opened the door. "*A gutte nacht*, my Faigeleh."

Suite 49

That Rachel woman from the fourth floor was in the elevator. As Lenny walked past, she fluttered her lavender lids. With her dyed black hair, she looked like a Liz Taylor knockoff. She looked deeply into his eyes as she walked out of the elevator. Lenny stepped out behind her.

It was seven sharp. He prided himself on his punctuality. Ringing the doorbell of Suite 49, he began, "Da, da, da, da, da—" but stopped himself. No one likes a six-foot singing canary.

Esther Fein opened the door. Lenny stood in her doorway, holding a pair of black wool slacks over his arm and his six-pack. He handed her the pants. "You offered," he said.

"Yes, I did," she answered, taking them from him.

Then he handed her the beer. "This is to express my heartfelt gratitude," he said like he'd memorized the phrase. "You look different."

"I'm not wearing my glasses," she told him. "I decided to try contact lenses."

He examined her in the doorway. "You have nice eyes."

Embarrassed, Esther smiled. "Come in."

"Maybe you should put the beer in the frigidaire," he suggested.

"Why not?"

Lenny followed the swish of Esther's muumuu that completely covered her body. Lenny strained to see where she might be within her floral tent—a waistline, perhaps, a buttock—but all he could see were her legs, which were very nice with surprisingly trim ankles, and white high-heeled sandals.

Looking around her digs, Lenny whistled. Somehow she had fit several upholstered chairs, fancy standing lamps, and a brown velvet sectional sofa, not to mention a crystal chandelier, into her suite. It was like a house in Queens! There were framed paintings on the wall and a small dining table, which was set with mats and cloth napkins.

"This is really classy!" he exclaimed. "And you're only two floors above me." He gave a whistle.

She laughed. "Can I get you something to drink?"

"Just the beer," he said brusquely, then added, "Hey, I'm a bridge and tunnel kind of guy, raised in Canarsie. I'm still mad the Dodgers left Brooklyn."

"I'm not impressed," she told him. "I grew up in Bensonhurst. I think I'll have a glass of rosé." She poured his beer.

"Thanks," he said, sitting down on a brocade chair with upholstered arms. There was a matching ottoman nearby. He put his feet up on it. Then he noticed his shoes were filthy. He dropped them hastily.

"Very nice indeed," he said, leaning back into the overstuffed chair.

Esther held a wine glass. "*Cin cin.*"

"Whatever you say."

"I fixed your jacket. Just a minute." Esther went into her alcove and brought it out. "Look."

He took it from her and studied the brown lining attached to the jacket with small, neat stitches.

"I don't know what to say," he said, truly touched. No one ever did anything like this for him, except his mother, Alice, who had passed away on Groundhog Day, '72.

"It's nothing." Esther shrugged. "I always used to fix Jerry's jackets and pants, sew his buttons, mend his socks. I miss doing things like that."

"Jerry was your husband?"

She nodded. "We were married for over thirty years. I lost him three years ago to lung cancer," she recited mechanically. "He smoked like a chimney on fire."

Lenny had been about to take out his cigar but thought better of it. "Sorry to hear that," he said. "Is that when you moved into this dump?"

She turned to him. "You don't mean that."

"Why don't you find yourself a one bedroom at Lincoln Towers?

"What? I have my friends," she declared. "I'm happy here."

"You make it look like a real home," Lenny said, looking down at the Persian rug, the fancy vase with cut flowers.

"Thanks," she said. "Besides, I like Saul."

"Me too. He's a total lunatic though."

"Who wouldn't be, after what he went through?"

Lenny nodded knowingly.

"Have you met his new wife?" she inquired.

"Luba?" He shook his head. "What about you?"

"I don't think she comes to the hotel."

"So you had a good marriage?"

"I met Jerry when I was eighteen. He was twenty-two, going to Brooklyn College on the GI bill. I was getting a degree in social work. We didn't have any children," she added.

"You a social worker?" he asked.

She nodded. "How long have you been driving a taxi?"

"Twenty three years, November, but I don't work for no fleet. I have my own car. Purchased my medallion ten years ago," he said proudly.

"Did you see that movie *Taxi Driver* with Robert DeNiro?"

"I didn't like it," he said. "Gives us cabbies a bad name. That *meshuggeh* shaving his head. I mean, not that there aren't some nut jobs out there. I've met them all, and I never met anyone like that guy. That movie was sick."

"It was an incredible character study though. Martin Scorcese is a genius—" she began.

"I don't mean to be rude, but,"—he gave her his winning smile—"I was promised something to eat."

She looked at him. "I'll check."

His eyes followed her path to the kitchenette. As she bent over to open the oven, he spied a hint of flesh above her knee-high stockings. Yeah, this was a big gal, but he had nothing against fleshiness, especially if it was in the right places.

All of a sudden, a cloud of beefy steakness rose from the oven, wafted across the room into Lenny's nostrils. He sat up as if struck. Esther carried in a silver platter and placed it on the table.

"I hope you like London broil," she said.

"With fried onions!" he exclaimed joyfully.

Lenny joined her at the table. It was set with real silver and good steak knives. He looked down at his fingernails, which were dirty. How had he missed them?

"Just a minute." She went back to the stove and returned with a blue serving bowl. "And potato kugel." She placed it in front of him.

"I died and went to heaven." Lenny sighed.

"Would you mind slicing the steak?" she asked as she sat down across from him.

Lenny worked at the task with concentration. He forked three slices of meat for himself. Esther helped herself to a thin slice of meat. They ate silently for a few moments.

"Dis is delicious," he said with his mouth full, steak sauce dripping from the side of his mouth. "Really!"

"I'm glad you like it," she said, using her napkin to wipe the sauce on Lenny's chin.

"I miss cooking," she continued. "Everyone I know goes to restaurants. So do I. But sometimes I like to use my own dishes and silverware."

"I miss eating good food like this," he said, chewing loudly. "Thanks for the wipe down. Well, you can cook for me anytime, Queen Esther."

"I wish you wouldn't call me that."

"Why?"

"Why do you call me that?" she asked.

"I can't help it, Esther. Your name makes me think of Purim. In our spiel, I was always Hamen. He's the one that everyone boos at."

"Did you like that?"

"I didn't mind."

"You're right, you know," Esther admitted. "I was chosen to be Queen Esther, but I wanted to be Vashti. The evil one who wouldn't dance for the king. She was actually the first feminist in the Bible."

Lenny tried to think of something to say that wouldn't sound uncouth or coarse. "Aren't you going to eat anymore?" he asked, eyeing the thin sliver on her plate.

"I'm on Weight Watchers," she answered. "I can only have four ounces of beef."

"But you look terrific!" Lenny said, gesticulating with his fork. "I like a woman who looks like a woman. I can't stand those skinny bags of bones." He took another bite, chewing loudly.

Esther took a tiny sip of wine. "More beer?" she asked, standing up.

"Sit." He put his arms on her shoulders. "I'll help myself."

When he returned, he noticed Esther's tears. "Are you crying?" he asked, staring at her.

She shook her head. "No. I'm just having trouble with my contacts. That's why I never wear them." She stood up. "I better get my eye drops."

Esther threw her head back, poising the dropper above one eye, then the other. She closed her eyes, but they continued to tear. "Oh, this is awful!"

"What's the matter?" He gave her his napkin.

"It burns."

"So take them out."

"I need two cups of water. Could you get them for me?"

"Sure," Lenny said, rushing into her kitchenette. "Where are they?"

"The cabinet above the stove."

He found two teacups, which he filled with water. Then he put them on the table in front of Esther. "Can I do anything else?"

She shook her head, keeping her eyes closed. Slowly, she bent over the cup, removing her right lens. As she did the same with the left, the lens slipped from her finger.

"Shit!" she cried. "Oh, excuse me!"

"What?"

"I dropped the lens."

"Where?"

"I think it's on my dress somewhere."

"Should I help you?" Lenny scanned the expansiveness of her tent.

She nodded. "I can't move or the contact will fall on the floor."

He approached her awkwardly. "What should I do?"

"I'm going to pick up my skirt so maybe it will fall into the center."

Lenny grinned happily as she raised the dark tent above her knees. Squinting, he patted the material, trying to find the tiny sliver of glass. There was much material and no lens.

"I don't see it," he said.

"Neither do I. Maybe it fell on the floor." Esther stood up, carefully shaking the dress.

"Are they insured?" Lenny asked.

She shook her head. "I'm going to check the carpet."

"I'll help you." Lenny lowered himself to the floor.

For several minutes, they crawled on the carpet, feeling for the lens with their fingertips. Next to Lenny, Esther looked slight, feminine, even delicate. Once their heads met. They gazed at each other on all fours. Esther burst into a fit of giggles. "Will you look at us? I feel so stupid."

"What about me?"

"It's so undignified," Esther cried.

"I'm almost sixty years old!" Lenny whooped.

"I'm no spring chicken either," Esther giggled helplessly.

"We're both much too old for this."

Shaking with laughter, they fell into each other's arms. Without a moment's hesitation, Lenny lunged at Esther, giving her a big, messy tongue kiss. She responded, throwing her arms around him, shutting her eyes. For several moments, they kissed. Slowly, his right hand wandered over the tent of her dress until he reached the bottom of it. As he tried to reach beneath, his hand was met with an iron clamp. She held it there. As they continued to kiss, his free hand found her breast within the tent.

"Whoa! Wait a minute!" She scrambled on the floor, pulling away from him. "What are you doing?"

"What do you think I'm doing?"

"You work kind of fast." Esther sat up, straightening her tent. "I'm not ready for this."

"For what?"

"Messing around." She combed her hair with her fingers.

"Huh?"

"You know, petting. One thing leads to another... "

"So kill me," he said. "I'm hot and bothered."

"I'm just not that modern," she said, standing up.

As he struggled to stand up, a loud, piercing sound escaped.

"Excuse me! I should find your little boy's room." Lenny rushed out of the room. The smell remained behind. Esther found lilac freshener and sprayed the room.

After fifteen minutes, Esther called, "Are you all right in there?"

"Do you have any Alka-Seltzer?"

"In the medicine cabinet."

"Must have been the kugel," he said as he joined her a few minutes later. Esther pointed to his open fly. "Lenny, your fiddle case..."

"I'm such a *shlemiel*," he said, zipping up. "You know, Yiddish has about a hundred ways to say shmuck, putz...They're all words for the penis."

"Like the Eskimos' words for snow," Esther interrupted. "Actually I'm the *shlemazel* for losing my lens."

"Did you find it?"

She shook her head. "I knew I shouldn't wear them."

"About before," he began. "It was just too tempting with both of us on the floor that way."

"Don't worry about it," Esther said.

"I'm really in no rush," he added. "Besides I have another pair of pants."

"Just bring them to me," she said passionately. "If you're missing buttons on your shirts and jackets or need me to let out a seam."

"Because you've done this for me," Lenny declared, "I want to do something for you."

"Yes?" Esther looked expectant.

"I know something about the horses," he began. "Been playing 'em for forty years. Anyway, I got a tip from a good source. Midnight Shadow. Favored to win, five to one. I know the jockey. He says she has a real chance."

"Are you saying I should put money on Midnight Shadow?"

"I'm placing my own two hundred."

"I see."

"Do you have any mad money, because you could lose it," Lenny said. "But you could make some real dinero."

Esther thought about it for a moment. "I've never gambled in my whole life."

"So live a little," he said.

"Why not, Lenny?" she said mischievously. "I never take any risks."

"Now you're talkin'!"

She pulled a black wallet from a desk drawer and counted ten crisp ten-dollar bills and handed them to him.

He whistled. "That's a lotta change."

"You only live once."

"You're not going to be in the poorhouse, right?" he asked. "'Cause nothing's ever a sure thing. But you could make some dough-re-mi."

"What happens if we win?" she asked.

"Don't count your chickens before you've been laid." He grinned at his own joke.

"So now I'll be a gambler." Esther smiled. "I like you, Lenny, but I don't believe in going all the way on the first date. Or at least, I didn't the last time I had a date, which was a long time ago." She touched his hand softly. "Please don't stop trying."

He grabbed her into his arms. She pulled away. "You said I shouldn't stop trying," he cried.

"Not now, silly," she giggled girlishly.

"We're only young once," he said.

"So young." She laughed.

"Two virgins." He grabbed her again.

"Hold your wild horses," Esther said, pushing him out by the shoulders.

"Speakin' of horses, I'll let you know about Midnight Shadow as soon as I know."

"I'm excited!"

"Hey, my jacket! The one you fixed! I almost forgot."

She handed his jacket to him. "I'll do your pants tomorrow."

He kissed her hand.

"*Bonne nuit,*" Esther said dreamily, opening the door for him.

He bowed out of the doorway like a goddamn prince. As he walked to the stairwell, Lenny started to hum. "Da, da, da, da, da…"

Penthouse

Leah awoke with a start. She'd been chased by a dark-skinned man with a bleeding gash across his cheek. Who was he? She caught her breath, looked out the window. Darkness. She glanced at the clock. 8:30—a.m. or p.m.? A thick film of soot covered the single window.

Moving slowly, shifting her head from side to side, she tried to rouse her aching body. Get the blood moving inside her head. Ouch! She stretched her legs. It had been a long night. Her neck and shoulders hurt like hell. The last stretch began Friday morning. All those hours stooped over galleys, poring over each article until she thought she'd collapse at her desk.

It was the perfect job for her. Twenty hours plus overtime. Thursday, Friday, Saturday till however long it took. She had worked at *Newsweek* for four years, having started out as a proofreader. Now she was a copy chief. Hers were the last pair of eyes that saw the copy before it went to the printer. This week's issue had not been put to bed till eight that morning. It was almost ten by the time Leah lay down on her bed, dead and a half.

She stretched out her arms and sighed. 9:10—p.m., she thought. She could fall back asleep in a snap. But if she hoped to cop anything, she'd have to get her act together. Kofi didn't like waiting around.

Leah reached for her black sweater, slipping into its sleeves. She still felt overweight, though she was a hundred and eight pounds. It was her tits she detested. People were always staring at them. She'd surgically reduce them if she had the money. She pulled down her leather pants, slung over the closet door. The black skin slithered over her skinny ass as she tucked herself in. Then she sat down on the bed and laced her black boots.

Opening the top drawer of her desk, she removed a small plastic tube and twisted the cap off. Two black beauties rolled into the palm of her hand: dark, shiny ovals that looked like capsules of India ink. She swallowed one with a swig from a bottle of Tab. Leah threw on her black trench, shielding her bloodshot eyes with Ray-Bans. The door locked automatically behind her.

She took the stairs to the sixth floor, then pressed for the elevator. It came immediately. Leah stepped in as the guy with his bicycle followed her. Always giving her the once-over. Leah looked down. How she hated when people stared at her. Why couldn't someone have privacy in her life?

She let him go out in front of her, peeking out from the elevator door, looking in both directions. The lobby was empty. Thankfully, she didn't see anyone she knew. Bad enough having to live at the hotel and being subject to appraisal in the elevator. She hated people nosing around her business. New York City, the biggest zoo in the world, and still she ran into people she didn't want to see. She crossed Columbus Avenue briskly.

Even at eleven on a weeknight, 72nd Street buzzed. She had told Kofi to meet her at the Nickel Bar, which was just down the block from Stone Free, a boutique. It was that kind of neighborhood.

From the outside, the Nickel Bar looked like the other Irish bars in the neighborhood. Plain on the outside, with *GUINNESS* flashing in red neon. But it attracted a heavy trade. An interracial scene, lots of black guys hitting on white women, who often wanted exactly that—but not always. There were fights, and someone had been shot at the Nickel Bar. Besides, everyone knew its name referred to a nickel bag of dope.

Tap-a-Keg, "A Hell of a Joint" on 75th and Columbus, had had a shooting too. And Tweed's, farther down 72nd, west of Broadway, was the site of the *Looking for Mr. Goodbar* pickup. The murder inspired a book and a movie too. It also led to a name change: the All-State Café. That sounded sufficiently generic. I could give a Murder and Mayhem Walking Tour of Manhattan, she thought.

It was dark inside the Nickel Bar. Leah dropped her shades on her nose to check out the scene. Hard-drinking patrons sat at the bar, covered in a cloud of smoke. She walked past them to a stool at the far end.

"What are you drinking?" asked Peggy, who'd once been a dancer with Martha Graham. She wore a long braid down her back, large silver and topaz jewelry.

"Tab with a slice of lemon."

"Sure," Peggy said, smoking a Newport as she squeezed the hose and filled a glass. "Here."

She forgot the lemon, but Leah didn't want to bother her. She was wide-hipped now, with a Down syndrome daughter.

For a few minutes, Leah stared into the mirror. The liquor bottles created a prism of colors. The opening bars of the Bee Gees' "More Than a Woman." Leah spun on her stool to face the lit-up dance area, surrounded by ruby and emerald glass beads. They made a lovely tinkling sound when someone entered the magic circle. A mirrored globe slowly spun, throwing dappled light on the walls and the smooth wooden floor, which was empty.

Eyes shut, she imagined entering the magic circle. The colored beads shimmered in raindrops of light, swishing around her. Her body slinking across the dance floor, a snake woman slowly uncoiled as Barry Gibb's falsetto ran through her veins: "How deep is your love…"

Leah felt his presence before she knew it. Startled, she opened her eyes. A fine-looking black Ras with long dreadlocks, a single glittering gold tooth set in the center of his white pearlies, sat down next to her at the bar.

"Kofi!" she cried out.

"What's with the shade shit?"

"I could ask you the same thing."

"I always wear my shades," he said. "So how ya doin'?"

"What's happening with you?"

"Same old," Kofi answered. "Did you hear about Cathy Jones?"

"No, what?"

"She got busted."

"You're kidding." Leah dropped her voice. "How?"

"A narc," he said. "Some long-haired prick who fucked her."

"No shit." She shook her head.

"She sold him two joints," he said. "Can you believe it? How fucked-up is that?"

"Speaking of fucked-up," she whispered in his ear.

"Powda room?"

Leah put two dollars on the bar, then made her way to the back. Closing the bathroom door behind her, she checked out her reflection. Her hair needed washing.

A light knock on the door. "Kofi?" She opened the door for him.

"Hey, babe!" he said, leaning against the sink.

"You have a nickel?"

When Kofi smiled, his gold tooth glowed like sunrise on a New York skyline. "Prices are up, babe," he said. "My nickels are dimes."

Kofi went into his Guatemalan knapsack and took out a plastic baggie. She inhaled its bouquet. "Smells good."

"Mexican."

"How much?"

"Twenty-five."

"Would you accept twenty?"

"No can do."

Leah dug into her Indian bag for her wallet. "Here." She handed him a twenty and five singles.

He pocketed the cash, then gave her an approving appraisal. "You're attractive for a dyke."

"You're not bad for a male." She stuck the baggie into the inside pocket of her trench. "I like your dreads." She smiled. "How often you wash 'em?"

He took out a rolled joint, lit it, drew on it, passed her the joint. Leah inhaled deeply. "Mmmm," she said, sighing.

"Every two months," he said, twirling a braid around his finger. "But I clean them every day with a toothbrush."

He took another hit, gave her the joint again. She breathed in the smoke, beginning to cough suddenly.

"Easy does it," Kofi said.

She took a sip of her Tab. "I'm okay." She passed the joint back to him.

"You ready?"

She nodded.

Opening the door, fumes escaped into the area. An older black patron in a Yankee cap looked like he'd been waiting for the toilet awhile. He was pissed. "What the hell you been doing in there?" he demanded.

Kofi shrugged. Leah just looked down, her best defense.

After the door slammed shut behind them, they cracked up and slapped each other five. "As if he didn't know," Leah said.

"He's probably in there shooting up."

Outside the Nickel Bar, Kofi asked, "Which way you walking?"

"I live across the street."

"Where?"

"The Last Hotel."

"That dive?"

"What are you talking about?"

"That old place on the corner?"

"It's not a dive."

"Whatever you say." He shrugged. "Babe, did you get off?"

"A little," she said.

He flashed his golden smile. "I'm performing my poetry at the Nuyorican Café in a few. Send you a flyer."

"Hey, thanks, man."

Kofi's tooth lit up for a moment. "No problem. I like to help my friends," he said. She watched as he walked down 72nd Street toward Broadway, his dreadlocks bouncing on top of his Guatemalan knapsack.

Leah entered the lobby, making a beeline to the elevator. She pressed the button impatiently. She really didn't want to see anyone. The door opened immediately. It was empty. Thank God for small favors. She pressed 6.

Stepping out of the elevator, she opened the stairwell door and walked up a flight of metal steps. The plaster dust rose in a cloud as she closed the door. There were cans of paint, and a ladder leaned against the wall. Leah coughed as she turned the key. Someone had a sense of humor. Calling an attic the penthouse. The ceiling slanted down to a narrow triangle, where a single bed huddled at the point. There was a chest of drawers, a table, a sink and toilet in a closet. She, the daughter of Holocaust survivors, lived in the attic like Anne Frank, and if that wasn't fucking ironic.

Leah switched on the single bare bulb that lit her cell. God, the place sucked. But she had it gratis, and everyone knew the best things in life were never free. She could buy a lampshade, she supposed, but this was only temporary, until she could pay off some of her bills. Then she'd find her own place.

In April, Angela had asked her to move out of her loft on Wooster. Just like that. Said she didn't want to live together anymore. They'd been together for two years. Said she wanted to be free. There was someone else, of course, younger, with "less baggage," as she had put it. As if one's life could fit in luggage, SML. Small. Medium. Large.

Leah was screwed, big time. Deep in credit card 17-percent-per-month hell. She'd pissed thousands of dollars following the itinerant Angela to the Dominican Republic, where she researched an article, to New Zealand, during her summer vacation, always paying her own fare while Angela's were freebies. Post-Angela, she couldn't even scratch together an extra month's deposit. Though she hated to do it, she had contacted her father at the hotel.

Leah had known about the attic room, having played there as a child. "I just need someplace to crash for a few months," she told him.

"What are you crazy?" her father yelled into the phone, exactly as she expected. "It's not a place for a decent person to live. Why don't you come back home," Saul said. "You can have your room in the house. No one will bother you."

When she didn't say anything, he started up. "It's a shit hole! That's why I've never rented it. Why would you want to stay there when you could be perfectly comfortable?"

"You're not using it for anything," Leah insisted. She wasn't giving up.

"It's not legal for anyone to live there." He hemmed and hawed. "Let me talk to Luba," he said finally.

That was it. "What did you say?" she demanded. "You're going to ask *her* whether your own daughter can live in a hotel her father owns?"

"You know I'm just a partner," he said densely.

She began to shake with fury. "How could you?" The unsaid words. "Luba?" She spat the name. "A Polish *shiksa*. Do you remember how Mom and you carried on if I ever went out with someone who wasn't Jewish?"

"Mom did more than I did."

"Well, you went along with it."

"I went along with a lot of stuff I shouldn't have with your mom." He paused, then said, "Luba's family helped my family during the war. I knew her when we were both children. Leah, you have to move on with your life."

"Well, you certainly have," she said, beginning to tear up.

Her father just couldn't wait to get married again. It was thrift—as Hamlet said. The wedding expenses could be saved by using the funeral canapés. Actually it had been more than the prohibited year, three years and change, but who was counting? It wasn't as if time had made her loss any easier.

Her mother's death had been so fast. There were the stomach aches and gas. "Who goes to the doctor with an upset stomach?" Ruth insisted. Finally she went to the emergency room. A few tests later, the diagnosis: pancreatic cancer. Too late for surgery. The doctor advised against chemo. Quality of life, he said. She had died exactly a year after the news.

"When can I have the key, Dad?" Leah demanded.

"I could get Henry to do some painting and fix it up a little."

"I need a place now," she said.

"Monday," he answered.

"Nobody will even know I'm there," she told him. "I usually work at night. Don't worry. I won't stay here long. I just need to save some money."

"Will you come home for the holidays?" he asked. "It would mean so much to us."

She stared at him. "You know when I'll do that, Dad? Never. Understand. Never. And don't think you can pull strings—"

"Leah, I know you loved Mom..." His voice trailed off. Then he said in that wisdom-of-the-ages way: "You're still so young. We can never know what will happen to us. How we will feel. I loved your mother. Then I was alone, and it was terrible. I have Luba now, thanks God."

Leah scrutinized her face in the mirror. She didn't look like either of her parents. Maybe she was born to one of those relatives who got gassed by Hitler. A refugee changeling. It probably wasn't true, but she never felt part of her own family.

Leah emptied her plastic baggie on a record jacket, Jimi's afro aflame like a black sun god. She started up her turntable. The small pile of weed cast its fragrance.

> *Purple haze all in my brain*
> *Lately things just don't seem the same...*

First she crushed the bud, removing twigs, stems, and seeds, then tilted the record jacket. Using a matchbook cover, she swept through the dope so the good stuff slid to the bottom. She pulled out two Bambu papers, licked them together, and rolled a perfect joint. She tongued her doobie and wrapped it in the matchbook. It would make a good traveler.

Here at home, Leah preferred her hand-blown glass hookah, which she filled with ginseng tea. She sprinkled several flakes and lit up, drawing deeply on the long tube until the liquid in the bowl began to boil. The smoke floated up, filling her lungs. Like Alice's Caterpillar, she sat on her lily pad, sucking on the hose of her hookah, blowing smoke rings in the air. The scent from the sacred plant filled the room.

Oh, how she loved it. Gentle and green. When Kofi asked whether she got off, she hadn't, actually. She rarely did—with another person. She was just being polite. Smoking was a solitary activity for her. It wasn't about parties or sex, though that was fun, of course. Mainly, she did it for herself, to herself, by herself. It was a lifeline. Having grown up with the psychos, her parents, she should have an IV pumped directly into her veins.

A mild buzz kept the doctor away, she mused. Most of the time. Dope allowed her to live. To imagine. To have time off from her demons. There had been times she let someone in her lair. Oh, Angela. You bitch, you cunt...

A cockroach scurried across the floor, followed by another one. "Gross!" Leah stood up and stomped on both of them. Good thing she was wearing her boots. Maybe they were a couple.

She sat down and lit the hookah again. Its magic smoke surrounded her. She thought of Angela's white milky thighs. She could live there forever.

I'm acting funny and don't know why
Excuse me, Miss, while I kiss the sky.

Leah heard something. She jolted to attention. Someone was outside. She strained to listen. Standing up, she walked over to the door. Listened again, holding her breath. Now it was quiet.

Slowly, she pulled open the door a crack. No one. She opened it wider. Looking down at her feet, she saw a stack of books and a pair of brown gloves. She stepped out into the hallway. No one. She picked up the books. Stories by John Updike. And *Birds of North America. The Women's Room.* And a pair of blue cashmere gloves. She sniffed the gloves. They smelled freshly washed. Confused but not displeased, she carried her gifts into the apartment.

Suite 62

The stomach-churning sound of traffic at 4:55, then the assault. "TEN-TEN WINS, TEN-TEN WINS NEW YORK, TEN-TEN WINS..."

"Shut the fuck up, Ten-Ten Wins!" Fred Janov slammed the radio alarm with his fist.

Though his window faced an airshaft, he could tell it was still dark outside. When did goddamn daylight savings kick in? God, he hated to get up at this ungodly hour. That's what he had to do if he wanted to find anything before it was picked over by vultures.

Slowly, Fred lumbered toward the sink, careful not to upset any of his stacks of books. He didn't quite make it to the toilet, which was in the hall. He let the monkey roar, pissing in his sink, then ran the water. Sure, his mother didn't teach him that. So what? He washed his hands and face, rinsed his mouth from the faucet.

Switching the light startled a colony of cockroaches. They scurried for their lives. Fred chased them, banging the floor with a rolled up *New York Post*. Casualties were heavy. A few still wiggled their legs. He put them out of their pain, crushing them with his heel.

Fred looked around, shaking his head. What a dump. But it was his dump. He had lived in this small, funky room for over eight years. That was a long time. His first and only place in New York City.

He'd grown up so near, yet so far away—in the suburbs, Woodmere, to be exact. One of Long Island's "five towns," land of manicured lawns and nails, digging in, everyone striving, driven by the fierce desire to have and achieve more than their neighbors. It was a nightmare of upward mobility.

Fred was definitely downwardly mobile. By design. His dump was *cheep, cheep*. There were only three rooms on the sixth floor and a bathroom at the end of the hallway. Pete, the Teamster guy, lived next door. What a drunk. And down the hall, Duc, a Samoan, who worked as a bouncer at Studio 54. They all shared one toilet. Duc was a slob, leaving his hairs everywhere. The light was always on the blink. Fred was the only one who ever bought toilet paper.

He made his way gingerly across the floor, where books were stacked in order of subject. Art books fetched the highest prices, followed by hardcover philosophic and political tomes. Lots of romantic and detective novels. He had even found first editions with authors' signatures. This weekend he would set up in front of Zabar's.

He bent over to avoid the clothesline strung across the room. Single gloves and mittens of every hue hung like laundry in a country backyard. He'd been collecting them for years.

He liked singles. Half a pair of mittens. He liked to imagine where the other half might be. Just like him. He was single, had always been single. A singlet. Was his other half floating around somewhere? Someone tried to match him up with a not very attractive female photographer, but he had standards.

Another line held mufflers and hats, women's brown suede gloves. His smaller collections were scattered around the room: glass jars filled with keys and key chains, single earrings, watches, and false teeth. A basket of combs and brushes. Hundreds of pens jammed into coffee cans. Piles of hair barrettes and elastics. Sunglasses. In the corner, a wooden box filled with red sticks of dynamite. All found on the streets of New York City.

Fred picked up yesterday's clothes from the floor. He slipped into a stained white T-shirt with a red Rolling Stone tongue, soiled jeans, and torn gray windbreaker. Gathering several shopping bags, he folded and attached them to his bicycle with a bungee cord. He grabbed two thick chains and a Kryptonite lock, then threw an empty oversized knapsack over his shoulders. Guiding his bike by the handlebar, he pressed the elevator button.

This was his morning ritual. Wednesdays were best, when supers put out their buildings' trash to be collected. Or individuals tossed what they considered trash, which could include TVs in perfect working order, stereo systems with speakers, washers, dryers, sewing machines. The most amazing things! Brand new stuff that still had price tags. An unopened bottle of Charlie cologne. A tossed Jean-Claude Killy ski jacket. Gloria Vanderbilt jeans. A one hundred percent cashmere cardigan. Valuable things that just needed to be washed.

New Yorkers had too much money. That's all. They were suckers. They put out for the latest, most overpriced piece of crap. Like the pet rock. That's why the streets were filled with treasures just waiting to be picked—there for the taking, for those who opened their eyes and hands.

Once Fred was heading uptown on Amsterdam Avenue when he spotted something green lying in a puddle in the gutter. He picked it up to discover a hundred-dollar bill! Turning stealthily, he checked to see if anyone looked like they had lost something. No one did. People never stopped their ceaseless rushing on the street. He pocketed the bill, of course. It had been in full view, and no one saw it. They were blind. Or they just didn't give a goddamn.

New Yorkers had gotten too rich for their own good. Wait till the economy tanked. "Drop Dead, New York," President Ford said. The city was bankrupt, a tiny fleck of insanity floating out there in the United States of Amerika.

As Fred led his bicycle into the elevator, he felt the presence of another person. The woman from the penthouse stood in the corner of the elevator. He bowed his head, giving her a friendly nod. After all, there weren't too many people out at this hour. She ignored him. That was a punch in the gut.

Fred had never gotten rid of his adolescent acne. There was a gray pallor to his skin, and he was painfully skinny, as if he didn't eat enough. His hair looked wired, bolting away from his head in brownish gray clumps. He stepped out of the elevator, rolling his bicycle behind her. She took off, not even holding the door for him.

On the street, Fred hopped on his bike. As soon as he started pedaling, the wind and car exhaust in his face, he got the feeling. He was totally free! Free as a NYC pigeon. Neither rain nor snow could keep him off his bicycle, the best, fastest, and cheapest way to get around the city.

He came to an abrupt stop at the end of the block, 1 West 72nd Street, in front of the gated entrance to the Dakota. Now this was a gold digger's dream. Not the kind who married money but someone like yours truly who could dig in the muck. His eyes sparkled greedily.

Iron railings surrounded the building with mythological griffins and sea monsters. Fred put on his black rubber gloves and began opening the plastic bags. He pulled out a few things, which didn't interest him, then sealed the first bag securely. He didn't want to piss off the doormen, who watched him with nose-twitching disdain from their metal outhouses.

As he was going through another bag, he noticed a young girl pulling a brown and white spotted beagle. The dog's collar had silver spikes.

"Come on, Ruby!" the girl called, yanking the leash. "I said come on." The dog yelped.

"What are you doing?" Fred startled the girl.

"Ruby won't budge," she answered, tugging the dog's leash again. "The dog trainer told us beagles are stubborn."

"Don't you realize you're hurting your dog? Those spikes go right into her skin."

The girl gave him an insolent stare. "She's my dog."

Fred's eyes grew large and furious. "So you're going to torture a living being because she belongs to you? How would you feel if someone did that to you?"

Suddenly the girl burst into tears, running into the arms of a tall woman with frosted blonde hair.

"How dare you talk to my daughter like that?" she demanded.

"Why don't you teach your daughter not to strangle her dog?" he said.

"Excuse me," she said icily, dragging her daughter by the arm as a doorman whistled for a cab. The dog followed after them.

"Just ignore the crazy man," she said, pulling the girl behind her into the taxi. "Come on, Megan! Pick the dog up and put her inside!"

"You people have no heart," Fred said, continuing his search in the black plastic garbage bags.

He found a toaster oven, which he stuck into his knapsack, and leaped onto his bicycle. Then he turned uptown at Central Park West.

Fred had a system. He rode down 73rd Street with the traffic till he got to the Ansonia Hotel, a white beaux arts elephant, which occupied the whole block on Broadway. Caruso had lived there. So had Babe Ruth and most of the Yankee team.

His sharp eyes caught sight of something. Parking his bicycle by the building, he began to tug at what turned out to be a Persian rug in excellent condition. He could sell it to Ahmed. Fred rolled it up and attached the rug to his bike with a bungee. Continuing down the street, he saw a matching couch and loveseat, but what could he do with that? Then he went up 74th Street, following the direction of the traffic. A standing lamp with a tacky plastic shade. Not for him. Down 75th, up 76th, when he spotted several paper bags filled with books. This was his bread and butter.

He leaned his bicycle against a brownstone stairway. 76th Street was a good block, though it had its bad element. But on this part, between Amsterdam and Columbus, the brownstones had been gutted and turned into fancy co-op apartments. Rich people were beginning to buy up the neighborhood. The local laundromat had to sell out to fat realtors. More homeless people. More hunger. The way of the world.

Fred began removing books. *Steppenwolf* and *Siddhartha* by Hermann Hesse. Aldous Huxley's *The Doors of Perception. The Prophet.* Very nice. Dante's *Inferno. The Way of Zen* by Alan Watts. What a haul! These would go in five minutes. In another bag, a philosophy text, a pocketbook edition of *The Prince* by Machiavelli. Fred had read most of the books in college.

He'd been a philosophy major with a minor in poli-sci at Cornell. His expensive college education, paid for by his parents, prepared him to be a fleet cabdriver, a bicycle messenger, or to take a job in the post office. He was nouveau poor or had been for the last fifteen years, and proud of it.

He could have joined his father's business. Diamonds. Jewelry. Watches. Julius Janov had a booth in a large storefront in the Diamond District on 47th Street. Fred had tried it for a few years and made money but hated every moment. How you had to talk to customers, convince them to buy, bullshit for eight hours a day. Not for him. He preferred to work outdoors.

As Fred made his way home with his stash, he stopped in front of the Éclair bakery and locked his bike to a parking sign.

How he loved the smell! It brought him back to being a boy and going with his father on weekends to pick up rye bread and bialys. On the way home, they shared bread slices. It was about the only time he recalled Julius relaxing.

Fred checked out the shelf with day-old bread. He picked up a bag of onion rolls. Then he looked at the pastries. Ah, seven-layer cake. He remembered as a child, separating the layers, licking the chocolate cream. "I'll take one slice of the seven-layer," he said.

"One dollar twenty-five," a white-haired woman said, "and three rolls, seventy-five cents. That makes two dollars."

He dug into his jean pockets and gave her a handful of change. She stared at him as he counted the coins, shaking her head in disapproval. He didn't notice.

Outside, he attached the bag to the back of his bike, which he walked down the street.

When Fred returned to the hotel, Saul was already seated in the lobby, reading his *New York Times*. He looked up. "*Veys mir!*" he exclaimed. "Fred, what do you have there?"

"The usual," he answered.

"I just don't understand where you keep everything," he said, perplexed. "You have such a small room."

"Don't worry," he said, pushing his bicycle past him. "I sell most of it."

"Let me know if you see some more chairs like the wooden one you found me. And Henry needs a TV. His junkie son stole it."

"I'll keep my eyes open. Saul, there was a couch and loveseat on 73rd Street," Fred told him, "but it's probably gone by now."

Saul shrugged. "There's always stuff on the streets. Hana, you know the writer in Suite 55. She found a nice mahogany night table."

Fred hesitated for a moment. "Hey Saul, I heard something."

"Yeah?"

"Anyone going to buy this hotel?"

"Fred, you have a big mouth. No one's buying the hotel as long as I'm here."

"It's just a rumor I heard."

It was almost nine when Fred unlocked his door, wheeling the bicycle to the far corner, where he hung the back wheel from a large hook. He washed his hands in the sink, dried them on his pants. Then he opened his mini fridge and took out a container of milk. He poured himself a glass.

Fred sat down in his green La-Z-Boy, salvaged from the 77th Street trash, and served himself seven-layer cake on a paper plate, a glass of milk next to it. He turned on the TV, also a gift from the street, as well as the VCR. He pressed PLAY.

There was a several moment gap, then the movie began. Time for milk and cookies, kids. Fred took a forkful of the cake, licking the chocolate cream with his tongue. Then a sip of cold milk. He leaned back in his La-Z-Boy, sighed, as a young woman in a gold thong screamed in the throes of orgasm.

Suite 36

The next Friday, as Pincus prepared for Shabbes, there was a knock.

He opened the door to discover Faye standing in his doorway.

"You came back to me, Faigeleh!"

"Well, I figured you wouldn't come to me."

"I'm bashful," he admitted, looking down.

"I know," she said.

He smiled. "I was hoping, of course. It's almost Shabbes." His excitement was like a young boy's.

"Can I come in?"

"Yes. Yes." He followed her in. "I was about to light the candles."

Pincus gave Faye the matches, and she lit one candle, then he lit the other candle. They recited the Shabbat prayer.

"I think we should say now the *Shehechiyanu*," Pincus said.

"I don't really know it," Faye admitted.

"Ooh, the *Shehechiyanu* is very important. This is the female diety."

"I didn't know Jews have a goddess."

"Yes, yes, the feminine principle. But the *Shehechiyanu* is what we say when we start something new, or do something for the first time. Even if we buy something. People say it for a new pair of shoes, a new car."

"It's not our first date anymore. If you call this a date."

"I call it a treasure to be here with a beautiful woman."

"I like that." Faye smiled.

"I like you." He paused. "Faigeleh, this is my first time with a woman since Sylvie."

"That's something." She melted into his arms. He pulled away.

"First, the *Shehechiyanu*."

They both stood up. Pincus began. "Repeat after me:

Baruch Ata Adonai, Eloheynu Melech haolam,
Shehecheyanu, Vekiymanu, Vehigianu lazman hazeh."

He recited the prayer three times. Faye repeated the words.

"Blessed are You, Universal Presence, who keeps us in life always, who supports the unfolding of our uniqueness, and who brings us to this very time of blessing. Amen."

Faye turned to him. "I'm glad we waited."

He was staring at her cleavage, which rose like loaves of bread from her doughy skin. He bowed his head into her bower. "No more *vaiting.*"

Pincus took Faye's hand, leading her to his small bed covered with a white nubby bedspread. The lights from the candles glowed softly, coating their bodies in a golden radiance. Faye took him in her strong arms.

"You know what the Kabbalists believe?" Pincus whispered.

"No."

"When a man and his wife make love on a Friday night, they unite the male and female parts of God."

"We're not married."

He smiled. "It's a *mitzvah*, Faigeleh. A blessing."

"Okay."

"I'm not a fooling around guy."

"I know, Pinkeleh."

How he loved her full brosts. A man could live on those brosts, which lay on her chest like boulders, but soft as pillows. He wanted to nurse on her large nipples. His skin, white as parchment, wrinkled, but firm against hers. Her stomach flaccid, her legs snaked by varicose veins. His thighs, hers, her pubic hair, thin and wiry, his. His petzeleh climbed between her *brosts* like a *vilde chaya*, a wild animal, after a long winter's hibernation.

Lobby

Saul looked up to see Pete Mahoney still sitting on the turquoise vinyl couch by the elevator. He'd been there for an hour, holding a brown paper bag.

"Why aren't you working, young man?" Saul approached him. It was a joke between them. Pete was in his fifties.

"They canned me last week." Pete took a sip from a straw in the bag.

"That construction company?"

Pete shrugged.

"You getting unemployment insurance?"

"You bet."

"What are you drinking?" Saul asked.

"Misery loves company." Pete took another sip from the straw. "It lasts longer this way." He began a slow-motion forward lean.

Saul approached him. "Pete, you know you can't sleep here."

"I'm not sleeping." He slid further into the couch.

Saul tried to rouse him. "Pete!" He shook him. "Come on, you can't sleep in the lobby of the hotel. Do you hear me? PETE!" He shook him a little rougher.

Still no response.

"Pete!"

Saul unlocked his office. Inside, he found a bottle of seltzer. He carried it over to Pete, who had begun snoring. "PETE!" he yelled. When he still didn't stir, Saul shook the bottle of seltzer. Then, a stream of seltzer exploded over Pete.

Startled, he shook his head. "Wha' the fuck?"

"Go to your own place if you want to sleep."

Pete stood up unsteadily. "It's the company I like, Saul." He wiped his face with a red cotton handkerchief from his back pocket. "That wasn't very nice of you."

"Get out of here before I call the cops."

"You wouldn't do that."

"You're right. But go somewhere. I don't want to see your face."

"What's wrong with my face?" Pete pressed the elevator button.

"The only face I want to see as often as I see your face is my wife's."

"My wife, less was better." He opened the elevator door and entered. "Never was best."

Saul smiled to himself. The residents in the hotel. One character more *meshuggeh* than the next. But he loved to come here every day. To put on a clean shirt, a tie. The place had been good to him. He picked up the business page of the *Times*. He was checking his stocks when he noticed two men in suits enter the lobby.

The younger one, fair-haired, with a pudgy face and tinted aviator glasses, introduced himself. "Mr. Ehrlich, I'm Jonah Last. Viktor's son."

"I remember you," Saul said, staring up at his face. "I was at your bar mitzvah."

Jonah grinned. "Leonard's in Great Neck, Long Island."

"I have still the yarmulke." He looked at the kid. "How old are you?"

"Twenty-five."

"You're a very young man to have such a valuable property thrown into your hands."

He nodded. "I know." He paused. "And this is Jesse Hellman." The other man was short with dark hair and narrow eyes. "Jesse's my old friend and lawyer."

"Hellman," Saul repeated. "Is that your original name?"

"No. Horowitz," he answered.

"Horovitz. I knew a Horovitz. Where is your family from?"

"Lithuania," he answered.

"You're both Holocaust kids," he said. "Like my daughter, Leah."

"I remember her," he said. "What's she up to these days?"

He shrugged. "Who knows? So?" Saul stood up, taller than both young men. "What's up?"

"We want to talk to you. We also want deli at Fine and Schapiro's across the street. Would you like to join us?"

Saul looked doubtful, then agreed. "I can get away for a few minutes."

As he walked behind them, he noticed that Jonah wore a black ski jacket with white passes attached to a metal square. Saul tried to imagine Viktor or any of them skiing down a mountain.

"Lean pastrami sandwich, please. And a cream soda," Jonah ordered from the elderly waiter, who appeared almost immediately.

"What about you, Saul?" Jonah asked. "This one's on me."

He shook his head. "I ate already."

Jesse ordered a corned beef sandwich and a Heineken.

"All right. A cup of tea with lemon for me," Saul added.

The waiter walked away with a slight limp.

Jesse plucked a sour pickle from a metal dish and took a bite. "I forgot what real pickles taste like."

Jonah began. "As you know, my father, Viktor, passed his share of the hotel to me. That's forty-five percent."

"Are you married?" Saul asked.

"No." He shook his head. "Not yet."

"Neither is my daughter," he said.

"Anyway, what we came to talk to you about is we're offering all the partners—"

"How is Viktor doing down there?" Saul asked.

"He loves Florida. Goes to the swimming pool. The Jacuzzi. He and my mom eat Early Bird Specials. The Chinese buffet. They're in heaven."

Saul shook his head. "Not until they put me in a box."

The waiter returned, leaning over to place Saul's tea in front of him. "Cream soda and Heineken," he mumbled.

"Still the same rude waiters," Jonah said, as the man walked away.

"It's part of the décor." Jesse took a sip of his beer.

"As I was saying," Jonah continued, "Viktor's share is 45 percent. There are four other partners, three with ten and you with your 15 percent."

Saul looked up. Ronald Reagan and his wife smiled from the TV set.

"Only in America can an actor run for president," Saul commented.

"He's got some good ideas," Jesse said.

"He's an ignoramus!" Saul said, raising his voice.

"All right," Jonah said. "Anyway Saul, we know you've done a good job as the manager. We are aware of that."

"Thank you." Why was he glad-handing this arrogant whippersnapper?

"And we want you to continue, of course. But we're making offers to all the partners. We want to buy out your share."

"Go on," Saul said, calculating numbers in his brain, betting on their generous offer. Ten thousand? Fifteen? Twenty? Fifty? Seventy-five?

"We know you paid ten thousand dollars."

"That was in 1960."

It had taken all his energy to save that amount. How he had worked overtime at the factory, into the early hours of the morning; how he had begun to play the stock market, studying the columns of numbers till he knew them by heart.

Jonah's voice brought him back. "What do you think your share is worth?"

"What I want to know is why you want to buy our shares," Saul said.

Jonah and his shrimp of a lawyer looked at each other.

At that moment, sandwiches arrived. Huge, over-stuffed, rye bread slices balanced on several inches of red meat. Cole slaw and potato salad on the side. Jonah took a rhinoceros-sized bite. Oh, those beautiful white teeth must have cost Viktor a pretty penny.

"I promised my father I would be generous to you. We're prepared to offer twenty-five thousand dollars."

"It's a substantial buy-out," Jesse added.

Saul nodded. "Well, I can retire and live on that."

"No one's talking about retiring. You're a good manager, and we want you to continue. Things won't change too much. And we'll keep Henry on, of course."

"Twenty-five thousand dollars is a lot of money."

"Yes, so?"

"Who's paying for this thing?"

Jesse interrupted. "I don't think that's your concern, sir."

"You want to sell the hotel, and you don't think that's my concern?"

Jonah looked at Jesse, who gave a slight shake of his head.

"We're not planning to do anything at this point."

"Why do you want our shares?"

"It's a business decision," Jesse the lawyer declared.

He could have bought the Last Hotel in 1972. Saul recalled that Otto Stern, the original owner, offered to sell it to Saul. "I can't take the aggravation no more," he had told him. He wanted a hundred and twenty-five thousand dollars in cash. It was a steal.

Saul could have raised the money, but he was afraid. And he had no family to help him with the business. Certainly not Leah, who was just going to college.

"What about the other partners?" he demanded.

"We've contacted them too."

"How come they didn't speak to me about it?"

"We told them it was confidential, just as we'll tell you," Jesse said.

"Listen, you. I could've bought the hotel a few years ago. They wanted twelve point five down in cash. Now it's worth over a million dollars. And you think you can buy my share for twenty-five thousand? Add another zero and we'll talk."

"I don't know where you get the figure of a million dollars. That's not happening yet on the West Side," Jesse said.

"It's a generous offer, Saul," Jonah said, smiling with his gorgeously straight, white American teeth.

"I'll think about it," Saul said, pushing his chair back.

"Don't think about it too long, please," Jonah said.

"What does that mean?"

The other man answered. "Mr. Ehrlich, with all due respect, we wish to finalize the matter."

"What about the hotel?"

He shrugged. "Residential hotels are going out of business all over New York. The city is broke. Unless you're the Plaza or Waldorf, it doesn't make sense anymore. People will pay hundreds of thousands of dollars for co-op apartments and condominiums. This property has an excellent location."

Saul stood up to his full six feet. "This isn't just a job, all these years. It isn't just a property. I've made the Last Hotel what it is. I installed an automatic elevator that saved thousands of dollars the hotel was spending on the elevator men." He paused for a moment. "What about the people who live in the hotel?"

"We'll have to see."

Saul peeled two dollars from his money clip. "That should cover my tea."

He walked out on 72nd, crossed the street, continuing to Columbus Avenue. Jonah. That awful son of Viktor's should only be swallowed by a whale. He would be swallowed soon because there were much bigger, shrewder fish out there in the ocean. As for himself, Saul thought, he was just a minnow, actually a slippery eel. How he had slithered through the camp on his stomach. That's all they were. Hungry stomachs. And he had bribed his way to work in the kitchen, where he traded food for favors. So he could live. For this. He stopped to catch his breath.

Suite 52

Amber sat down on her brass-post bed to pull on her stockings. She leaned back against a pink satin pillow. A white fur had been thrown over the headboard. A large mirror in a gilt frame dominated one wall.

She wriggled as she tucked her shirt into a black silk skirt, slit up the front leg to reveal sheer black hose and fuck-me high heels. Underneath her Henri Bendel beige gauze shirt, Amber wore a flesh-colored lace brassiere adorned with lilac tulle. So girlie. Spraying a cloud of Parfum de Joy, she grabbed her Burberry trench and umbrella, in case.

Her chariot descended five floors. As she clip-clopped past Saul, who was sitting at his desk, she gave him a flirtatious wave of her head, her honey-dipped auburn hair spilling over her shoulders.

"How you doing, Saulie?"

As she waited for him to look up from his newspaper, she wondered whether he knew. The only one she'd ever told was Hana, who lived next door. She said, "I don't care. You're my girlfriend."

"You don't look so good," she told him.

"The hotel." He shook his head.

"What?"

Saul lowered his voice. "My partner passed onto his son his share. He's the big man, Viktor. So he moved down to Fort Lauderdale. And now the son's buying the partners out." He looked around the lobby. "They're turning all this to garbage."

"That's terrible."

"They want to buy me out. After all I've done."

"What a crying shame," Amber said. "I like it here. Everyone likes it here, Saul."

"Look, for the time being, things are supposed to stay the same, but I wouldn't count on it."

She shook her head. "Can't we do anything?"

"You have weekly rentals. And no lease," he said. "It's a hotel."

"There's a man I know," she began thoughtfully. "Lots of money. Kind of a sugar daddy type, not that he's my sugar daddy."

"Forget about it. It's a done deal."

"Well, I guess I have to start to look around, Saul. Thanks for the heads up." She looked at him. "How sad. The Last Hotel is a lovely place. I'm really sorry."

"That little stinker," he said. "I was at his bar mitzvah."

"The younger generation is lazy and shiftless," Amber said as she walked out the door. "I know with the girls I manage at the store."

"Have you talked to Duc yet?" he asked, following her out.

She shook her head. "I never see him."

"He told me he works at a place called Studio 54. You ever heard of it?"

"Oh, it's very famous. Mick Jagger goes there."

"Who?"

"Andy Warhol."

"The one who paints the soup cans?"

She nodded as she walked through the lobby.

Outside, a cab careened down 72nd Street. Amber hailed it. "Lord and Taylor, please." As she sat back in the seat, she said to herself, Studio 54, huh?

Not in her wildest daydreams in Butte, the butt of her Montana childhood, had she ever imagined that her days would be spent in a pouf of gossamer lace, draping straps with pearly swans. So soft, so silky. Black lace bustiers with shimmery satin ribbons, hothouse-hued bikini panties that seemed to have a life of their own, fluttering before her eyes like antic butterflies. This was female heaven. The Intimate Apparel department of Lord & Taylor.

She used to work on the main floor in Fragrances, ambushing innocent women with showers of Shalimar, sprays of Tabu, My Sin, and Madame La Roche. Carlo had manned the Brut counter. A lovely young gay boy, he wore tight muscle shirts, gold jewelry, sideburns like Tom Jones. He called her "mi bonita." They dished for hours. Then he got a job at Chippendales, where suburban wives stuffed twenty-dollar bills in his golden jockstrap. Adios, my sweet.

Her nose perked up. Amber was definitely olfactory by nature. Such a strange, ugly word for that most acute and ancient sense. So many, too many scents surrounded her, but her favorite was still Joy. She was loyal. Parfum, of course. Never eau de toilette. What a horrible expression. She sniffed her wrist—the scent of white roses on a cool winter's day.

With her flaming auburn tresses, her glittering emerald eyes, Amber was empress of the shop. There were salesgirls on the floor who wore icky blue badges with their names and *HOW CAN I HELP YOU?* Not Ms. Amber, manager of the department.

Some customers came especially to see her. They regarded Amber as a sorceress with magic powers and brought her their problems of the heart. She prescribed lingerie and fragrances to fan wandering lovers' flames.

How strange life was when you were all female except in a few but significant ways. What did it mean to be female? To be a circle with a cross rather than possessing the trajectory of an arrow? Amber was both and had been since she realized she wanted to go to her senior prom as a girl.

Now she was Cinderella awaiting the transformation, but she didn't have to go to a ball, get kissed by a prince, fit into a shoe. Doing it herself for herself. Just be the woman she had always been, though everyone tried to convince, cajole, punish her for this fact of her life.

Dr. Tannenbaum once asked her if she ever worried that she might change her mind. Never! She was absolutely, positively sure that she had zero desire to live in a smelly, hairy, disgusting male body again. Just the thought of it was revolting. But that didn't mean she would mind having one inside of her.

She knew how men were, having been one herself. The messy, chauvinistic beasts! Yet she couldn't help loving them anyway. Not as a faggot, mind you, but as a passionate, loving woman!

She knew women through her heart and sympathies, even if her face had a late afternoon shadow if she didn't shave. Electrolysis, depilatories—ugly, ugly, ugly. It wasn't easy being a girl. Especially when you were born missing certain things and endowed with too much of other things. Never mind that.

Thank God for reconstructive surgery. Amber checked the mirror, smiling at her reflection, then she rehung a rose-colored nightgown with a matching robe, white rabbit fur on the hem.

Amber never understood why some TVs went through all the hormones, the injections, the operation—only to become matronly drones, donning thick wool suits, chunky shoes, support hose, and pearls. You might as well be an ugly guy. That way you could at least shtupp your ugly wife.

Did clothes make the man or woman, as the case may be? She glanced over at the Lady Marlene counter, Bali, Lilyette, Maidenform, Olga, and the Oscar de la Renta sleepwear collection. "It is better to look good than feel good," said Oscar Wilde. She wanted both.

The good doctor had asked her if she thought about having a child. Some transsexuals found themselves wanting to adopt. "Not me," she told him. "I want to take care of my own feminine self for a while."

What did she really aspire to in her life—besides cutting off her dick? Though no one knew it, not even the shrink, Amber studied photography at The New School.

She has been documenting her alteration. Over the last nine months, once a week, Sunday mornings, at the same time her family went to St. Agatha's Passion in Butte, Montana, she stood naked against a white wall as a Leica mounted on a tripod snapped shots.

Once, she had arranged several pillows on the floor so she seemed to rise out of the sea like Venus. It was all on film: the new curves, her breasts as they blossomed out of her chest (with a little help from the surgeon), her testicles as they receded. Like filming her own birth. She was her own creator and creation.

The hormones made her crazy, of course. Do you know how to make a whore moan? Don't pay her. She used to be a gentle guy; now she was a fucking femme fatale!

A dark-haired young woman in blue jeans strode past her. She reminded her of Hana, her next door neighbor at the hotel, who dressed like she was still in college. Now that was a case. She could be attractive if she did something like wear a bra. Floppy, floppy. Brassieres just give you a better line, she told Hana. It's not like she had tight little buttons either. They were C cups that dangled like loose sacks. Hana's answer: breasts are meant to roam free. What's wrong with a little bounce? That kind of attitude could put the Intimate Apparel department out of business.

Once Amber even brought Hana a flesh-toned Vanity Fair bra that hooked in the front. Hana thanked her, said she loved the gesture, but did she wear the bra? Not that Amber could see. Floppy, floppy. Ms. Natural with disgusting hairy pits. Luckily Hana shaved her legs because with her dark hair, she'd look like a gorilla.

Amber shook her head. Monica, the soap opera star from the fourth floor, bought out the shop the other day. A regular shopaholic. What was her story? She was a beautiful woman but a lousy actress. Amber couldn't stand her in *Forgive Us Our Passions*. She paced. She had to think about something as she stood there, looking gorgeous, trying to lure some unsuspecting gal into her lair of feminine fantasy. That's when she spotted her next victim, swiftly approaching.

They'd been together all night! Faye was floating on a cloud of post-coital intoxication. She'd forgotten the power of eros. How was that possible? Faye felt like Sleeping Beauty arising from a long sleep, covered with brambles and thistles. Rapunzel, let down your hair! An aging romantic. That's what she was. And how absurd was that?

"Excuse me," she said breathlessly to Amber. "Can you help me?"

"Don't I know you?" Amber asked.

"You live in the hotel, don't you?"

"Oh, yes. What's your suite number?"

"Thirty-two. And yours?"

"Fifty-two," Amber answered.

Faye looked embarrassed. "I need a…uh…an undergarment. But it's been so long, I don't know what to buy. Really, I don't know who I am—in that way. Do you know what I mean?" She was flustered. "Especially with my new…" She hesitated, then sighed with emotion. "My new lover!"

"Ooooh," Amber crooned, surprised that this older woman was even having sex. "Lucky you. Anyone I know?"

Faye looked down mysteriously.

"Does he live in the hotel?" Amber guessed.

She nodded.

"Well?"

"Can you keep a secret?"

Amber grinned. "To my death, and beyond."

"You've seen him."

"Not the taxi driver!" Amber cried out.

"Lenny?" she said in disbelief. "God forbid."

"Who?" Amber asked.

"Pincus," she whispered his name. "Please don't tell anyone."

"You mean the old Yiddish guy?"

She exploded with a passion that could not be suppressed. "He's a god! Sexier than men thirty years younger."

"You take my breath away!" Amber said.

"And such a gentleman! My heart is full! I've been dying to tell someone. But please, swear to me, not a word to anyone."

"My lips are sealed."

"Pincus is a widower," Faye continued confidentially. "His wife died eleven years ago, but he still mourns her."

"How sweet is that."

"I know. I was really touched."

"What did you do? I mean, how'd you get together?"

"I brought him my beef brisket."

"What?"

"I made a brisket and brought it to him. Single men don't get home-cooked meals," she added.

Once again, humanity astonished her. Who would've thought it? She looked at Faye's cheap dye job, her creased face, very generous ass. She could have been attractive in her youth, but now she was well past her first and second bloom. Yet, somehow, despite life's cruel tricks, she was still out there, playing her best hand. It was inspiring, really!

Faye picked up a black chiffon camisole, fingering the straps.

"This is a popular style," Amber said.

Faye checked the price tag.

"Sixty-five dollars! That's too popular for me," Faye said. "Besides what I need is a brassiere. Sexy, but not too. Not X-rated, if you know what I mean."

Amber stared at her. Did she miss something? What movie was she talking about?

"One that hooks in the front," Faye continued. "That maybe has lots of hooks?"

"Do you know your size?" Amber asked, taking a tape measure out of her pocket.

"Thirty-eight C."

"An underwire?"

She nodded wryly. "I'm afraid so."

"Here's something for you," Amber suggested, showing her a coffee-colored silk bra with beige lace trim. Faye looked at the price tag. "I don't think so. Is anything on sale?"

"Sure. On the table in the corner. Why don't you see if you like something. Then I'll try to find it in your size."

"Great." That's what rang her bell. Faye never met a SALE sign she could walk past. Fifty percent off was an aphrodisiac. She walked off, swinging her large hips. Though she could afford to lose twenty pounds, Faye had an appealing sensuality.

Amber gave her a few minutes, then approached. "Did you find anything?"

"I love this one!" Faye exclaimed, handing it to Amber.

The brassiere was right out of *The Story of O*. A black lace push-up with six hooks in front and a red satin ribbon. "Pincus will like this one," Faye whispered.

"Just don't give the poor man a heart attack!" Amber teased.

Faye grinned sheepishly.

"Let me see if I can find it in your size."

In a few moments, Amber returned. "You're lucky. We have it." She handed her a black brassiere with trailing purple ribbons. "Is purple all right?"

"Oooooh!" Faye shivered with delight.

"He will love it," Amber said.

"So will I!" Then she looked down at the price tag and was stricken. Thirty-five dollars. "Oh," she said. "I thought it was on sale."

"It is," answered Amber. "It was originally seventy-five dollars."

"I can't." Faye shook her head.

"Why?"

"I've just never bought anything like this," Faye said. "It's such an extravagance."

"I can't do anything about the price," Amber said. "Go on. Try it on."

"What can I say?" She shrugged. "It's not who I am to spend so much on something like that. I wish I could."

"You could ask yourself what's it worth to you."

"A bra?"

"A feeling."

"Feeling, shmeeling. Thirty-five dollars? There are homeless people in the subway," Faye declared.

What was anything worth? Amber could go through law school and then some with what she was spending on the operation. And it wasn't covered by medical insurance. Elective surgery. Ha! More like a birth defect.

"Just try it on. See what it looks like," Amber suggested.

She led Faye to a mirrored room and closed the curtain. Faye unhinged her white cotton brassiere, yellowed and stretched out from too many washings. She studied the black lace push-up with six hooks in front and a purple satin ribbon.

Slowly, she slipped the black lace over her pendulous breasts, inhaling as she snapped the silver hooks. She took another breath before opening her eyes. There she was in the full-length mirror. For a moment, she didn't recognize her own breasts. The purple satin ribbons glowed, and she had a lovely dipping cleavage.

"Oh, to be a sexual siren at sixty..." she told her reflection. "Not being put out to pasture quite yet. Keeping it up, pulling it in, the body...Oh!" She thought of Pincus.

"Very nice, indeed," Amber said when Faye opened the curtain.

"Amazing, actually," Faye said. "I don't think I should."

"Listen, why don't you take the bra home with you? Show it to Pincus!" Amber proposed. "Model it for him."

"I will!" Faye gasped with pleasure.

"If you don't want to keep it, you can have your money back. Just hold on to the receipt."

Faye's face flushed with pleasure and a little shame as she passed the contraband black brassiere with trailing purple ribbons to a gum-chewing girl with black talons. She didn't bother to notice her customer as she rang up a major purchase in Faye's life.

"Enjoy," Amber said.

Their eyes met. Faye raised her forefinger to her mouth. Amber nodded knowingly, sealing the zipper of her magenta lips.

She thought of Saul. What a matchmaker. But she had noticed Duc on the elevator. How could she not? He was at least 6'6" with latte skin and black hair to his waist. What a total hunk of fine maleness!

Lobby

Saul unlocked his office and went inside. He picked up his old black phone and dialed Bolek. "When did they contact you?"

"You don't say hello first?"

"When did they contact you?"

"A while ago."

"When, Bolek? Tell me," Saul demanded.

"A few weeks ago. Then they called again. We can't do nothing about it."

"And you didn't tell me?"

"I thought you knew," Bolek said, sounding sheepish. "They told us not to talk about it."

"And you listened?"

"You know, the hotel hasn't been doing so good."

"What's wrong with you? Don't you see what's going on? They want to buy our shares and sell the building."

"It's a decent offer. Frankly, Saul, I need the money. Vanda hasn't been so healthy. We have doctor bills."

"How much?" Saul demanded.

"How much you?"

He grumped.

"The number, Bolek."

"You."

There was a moment's silence at both ends of the phone.

Thirty-five years ago, Saul and Bolek had dealt deutsch marks in Berlin's black market after the war. Both had shared a jail cell for six months. Bolek had been in Treblinka; Viktor, Bergen-Belsen. Janusz had some story of several different camps, finally dumped in Sobibor. Heniek, Auschwitz. All were alumni of the same universe.

The Survivors. They had been viewed as victims when they first arrived in the early fifties. Nothing in their pockets. Distant relatives but no real family. They were awkward, nervous, grasping. Their English wasn't good. Refugees. Greenhorns. Dirty, possibly diseased Jews, who had suffered terribly. No one really wanted to look at them or know their stories.

The men got together on Friday nights. Seated at a card table in one of their living rooms, they pitched quarters, dealt cards, spoke Yiddish. Summers, they installed their families in bungalow colonies with names like Blue Paradise in the Catskills. During the week, they sweated in the city. But there was fresh air for their wives and children. Later, they went into real estate together, bought brownstones uptown and finally, the Last Hotel.

"Did you talk to Janusz?"

"He's happy to take the money and run away. Janusz is living with his daughter in Petah Tikvah. They contacted his lawyer."

How could he have not known this? It was like during the war. People didn't stick together. That was a fairy tale. They stole from each other. Every crumb of bread, meat, bone. Bolek, who he'd known since the ghetto.

"How much did they offer you?" Saul asked again.

"Okay. Ten thousand."

"I see. Did you sign something?"

"Yes," he admitted reluctantly. "They gave us bonuses to sign within twenty-four hours."

"How much?"

"Five thousand."

"And you didn't talk to me?" he demanded. "Idiots! IDIOTS! That's what you are. Do you have any idea how much the hotel is worth?"

"Who told you they were selling it?"

"Grow up, Bolek. I made a mistake. I thought you were an intelligent man."

"Vanda is ill. We need the money," he repeated.

"The hotel is worth close to a million dollars! A million dollars. And he gives you fifteen thousand?" Saul laughed.

"What did he offer you?"

"More, because I have 15 percent and manage the hotel."

"How much?" Bolek demanded.

"Twenty-five."

"The bastards."

"They bought you cheap," he said. "Not me! Not those wet-around-the-ear little Hitlers. I'm not going to just roll over. Not me!" Saul dropped the receiver with a loud bang.

Oh no! He picked it up. There was a crack in the plastic. He'd have to replace it. A phone wouldn't cost so much. Why was he worried about the hotel's phone? He wanted to smash it into smithereens.

It was over. The change wouldn't happen right away, but he could feel it. This was the beginning. His life floating away from him.

At that moment, Hana from Suite 55 entered, holding a bag of groceries from Pioneer. "Are you all right, Saul?" she asked gently.

"Why shouldn't I be?" he demanded.

"It's just that—"

"It's just that it's none of your business," he barked, picking up his newspaper. "Everyone in America wants to know how you feel." The pages shook in his hands. "Their stupid smile buttons. Have a great day."

Hana said nothing as she pressed the elevator button.

After a few minutes, Saul stood up. Picked up his phone book, flicking through the pages. Lamm. Lap. Last. He would make the call. Even though it was long distance. He would speak to Viktor. Though he hadn't seen him in several months, they could always talk honestly. Did he know what his son was doing? Viktor Last started the hotel with Saul. It was goddamn named after him.

Viktor picked up immediately. "So how are you, Shlomo?" He called him by his Yiddish name.

"How do you think I am? Don't tell me you don't know what's going on with your son and that lawyer of his."

"Say hello, how are you, you bondit. You think I'm happy with the mess he's making? My Jonah. Trying to be a big businessman. Between us, he don't know nothing."

"Why, Viktor? We built the Last Hotel together. Remember when Anthony Quinn used to come to visit his sweetie? And it made money for us."

"Sorry, Saul. It's his business now. I signed the papers over, and I'm not putting my nose into it. I told him, 'Jonah, don't take a good business and turn it into shit.'"

He coughed loudly. "You see, my lungs aren't what they were. I have a heart murmur. I can't do it no more. Too much stress. After what we went through. So who else could I pass on my business to?"

"Why didn't you talk to me?"

"First of all, you're not so easy to talk to. You'd be screaming your head off!"

"I am screaming my head off, but the volume is turned down. How could you do such a thing without telling me?"

"You of all people should understand. He's my blood. I'm taking it easy. Why not? The weather is beautiful here."

"He's bought the other partners out. And he wants to buy my share."

"Shlomo, this is the future you're looking at. People don't care about residential hotels no more. They don't make sense anymore. Either you have a residence, or you stay in a hotel."

"Enough already, Viktor. You've slit my throat, thank you very much."

He hung up the broken phone receiver.

Suite 21

He'd called her twice. Monica liked his persistence. She would just pay Dr. Tannenbaum a neighborly visit. He was her neighbor. A psychotherapist. Since she was on a diet, she would withhold her favors.

She slipped into her turquoise and black striped Betsey Johnson one-piece jumpsuit, snapping closed the myriad of hooks from neck to crotch. She had worn it to Studio 54, where she met Enrico. It was her version of a chastity belt. She spritzed herself with Obsession.

After her therapist, Pauline, had listened to her most recent miserable romance, she insisted that Monica go on a diet. No men allowed. "Every time we build up your self-esteem and you're functioning well, some man comes along, who you allow to rip the foundation we've worked so hard to build. Then we have to start all over again." She had looked hard at her. "Monica, the only power a woman has is in her work."

"*Voulez-vous couchez avec moi ce soir...*" crooned the radio. "We have nothing to be guilty for our love..."

It was the end of the seventies, when everyone fucked anyone if they danced well or had a nice smile. Out of curiosity, as a form of knowledge, recreational exercise, and free entertainment.

Hey, it might be nice to have a friendly neighbor at the hotel. That way she could borrow more than a cup of sugar. But would she have to tell Pauline? Someone was holding the elevator upstairs. She pressed the button again.

When the elevator finally arrived, the door slid open. The woman from the penthouse stood against the far wall in her dark glasses, black trench, and fedora getup. She didn't look up.

"Hi," Monica said as she entered.

The woman glanced at her momentarily, then down at her feet. She wore high black lace-up boots. Who was she? And why was she so unfriendly? The elevator stopped on the second floor. Monica walked out. The woman looked away as the door shut.

Monica examined the brass plate. Rang the doorbell. After a few moments, Dr. T. opened the door.

"Well, hi ..." he said, checking out her snug jumpsuit. A big smile spread across his face. He wore a loose-fitting Indian gauze shirt, red Guatemalan sash, and white drawstring pants with no underwear.

"Hi," she said, hesitating in the doorway. She was used to seeing him dressed in a sport jacket and pants. It was better than a leisure suit, she supposed. She wondered what Pauline would think of this.

"Come in, come in. I'd given up hope," he said.

"I had my doubts. I mean, we don't know each other."

"So you took a risk, Monica," he responded.

"Said like a therapist."

"Actually, I'm a psychologist."

She'd been curious about him, but now she felt self-conscious as she followed him inside his suite.

"I have a nice bottle of wine for us," he said, ducking into his tiny kitchenette, which looked just like hers: a double-burner hotplate, half fridge, small sink.

She walked into the inner sanctum: his office. There were framed diplomas on the wall. *RONALD TANNENBAUM, Ph. D., ADELPHI UNIVERSITY. RONALD TANNENBAUM, M.S.W., HOFSTRA UNIVERSITY.* Standard shrink décor with minor variations: black leather Eames chair with matching ottoman, the patient's chair, a smaller version, like Momma Bear's. Glass coffee table, chrome legs. Art deco ashtray. The jumbo tissue box.

That got to her. How many tissue boxes had she emptied during her sessions with Pauline. When she asked her whether it was normal to cry so much in a session, Pauline had said, "When I was in treatment, my analyst said, 'If you get us a pair of oars, we can row out of here.'"

As she wandered around the room, she glanced at his books: *The Neurotic Personality of Our Time*: *I'm Okay, You're Okay*; *The Primal Scream*; *Between Analyst and Analysand*; *Dynamics of Group Therapy*. It made her nervous, but curiously turned her on too.

And the shrink couch covered in a colorfully knitted Afghan with a white cloth napkin and pillow for the patient's head. She sat on it, then stood up again.

He brought out a bottle of wine. With much ceremony, he uncorked the bottle.

He raised the cork to his right nostril and sniffed with discrimination. Then he passed the cork to Monica. "Chateau Sainte Colombe Cotes de Castillon. Take a whiff," he said.

She did. "I don't really know wine."

He poured the wine into two cut crystal glasses he had placed on the wooden table. "Here we are." He handed her a glass. It had a rich ruby sheen. "Skol."

They clinked glasses.

She took a sip and licked her lips. "Mmm."

"I visited the vineyard in Bordeaux. A beautiful villa with grapevines overhanging the balcony. They served the most amazing brie."

"Very nice," she said, looking around. "Do you have another room?"

"Come see my boudoir," he said, taking her hand. They entered a small room, darkened with rice-paper shades. A waterbed with black satin sheets took up most of the space, mirror on the ceiling. There were lit candles on a wooden mantle. It was almost religious.

"Is this where you conduct séances?" she asked.

"Did you know when two people go to bed with each other, there are at least four other people in the bed, usually more." He sat down on the bed. The waves whooshed behind him.

"Past lovers," she said.

"Our parents. They always hover over the bed." He drew Monica to him on the bed. She rose on a wave, then fell as the bed rippled.

"I should have brought my bathing suit."

"You can go skinny-dipping."

"I don't think so."

"I like you," he said, reaching for her hand.

"You don't know me."

"I've seen you on the elevator for months."

"I've seen a lot of people on the elevator," she said, trying to stand. The undertow of the bed held her as she tried to find a solid spot to hold. "But I don't get into bed with them. That's not why I came here." She grabbed the frame of the bed and shot up.

"Hey," he called after her. "I just wanted to show it to you."

"I saw it."

Back in his office, she went for the larger chair and sat down. "That's my chair!" he said.

"Why don't you sit in the patient's chair," she said, putting her feet on the ottoman. "For a change of pace."

"How does it feel?" he asked.

"Like I could charge seventy-five bucks an hour," she answered, leaning back. "I could definitely grow to like this." She turned to him seriously. "So tell me about yourself."

"What do you want to know?"

"What do you want to tell me?"

"Good," he said.

"Are you single?" she asked.

"I am now," he said. "I was married for a few years. And you?"

"Never married."

"Have you been at the hotel long?" he asked.

"About a year and a half. When I got my role on the soap, I wanted to be able to walk to work."

"Would you like another glass of wine?"

She nodded. "Why not? I don't have to drive."

He filled their glasses. Feeling nervous, she gulped it down. He refilled her glass.

"Why did you become a shrink?"

"I have to tell you I detest that term."

"Okay. What do you call yourself?"

"A clinical psychologist."

"I'm in therapy," she volunteered brightly.

"Why?" he asked.

The words were out of her mouth before she knew it. "Because I have trouble with men."

He smiled like the Big Bad Wolf. "What does that mean?"

Little Red Riding Hood suddenly realized she was in trouble. "Can we change the subject?"

"Of course."

"Where's that little elephant?" she asked.

He grinned at her. "Why not?"

He pulled out the white ceramic elephant from his pocket and handed it to her. The pipe had a lovely stone coolness, or was it stoned coolness? She caressed it with her fingers. "Where'd you get this?"

"India," he told her. "I was there when the Beatles were."

"What were you doing?"

"Meditation. I had a guru. You know…the George Harrison trip."

"I visited Mikonos once and stayed there for a few months. That's when I dropped out of U. Conn. Then I got a job doing cruises," she offered.

"And here we both are at the Last Hotel."

"Two floors apart."

They looked at each other.

"What do you smoke?" she asked.

"Top-grade Moroccan hash," he said. "Dark as bitter chocolate."

"You sound like a connoisseur."

"I've spent time in Istanbul."

He took a lump of silver foil out of his wallet, unfolded it. Using a tiny knife with an ivory handle, he sliced pieces off the rock and stuck a few brown crumbs into the pipe. "Here." He stood up, passing the pipe to her with a lighter.

"No, you first," she said.

"One minute." He moved toward the window and cracked it open. Then he placed a rolled up towel under the door. He sat down next to her.

Lighting the pipe, he inhaled deeply and passed it to her. He held the smoke in his chest as she inhaled through her nose and mouth. Mmmmm. It tasted delightful. The scent of coffee, musk, fudge, earth. She could feel the top of her head. Oh, oh! It was starting to take flight.

He lit up again, inhaled deeply, then passed the elephant to her. As he exhaled, the smoke sweeping over her like a veil, he leaned over and kissed her neck. "How do you feel?"

"Hmmmm." She sighed with contentment.

He rolled the ottoman closer and sat on it, at her knees. "I'm glad you're here."

"Me too."

She could imagine him as a therapist. He had a soft speaking style, which was incredibly soothing. She could tell him all her secrets. Yikes! That was the problem with dope. It made you want to tell all, do it all. A lifetime in one night. But she wasn't supposed to do that.

"You're a very beautiful woman," he said, staring intently at her. "But you know that already."

"Not really."

"Are you kidding! You're a shiksa goddess! Catnip for a Jewish guy like me from Brooklyn. We never saw anyone who looked like you except in the movies."

"I didn't think you even noticed me."

"I'm usually so preoccupied with work that I hardly see anything." He continued to stare at her, his eyeballs hyperactive black dots like Betty Boop's. "I see you now."

"What do you see?"

"I see you looking at me," he teased.

"As you were saying..." She paused, suddenly lost in the forest. "What were we talking about?"

He laughed. "I don't remember."

"I guess I must be stoned," she said. "Are you?"

"Of course," he said.

"Do you think it's bad, psychologically speaking? You're a professional. Do you think smoking kills brain cells and could become an emotional crotch, I mean, crutch, or something?" She began to giggle.

He shook his head. "Not at all."

"Well, pass the peep, I mean, pipe, por favor." She inhaled happily.

He turned the radio to the jazz station. Billie Holiday.

"You're very yummy," he said, drawing closer to her.

"What's yummy about me?"

"If you give up my chair and let me take you into my bedroom, I'll show you."

She began to giggle. She was feeling quite giddy and light-headed. "I don't think I can stand up."

"I'll help you."

He was strong. He pulled her up by the arms and led her into the bedroom.

"Just a minute," she said, holding back. "I hardly know you."

"What do you want to know?"

She thought hard. "What do you do when you're not working?"

"All kind of things," he said.

"Like?"

"Have you ever been to Plato's Retreat?"

"The sex club?" she asked.

"It's right down the block at the Ansonia. I've gone in a few times just to see what it's like."

"What's it like?"

"Well, there's no alcohol, just fruit juice, which is a turn-off. A lot of middle-aged people in white towels that don't quite cover their privates. A swimming pool."

"Why'd you go then?"

"Curiosity. Just like I'm curious about you," he said, leaning over her.

"I just want to know you a little before—"

"Before what?"

"Before we go to bed," she said softly.

"Aren't you being presumptuous? Just because we go into the bedroom doesn't mean anything. I haven't decided if I'll fuck you." He took her hand. "Are you attracted to me?"

She studied his body, appreciating his health club ass and legs, a good physical specimen. "Awfully," she admitted, then blurted out: "But, actually—" She paused, realizing how stupid she sounded. "I'm on a diet."

He looked bewildered. "What kind of diet?"

"I'm trying to build my self-esteem. My therapist thinks that I should refrain from relationships and—"

"Take off your clothes."

"Why don't you take off your clothes?"

He leaned over and began to unsnap the multiple snaps of her jumpsuit. After a few minutes of futile fumbling, he cried, "Help me, Monica!"

She laughed, sliding on the rolling waves as she rolled the top down, slipped out of its sleeves, then the pants.

"What beautiful breasts you have!" he cried out in pleasure.

"Thanks," she answered, not knowing what else to say. She peeked up at the mirror on the ceiling. There was a porn star in red panties staring back at her on an undulating bed.

"Those too," he said, pointing. "Off."

"What about you?"

He sat down next to her on the bed. The water pushed her away from him. He held her. "You know, Monica, when you're dancing, somebody's got to lead. Let me lead this time."

"What do you want me to do?"

"Relax." He untied his pants, slipped out of them. He had dark black hair all over his toned body.

She reached to touch him. He removed her hand as if he didn't need her assistance.

"Cup your breasts for me."

She felt shy.

"Go on, I want you to caress those beautiful breasts of yours."

He reached over and placed her hands on her breasts. "Go on. Show me how you like it."

Monica hesitated.

"Come on," he beseeched. "I want to see you play with those breasts of yours. So lovely," he said. "Pinch those nipples. Yes, like that."

He kept watching her. "That's it. Yes. You like it, don't you?"

She wasn't sure. She tried to reach for him again. He held back.

"Now I want you to play with yourself." He put her hands on herself. "Show me how you like it."

She hesitated.

"Come on," he said. "It's so exciting to watch you excite yourself." He was stroking himself.

Looking up at the mirrored ceiling, she saw a pornographic film that was her. It fascinated her. She couldn't stop watching herself.

"Come to me," she demanded, pulling him to her. "I want you."

He resisted. "Not yet, darling. First, I want you to bring yourself to orgasm."

"I can't!" she cried out. "I have trouble having orgasms…"

He looked bewildered. "Why's that?"

She shook her head.

"Show me how you like it, little pussy. Nice, little pussy. That's right," he crooned. "Show me your pretty thing. Yes. Let's see. Oh, so very pretty. Open it up for me. Yes, that's it. Show me your pearl. Look how wet it's getting. Oh, God! God! Yes, keep doing it. Don't stop. Oh, you're so sexy!"

As Monica listened to his voice, her whole body felt like it was about to explode. The water swelled in a wave, throwing her against him. "My God!" she screamed. Was she peeing in his bed?

"Shhh!" He put his hand over her mouth. "The neighbors."

"I'm sorry," she whispered breathlessly.

He stopped moving.

"What?" she asked. "Is anything wrong?"

"You mustn't talk about us to anyone," he demanded.

"I know that," she said. "I won't."

"This is private and just between us."

"Yes, yes," she said.

"Good," his voice softened.

Then he began to grind against her thigh. His erection felt like a blade.

"Just a minute," she said. "I need protection."

"Don't worry. I have something very special."

He took out a foil package from his night table. *ONYX*: silver letters on a black package. The condom was shiny black with small ridges.

All that black hair and then a jet black cock!

He lowered himself on top of her. "How deep can I penetrate?" he whispered.

Afterward, they lay together, sharing a bowl of hashish in his ceramic elephant.

He leaned over to her. "Was it good for you?"

"Do you need to ask? I made too much noise, didn't I?"

"I loved every moment of it, but I don't know what my neighbor Lenny thought."

"Do you really think he could hear us?"

"Next time, we'll go somewhere else."

He reached over to his night table. "Here." He handed Monica a legal-looking document. "I hope you won't mind."

"What is this?"

"It's a consensual confidentiality agreement," he said.

Monica looked bewildered as she read. "I don't understand."

"All it says is that you are not allowed to talk about anything that happens between us."

"I wouldn't talk," Monica said angrily.

"I have to be careful, you know, my profession. It's not personal."

There had been the problem at the Long Island Psych Center. The girl had stalked him, waiting for him after work. He wasn't her therapist. But they had still let him go. And now he was on probation.

"This is weird." She signed the form and returned his Mont Blanc pen.

They walked to the door. "You're almost too beautiful," he said. "You know that? I can't quite believe you're real."

"Oh, I'm real," she said, kissing him. "Really."

"My beauty, I'll call you," he said as he shut the door. Then he locked it.

Suite 55

The red IBM Selectric typewriter occupied the center of the desk like a cross-legged Buddha, Korectype and White-Out its handmaidens. So macho, it had once almost choked Hana when she leaned over to make a correction and her necklace got caught in the carriage. Now the silver globe glowed innocently in its cradle of letters. She looked up and stared out at her slivered view.

Hana stood up to turn on the stereo. Ejected Pink Floyd's *The Wall*, slipping in a cassette of the Rolling Stones. Something to get her going. She needed music with a loud, angry, driving bass to goad her into action. To get the bossy, prissy part of her brain to shut up. Keith's bass enveloped her. She stood up, her body snaking to the music.

What she really wanted to do was escape her cell and head to O'Neal Brothers bar around the corner on Columbus. All her friends were there, sitting at the round wooden table. People would kiss and hug her when she arrived. They'd move over to make room, buy her a drink.

This was her new Manhattan life. These were her new Manhattan friends. Having grown up in that most mediocre, ignominious of boroughs, she had craved just such bright lights. Her new friends worked in publishing, advertising; they were actor/waiters, apprentice filmmakers. Alex, a screenwriter, knew the director, year, and stars of every film, obscure and popular. He worked as an accountant from January through June and spent the rest of the time writing scripts and trying to sell them. Steve, who cared for his elderly mother, always carried thick library tomes of Gorky, Dostoevsky, Tolstoy. He had published a short story about having sex in the hospital with a woman visiting her ailing father.

All of them were aspirants more than actuals—so far. They told heroic stories of a friend of a friend, a producer who had agreed to check out an Off-

Off-Broadway production on Avenue C. Someone knew someone who could get a script to an agent at William Morris. An editor at the *Paris Review*. An audition for Woody Allen.

She knew most of it probably wouldn't happen, but the insider talk thrilled her. Friends gave her comps for screenings at the Elgin and New Yorker theaters. She went to art gallery openings. Experimental music. The Living Theater in the East Village. La Mama. And then afterward, just as she had imagined her life in the city, everyone sat around in dimly lit bars, bumming cigarettes, drinking cheap red wine, dipping whoever's french fries into a communal red blob while describing projects and patents for inventions, plotting their futures, instead of doing any real work.

An artist must practice discipline, she reminded herself. That's why she was sitting in her desk chair, death chair, like a prisoner of war. She'd been out nearly every evening. You're not going anywhere until you write at least a thousand words. At least turn on the damn Selectric.

Trembling, she picked up the manila folder. She was afraid to open it. Real writers wrote like angels, like poets, like professors. If she was a truly creative, sensitive artist, she would be dead already. Like John Keats. Janis Joplin. Jimi Hendrix.

Who wants to read about a Jewish girl growing up in Queens? After seven years, Feingold's words still lived in her system like an amoebic infection.

Junior year of college. 1972. City University. Two more years of being stuck in Flushing at the Queens campus, living at home.

Gabriel Feingold was an adjunct professor in the English department. She actually thought *adjunct* was an honorific title. Whatever he was, it was as if an Ivy League god, Yale '68, had magically settled on the campus of Queens College, sporting a tweed jacket with caramel-colored suede patches, his thick hair long, combed behind his ears, aviator glasses, well-fitting blue jeans, Frye boots.

She was an English major in need of a muse, a mentor, preferably male. Anaïs Nin had Henry Miller. Simone de Beauvoir had Sartre. In Shakespeare 41, Feingold had introduced Freud's idea of incest in Hamlet as popularized by Ernest Jones. Talking dirty about the classics! Now that was sexy.

Feingold had a reputation for making girls cry. With foolhardy confidence, Hana had registered for an elective one-on-one tutorial with him. The challenge was irresistible.

With excruciating effort, she had managed three single-spaced typed pages. They were about her mother's living room and the avocado velour couch, covered by clear plastic. Somewhere to start. A July afternoon, when her Aunt Shosh had tried to rise from the couch and discovered her considerable thighs were stuck to the plastic. The sound she made as she finally stood up to go to the toilet.

Feinstein had returned it without comment. She had stayed afterward, hoping he'd say something. They were the only ones in the classroom.

"So what do you think of Bellow's *Augie March*?" he asked.

She told him she preferred Grace Paley. "What about my writing?" she demanded silently.

He said nothing.

She waited until their next meeting, then finally asked, "What did you think of my story?"

He stared at her through his tinted aviator glasses.

"Hana, I feel I have to be honest with you. Otherwise, we're wasting each other's time." He paused. "You can write."

She sighed with relief. "Thanks so—"

He interrupted her. "A lot of people can write." Then he shook his head as though the diagnosis was fatal. "I don't know how to say this…" He wrinkled his patrician brow as if he detected a bad smell. "Who in the world do you think would be interested in reading about a Jewish girl growing up in Queens?"

How did he know how to pick the spot most tender, most likely to bleed, and stick the dagger of his upper class blade? What's the opposite of a mentor? A destroyer. And Feingold was Jewish himself! She wrote what she knew. She could still hear his snobbish, Ivy-educated voice. Who wants to read about a Jewish girl growing up in Queens?

She opened the folder, which had her notes. She flipped the switch. A red light beamed. *Vroom!* The Selectric revved to life. Fingers poised over the keyboard, she recited her mantra: "Fuck you, Gabriel Feingold." The silver globe began to spin, stamping black letters, words, sentences, across the white page.

She'd read the story in the *New York Post*. Hana retyped her poem in progress.

DEATH OF A GRAFFITI ARTIST

Before he slipped, he was spraying
Hot and spangly colors, naked whores
Sassing in diamond studded brassieres
The paint just shooting out like jive
From the spray gun held in his hand.

His lightning legs lost their grease
Oozing from the edge into darkness.
Hell's yellow eye burned like fever
Until the light turned red. The train
Thundering loud as God's wrath.

The woman followed after the policeman
To where her daughter Opal's son lay
His skinny rib cage crushed like ice.

Suite 49

Residents weren't supposed to entertain in their hotel suites. The rooms were too small. A fire hazard. Saul wouldn't be pleased. But what he didn't know… With great secrecy, Esther invited a few people "to greet the New Year and New Decade." BYOB. Lenny would bring beer; Faye, Almaden burgundy and Pincus; Rachel, a bottle of champagne. Esther had slipped an invitation under Reardon's door but doubted he would come.

It was almost time. Esther placed the baked brie wrapped in phyllo dough in a chafing dish. (From Fairway, on Broadway and 74th, which had everything, cheaper than it cost to make herself.) She also prepared a chocolate fondue with fruit slices. Esther hummed as she placed an embroidered tablecloth over a small glass table and lit a pair of candles.

Was she falling in love with Lenny? How could that be? Lenny: the taxi driver, horse gambler, beer drinker, slob. And yet, she enjoyed him greatly. Esther poured herself a glass of seltzer. Her stomach was nervous.

Lenny arrived at seven carrying a Budweiser six-pack in each arm. He wore a collared shirt of silvery gray silk and dark flair slacks. His hair was slicked back.

"Da, da, da, da…" He hummed.

"You look so…" she burbled, "handsome!"

"Aren't I your gigolo?" He embraced Esther. "You dress me up and take me out. But don't forget that's not who I *yam*." He emphasized the word.

"I'll put the beer in the fridge."

"Very nice," he said, looking at the table. "So where is everybody?"

"It's early. Do you want something?" Esther asked.

"I'll have a Bud. But don't move. I'll get it." He walked to Esther's refrigerator. When he returned, he sat down next to her on the couch, clinking his can against her glass. "Hi, you."

He was so nice to her. And she never had to say a word.

"Why you looking at me like that?" he asked.

"I guess I'm happy to spend New Year's with you."

"Me too." He snuggled her.

She kissed him on his sensitive spot, running her tongue over his neck.

"Stop!" he cried out. "I almost dropped my beer."

"God, we're too old to be having so much fun."

That's when the bell rang. Esther opened the door. Faye stood there with Pincus. "Come in, come in," Esther said, peering down the hallway. "I don't want anyone to see."

Faye put the bottle of wine down on the table.

"Hello, Lenny," said Pincus, shaking his hand. "Happy New Year."

"Not yet."

"Soon." He handed Lenny a large tin of salted peanuts. "Have some peanuts," he offered Lenny, opening the plastic lid. Then he popped a few in his mouth.

"Wine for you, Faye?"

She nodded. Pincus sat down next to Faye. "The same for me, please."

"The same for me, please," Faye teased.

He gave her a pretend punch in the jaw, which turned out to be a smooch.

"Who else are you expecting?" Faye asked.

"I had to invite Rachel," Esther said. "She might bring a date."

"In her dreams," Faye said. "Estie, can I have a glass of wine, please."

"Estie?" Lenny demanded.

"We knew each other at City College. That's what we called her, Estie."

"And you?" Lenny asked.

Faye smiled. "Faigeleh. Actually that's what Pincus calls me." They exchanged meaningful glances.

"Since we had a lot of Italians in Bensonhurst, I was Leonardo."

"I vos always Pincus, except," he recalled, "except my wife called me Pinkeleh." He paused, a dark crimson spot appearing on his face. "And now Faigeleh calls me that."

"I feel like I fell into a shtetl."

"We live in a *shtetl*," Faye declared.

"The hotel?"

"Look, all of us in this room are Jewish, so is Saul, Dr. T."

"Well, I'm sure Monica isn't."

"Probably Fred, the scavenger."

"And Reardon certainly—"

"Of course, of course," Faye said. "But it's not a matter of religion. Though Lenny Bruce said, 'If you live in New York, even if you're Italian, you're Jewish.'"

Pincus laughed.

"The Last Hotel is a vertical shtetl," Faye continued. The way we live in our little rooms, how we go up and down the elevator, and meet in the lobby."

"And who's Saul?" Esther asked.

"The mayor, of course."

"Have you heard anything about what's going on with the hotel?"

"What?"

"Pete said that he heard Saul talking on the phone about the hotel being sold."

Esther gasped. "Oh, no. I don't know anything about it."

"I heard something, but I'd check my information if it comes from Pete. He was probably soused," Lenny said. "Let's see what's happening in the world!"

He pressed the remote control button for the TV, a small RCA color. He flicked through several channels until he stopped. Dazzling lights, musical flares, people holding cocktail glasses. A reporter held a mic as a man in top hat and black tuxedo spoke.

"1979. A year to forget," he declared. "New York subway strike. Soviets invade Afghanistan. And Ronald Reagan is running for president? God help us!" Dick Clark cut him off with an icy smile, then turned to the viewers: "Live from Times Square in New York City."

"Do you really think Reagan can get elected?" Esther asked.

"Not a chance," Lenny said.

He leaned back on the couch, threw his arm around Esther's shoulders. "This was a great idea, Estie. A party at the Last Hotel. As long as I've been here, I've never heard about anyone having a party here."

"It's good to be around friends," Pincus said, smiling. He wore a new pair of blue jeans and a sports shirt.

"Eat something, guys," Esther said. "There's chocolate fondue with strawberries and pear slices, and brie baked in phyllo dough."

"Ever the gourmet," Faye commented.

Esther dipped a long fork with a pear slice into the boiling chocolate sauce. "Mmmmm," she said. "Come on! Leonard, can I make you one?"

"Sure."

"Me too!" Faye demanded.

Esther passed him a chocolate-coated pear slice with a napkin.

As Lenny took a bite, the chocolate dripped on his napkin, onto his pants.

"Oh, no! My new pants!"

"Just a minute." Esther ran to her kitchen and returned with a damp dish towel. "Here, let me." She bent down, on her knees, rubbing a spot curiously close to his crotch.

Lenny had a big smile on his face.

Pincus squeezed Faye.

"What you do to me," he said.

Esther stood up. "I don't think it'll leave a spot. Anyone else for fondue?"

"Which reminds me of a joke," Lenny began.

Everyone groaned.

"It's a little gross, but we're all adults here, right?"

"Uh-oh," Esther said, shaking her head.

"Well, it goes like this. This guy, let's call him Max, is married to Madge. Okay? One day, Max runs into Frank, Madge's first husband. Frank calls Max over and says, 'I guess you've gotten used to the stretched out part—where I used to be.'"

"Oh, Leonard!" Esther made a face.

"Go on," Faye said, grinning.

"You know what I think?" Pincus said. "You're depraved!"

"I warned you. Anyway..." Lenny paused, a glint in his eye. "Max looks at Frank, his wife's ex, who is trying to insult her and him. He smiles, answering, 'Well, you know, when I get past the part where you were, it's tight and juicy.'"

"That is truly gross, Leonard," Esther said.

At that moment, the doorbell rang. Esther opened the door. Rachel's perfume entered before she did. She wore a mink coat over a low-cut black dress and carried a bottle of champagne. "Happy New Year," she said, looking around.

Everyone greeted her.

"Are you coming from somewhere?" Faye asked.

"A party on East 86th Street. Beautiful duplex apartment. But I decided I wanted to be closer to home. At the Last Hotel with my friends."

"We were saying that before. The hotel being a good place," Esther said. "Though Saul would have a cow if he saw you all here."

"Did you hear?" Rachel asked. "Saul stormed out of the hotel earlier. He had been on the phone. Gittel said he was screaming on the phone."

"That doesn't sound good," Lenny said.

"I heard that one of the partners passed his share onto his son and retired to Florida."

"But that shouldn't matter."

"You know, Saul. He screams about everything." Rachel popped open the champagne. "Some French bubbly?" She poured herself a glass, then raised it. "Anyone?"

"What time is it?" Pincus asked.

"Too late," Faye answered.

"Too late for what?"

"Can you believe the seventies are over?"

"I can't believe the sixties are over," Lenny said. "Or even the fifties. That was my era."

"We're *alte cockers*," Pincus said.

"Maybe you are," he said. "I'm going strong." He winked at Esther.

"It's almost the eighties," Faye continued, rising to her subject. "It's so futuristic sounding. I keep thinking how we're getting closer to Orwell's 1984. Big Brother...M-C-M-L triple X. Those are creepy Roman numerals."

"You're such an intellectual," Pincus said, poking her affectionately.

Rachel rolled her eyes. Since her lids were surgically lifted, her eyeballs appeared to fall out of her lavender-slicked sockets.

On the TV, hundreds of thousands of carousers stood at Times Square, looking up, waiting for the giant ball to drop. There were still a few more minutes.

"Glad I'm not there," Esther said.

"Where's the champagne?" Faye asked.

Rachel stood up. "Who needs a glass?"

They all sat down to watch the TV. A group of drunken teenagers screamed into the camera.

After Rachel had poured champagne in five glasses, she said, "Let's make a toast."

Pincus and Faye stood together, holding their glasses, Lenny and Esther next to them. Rachel held up her glass. "What should we toast?"

"The New Year, of course."

"Okay, bottoms up!" Lenny cried.

At that moment though, something ran across the floor.

"Did you see that?" Esther asked.

"What?"

"I didn't see anything."

"Look!" she screamed. "Oh, my God!"

It was some kind of animal. A huge monster of a rat stood there, beady eyes staring at them. It scurried across the room again.

Esther leaped onto a dining chair, hiding her eyes. "I can't look at it."

"Come on," Rachel urged. "It's just a rat."

"It's not in your apartment."

"It's so big!"

"Vot should we do?" Pincus asked. "I never saw such a rat," he said.

"Hogwash," Lenny said.

"It's not like you can use a fly swatter or anything."

"How about we open the door, and try to chase it out?" Faye suggested.

"How you going to get it out the door?" Rachel said.

The rat made a squeaking sound, then burrowed its body under the skirt of the couch.

Esther unshielded her eyes. "I could call Henry."

"Let him have his New Years Eve in peace." Lenny stood up. "I have to get something from my place. I'll be right back."

"What?"

He ran out the door.

"What's he doing?" Rachel asked.

"Maybe he has a special spray?" Pincus said.

"This is an evil omen of the coming year," Faye said.

"The year of the rat," Esther said, still standing on the chair.

A few moments later, Lenny rushed back into the room, holding a silver pistol.

"You have a real gun?" Pincus demanded.

"Smith Wesson." He showed him the gun. "Where I drive, I have to have protection."

"Are you *meshuggeh?*"

"Look, the countdown's begun," Faye said, pointing to the TV.

"TEN...- NINE...- EIGHT..."- "

"Has it moved?" Lenny asked.

"No, it's still under the couch."

Crawling on all fours, Lenny approached the couch. He raised its skirt and peered underneath. "It's the year of the dead rat," he said, taking aim.

"SEVEN...- SIX..."

Lenny peered into the rat's shiny, beady eyes, staring back at him.

"You're *dead* meat."

"Oh my God!" Esther screamed.

"FIVE...FOUR...THREE..."

Lenny crawled farther underneath the couch.

"TWO...ONE! "

"HAPPY NEW YEAR!"

The Times Square ball dropped in a burst of light.

The gun fired.

Glowing on the TV screen:

1980

Basement

The first day of the year and he had this to deal with. Phone ringing at 7 a.m. Bessie still asleep. "No way!" Henry groaned as he reached for the phone.

"Sorry to call so early." It was Lenny. "I have a pickup at LaGuardia. Anyway, could you meet me upstairs on the fourth floor? I have to show you something."

Henry knew there was trouble. Like the time Dr. T.'s waterbed started leaking downstairs. What a mess. And when Gittel left a pot on her hot plate and almost burned the place down. And Reardon's espresso maker. What was it going to be? He could hardly wait.

Now he stood with Lenny, staring at the round bullet hole in the fourth floor hallway wall.

"You said what?" Henry asked.

"You wouldn't believe the size of this rat," Lenny told him, spreading his hands apart.

"You shot a rat?" he asked in disbelief.

"It was a mutant! I couldn't think of anything else to do."

"You could've killed somebody walking in the hallway."

"You're right," Lenny said. "I didn't think the bullet could go through these plaster walls."

"Was it a twenty-two?"

Lenny nodded. "Smith and Wesson."

Henry shook his head. "Ya gotta be careful with those."

"Where I drive and the weirdos that I pick up, I always carry a gun."

Henry bent down, running his finger over the hole.

"I guess I'll plaster it, then cover it with paint."

"I wouldn't share this with Saul," Lenny said.

"Uh-uh." Henry shook his head. "Not a chance."

Lenny handed him a twenty-dollar bill.

He pocketed it, looking down.

"I 'preciate it," Lenny said, then led him to Suite 49. He opened the door with a key.

"The hole is behind the couch." He pointed to the wall.

Henry turned to him. "Wha'd you do with the rat?"

"I got Esther's rubber gloves, picked it up, and threw him in a plastic bag. He must have weighed at least seven pounds."

Lenny handed him the bag.

"I'll bring it downstairs," Henry said.

Esther came out in a red terrycloth bathrobe. "I don't know what we'd do without you, Henry."

"Thanks," Lenny said. "I'll remember this."

"Don't worry. I'll take care of it."

Henry was the take care guy. The residents came to him with their everything. Sometimes it was hanging a lamp, installing electric outlets, putting air conditioners in, taking them out, changing a fuse, even helping the older ones reach things on the top shelf of the closet. They paid well, and he liked the people.

He was out of sorts though. First day of a new decade. 1980. The bullet hole unnerved him. Henry grumbled as he collected his pail, a bag of patching plaster, joint compound, and his tools.

Bessie, tying the back of her housedress, looked in on him. "Where are you going?"

Henry sighed. "I have to plaster a bullet hole in the fourth floor hallway."

"Say what?"

"You heard me. You know Lenny, Suite 22? Anyway, he was at Esther Fein's, Suite 49, and a big rat came out."

"And Lenny shot it?"

Henry nodded. "Why are white people so dumb?"

"Why are white people so useless?"

"Didn't he ever hear of a mouse trap?"

"Remember when we found that gun in Henry Jr.'s backpack?" Bessie asked suddenly.

"Don't talk to me about him," he said, clutching his heart.

Henry pressed the elevator button. When he got out, it continued upward. He walked down the hallway and found the spot. He laid down a small drop cloth and kneeled on it, in front of the bullet hole. He used an all-purpose putty knife to carve out the hole. Then he mixed a little water into the patching plaster and began to spread it with a spackling knife.

As he was on his knees, he saw a pair of yellow leather high-top sneakers stop next to him. He looked up to discover Monica Parker, the TV actress, though Bessie thought she was lousy on that soap opera.

"Hi, Henry," she said, smiling. "Happy New Year."

"You too, Miss Parker."

"Thanks, Henry." She stomped past him, her gym bag bouncing on her back.

As Henry worked, something caught his attention. Sticking out from his peripheral vision. He squinted. In the corner. Something gold. He crawled across the floor, turning to look in both directions to make sure no one saw him. When he picked it up, he immediately recognized it. A bullet cartridge.

Running his fingers over the smooth casing, he thought about when he'd last touched one of these things. Yes, he'd enlisted right after graduation. Got his high school degree like he promised his mother. First, he was in Texas for a few months, then France, and finally, Poland.

He'd been sent to Buchenwald. He'd seen the liberated Jews in their rags, so skinny, starved, sick, disgusting in their suffering. He couldn't look at them as he passed out boxes of food and drinks. The way they grabbed, those thin, filthy, diseased fingers, the torn fingernails, the bleeding cuts...

And now he worked for one of them. Saul, survivor of Auschwitz, was his boss, who yelled at him all the time. But Henry knew he couldn't help himself.

He tried to talk to him. "Mr. E., don't sweat the small things."

Saul answered, "That's all I can do."

Henry understood. He knew Saul was a kind man, a fair person, generous, and very stingy.

Henry would sometimes look at Saul and try to imagine him back there. Thirty-five years ago. Behind the barbed wire, when the gates were unlocked, when the remaining Germans were marched out to a waiting American transport.

Henry pocketed the cartridge. "He coulda killed someone with this." Henry picked up the pail with the plaster and gave the hole a final swipe with the spackling knife. Afterward, he knocked on the door of Suite 49. Esther answered. This time she wore a loose shirt and slacks.

"I need to fix the hole behind your couch," Henry said.

"Let me help you move it."

They each took one side of the couch and pushed it away from the wall. "Just a little bit more," Henry said.

"One, two, three," Esther called. "Let's do it."

They shoved the couch a few more inches from the wall. "That's okay," Henry said.

"I made some muffins with fresh blueberries. They're still warm."

Henry grinned. Whenever he did any work for Esther, she always had something delicious to offer him.

A few minutes later, he stood up. "This should do it."

"You can wash your hands in the bathroom."

"Thanks," he said, peeking into her bedroom as he walked past.

"Sit down," she said when he returned. "A cup of coffee?"

"Okay, but I can't stay long. You know Saul is going to be yelling for me any minute."

"He does scream a lot," she said, sitting opposite him at the table.

Henry shrugged.

"Does he seem more stressed out than usual to you?"

"He's always stressed out," Henry said. "That's how he is."

"Do you know anything?" she asked him. "About the sale of the hotel?"

"People talk. Saul hasn't said anything."

"Thanks for taking care of everything, Henry. I can't tell you how much we appreciate it." She paused, looking down for a moment. "I nearly died when I saw that rat. It was so huge. Really. Bigger than a cat. And then when Lenny walked in with that gun, and I thought, I didn't know what to think. But I have to tell you,"—she broke into a smile—"it was exciting."

Henry took a bite of the muffin. "Very good," he said.

"I still tremble when I think of it," she continued. "Lenny holding the gun. The craziest thing I've ever seen since I moved into the hotel."

"Lenny's a wild one."

"You don't know." She dropped her voice. "Can I tell you a secret?" She giggled. "That you can't tell anyone?"

Henry looked at her. White women, he thought.

"I'm falling in love, Henry," she exulted. "At my age."

"Oh, you're not old."

"Sixty's not too far away for me."

"Sixty's a memory for me," he said.

"Please don't tell anyone."

Henry smiled his pearly smile.

She opened the door.

Suite 42

As Rachel entered the lobby, she could feel tension in the air. Saul sat at his table, head buried in the *New York Times*, eagle-eyeing the stock listings. His small black notebook, where he wrote names and numerals, was open. But the newspaper shook.

"Hi, Saul."

"What do you want?" he demanded, eyes filled with rage.

"I…just…wanted to say hello."

"Hello!" he yelled.

Rachel's high heels clomped quickly as she stalked away.

"Mrs. Weinstein, I'm sorry." Then he added. "I have some problems."

Rachel stopped. "With your family?"

"No, no. Do you ever see a young woman with dark hair? She lives in the penthouse."

"Sometimes."

He nodded. "Does she seem all right?"

"She's not too friendly."

Saul nodded ruefully.

Rachel started to walk again, but Saul followed her. "Something's happening to the hotel," he said, lowering his voice.

"What do you mean?"

"I'm not sure what these people have in mind. They bought the other partners' shares and want to buy mine. You and the other tenants should keep your ears open."

As she rode up in the elevator, Rachel moaned. "Why me?" She didn't want to get involved. What a pain. She'd have to find another place. The elevator stopped at the fourth floor.

Rachel raised the lid of a steaming iron pot. A cloud of meat scent rose, steaming the window. She stuck a fork into the pot, blew, then took a dainty nibble. "Aaah!" She sighed.

Simmering in a thick iron pot overnight, the potatoes, onions, garlic and kidney beans had melted with the beef, creating a cholesterol paste made for masonry, not a mortal mouth. Chicken *shmaltz* was the secret ingredient in her *cholent*. Use a piece of steak, never mind what cut. A shank bone. How her grandfather Abe loved to suck the marrow. Sadie had passed the recipe to her granddaughter in a veil of deep secrecy. "Few can resist," she warned. "Beware of its power."

That's how she got Harvey to marry her. Harvey Fox sported a diamond-studded, six-inch mezuzah on his hairy chest. He took her out every Saturday night, usually for dinner and an overnight tête-à-tête.

One chilly December night, when she still lived in the Larchmont house, a Victorian inherited from husband number two, she prepared her *cholent*. Harvey took a little piece of beef on his fork. He wasn't a *chazzer*. He breathed in the aroma. Then another bite. Losing his cool completely, he dove into his plate. Smacking his lips, he cried out, "A masterpiece! Soft, onions...I never ate such a thing!"

That night, Harvey got down on his knees. After he made her come, not once but twice, he popped the question. What Rachel insisted on was a diamond that was a boulder, not a little pencil tip. They'd had a good time together for ten years, but that was over. Kaput. Six years ago, Harvey keeled over dead. Was the stroke from her *cholent*?

She didn't really miss him, but sometimes she wanted to be with a man. She still had the *yetz*. The desire.

That's why Rachel had decided to strike while her friend Faye was in Baltimore for some sort of conference. He'd never be able to resist her grandmother's legacy. Besides, a man becomes lonely when he gets used to getting it. Especially if Pincus was such a stud. Rachel had nothing to lose. And she would finally get even with Faye for Ahmet. Even if it didn't work out, it'd be pure mischief. Seduction. The game enticed her. Even at her advanced age.

It was Faye's own damn fault. Hadn't anyone ever told her to keep a good thing to herself? "Pincus is a god in bed. His touch, like a piano tuner. He just knows how to pluck my strings."

Yech! Rachel wanted to puke. Faye just went on, glowing like a naked bulb. "It's so wonderful to wake up with Pincus in the morning. That's our favorite time to make love…"

As far as Rachel could see, Pincus was an old geezer. He worked for the *Jewish Forward* and looked like one of those European intellectuals. But she had to admit that Faye's skin had a glow.

She and Faye had been friends for thirty years, at least. They were the red and black. Faye, an unnatural redhead. Everything about her—her long creepy nails, her vampire rouge and lipstick—was red. Some people think they have to look like a red alert to get some attention.

Rachel styled herself as a Liz Taylor brunette, turquoise eye shadow over black-kohled eyes, a black beauty mark painted on her right cheek.

Loose lips sink ships. Don't advertise your man! Especially in NYC, land of no parking spaces, no good men. A war zone of single women, divorcees, and widows, especially ripe, mature ones like herself. As for "eligible bachelors," they were the never-married *zhlubs*, who live like pigs—divorced losers and sickly widowers, looking for a nurse. Not me, sweetie. A decent man was hard to find. A hard one, forget it! If you happened to find one, keep it under your wig. Otherwise, you just never know what might happen…

There was the time Rachel had met the Turk. Ahmet. Between number two and three. He wasn't actually her type—too chunky—but in bed, he became sleek as a seal. Rachel had made the mistake of telling Faye, just before flying out to California. When she returned, Faye couldn't look her in the eye. She had sampled her specimen.

Rachel had outlived three husbands, two younger than she. Her secret? Lots of money, good bones, daily rides on her stationary bicycle, and an occasional discreet injection, here and there. After the collagen got rid of the dark circles under her eyes, she looked ten years younger. Everyone said so. And her natural gift for fellatio. That was what Mama Gabor had taught her daughters. Zsa Zsa and Eva were legendary in the Hollywood Hills.

Rachel sold real estate. Whenever one of her friends decided to give up her Westchester place and move to the city, Rachel sold it, taking a percentage for herself. Then she helped her find a co-op in Manhattan, and there was another fee.

"I'm a sinner. A total, unrepentant sinner. I love to be bad. It makes me feel alive," she told her reflection in a gilt frame. And yet, Rachel fasted on Yom Kippur and gave herself over to the ritual breast-beating. "I cheat, I lie, I steal, I am cruel..." Repeated over and over. Chanting it, she prostrated herself.

Now she slipped into a simple but costly black dress, humming "Love Me or Leave Me" and slipped out of her underwear. As she was about to leave, she sprayed herself with Chanel No. 5. Yes, down there too. Why not? They weren't children. She threw her keys into her pocketbook and grabbed a pair of red oven mitts to carry the pot of *cholent*, wrapped in a blue and white checkered kitchen towel.

Basement

Leah took the elevator to B. It was after six. Her father had already left. She knocked on Henry's door.

Bessie, wearing a flowered housecoat, answered. In the background, she could hear the TV.

"Is Henry around?" she asked.

Bessie shook her head.

"I wanted to ask him something."

"I don't know where he is. Can I help?"

Leah looked down. Embarrassed somehow. "Someone's leaving things at my door."

"What kind of things?"

"Books. Music cassettes. A pair of brown cashmere gloves that were washed." She smiled slightly, then frowned. "I don't know who's behind this."

At first, Leah had thought maybe they were from Angela. When she called, Angela's answering machine picked up. "We're in Istanbul right now. Leave a message and I'll get back to you when we return." Leah had slammed the phone down.

Then she had wondered if it could be Kofi. But he didn't know her apartment. And why would he leave her these things?

"Not Saul?" Bessie asked.

"He wouldn't leave me *Birds of America* by Mary McCarthy."

Bessie smiled. "No one ever leaves me gifts."

"I just don't know who'd do that."

"Maybe you have a secret admirer."

"Would you tell Henry? I think it's someone in the building."

Bessie studied her. "I don't understand. You want it to stop?"

"Yes," Leah answered vehemently. "I do."

Bessie started to speak, then stopped herself for a moment. "Have you talked to your father?"

Leah looked down. "No."

"I don't usually meddle in people's business—"

"Then don't, Bessie."

"Your dad ain't easy. I'll give you that. But he's a good man, and I know he asks Henry about you."

"I'm not ready," Leah said.

"Not ready. When you going to be ready? It's not for me to say, but you been living in the hotel. Would it be so terrible to just say hello to your father?"

Leah moved from the doorway. "Please tell Henry, okay?"

"Saul don't talk about soft things. But this silence between you is not good. Not good for him, not good for you."

"Bessie, let's not talk about this now."

She rang for the elevator. It stopped on the first floor. Fred wheeled in his bicycle, which had several plastic bags of books on the back rack.

Leah looked at the stuff curiously, then at Fred. His acne-scarred face, frizzy graying hair, filthy jeans.

"I left you some things I thought you'd like," he said, staring down at the floor.

"Why?"

"You look like you like books."

"Of course I like books. I love books," she said. "But it's such a surprise."

"There's so much stuff out there. I always wash the things first. Did the gloves fit?"

She nodded. "They're nice."

"New York streets are full of shit. People are so rich they don't even notice if they drop their gloves as they step out of a cab."

"I hate rich people too," she said.

The elevator stopped at 6.

"Well, thanks."

"My name is Fred."

"Leah," she mumbled.

"I guess, uh, I'll see you around," he said, wheeling his bicycle out.

Leah walked to the stairwell and up the stairs to the penthouse. She unlocked her door. Walked in and fell face-first on her bed. She began to weep. Maybe the world wasn't totally cold and cruel. Maybe Fred thought he could get laid. She wept till she fell asleep, snoring softly.

Suite 36

Pincus was sitting down to a humble repast of Campbell's chicken soup with rice when he heard a soft knock on his door. Who could it be? Faye was in Baltimore. He stood up.

"Who is it?" he asked through the door.

"A neighbor," a feminine voice answered.

He opened the door to discover a woman he recognized from the building. Rachel was beaming at him. He looked down at a pair of red over-sized oven mitts holding a steaming pot.

He looked confused. "Can I help you with something?"

"You could tell me where I should put this," Rachel said. "I made a *cholent*. There's too much for one person…"

"*Cholent?*" Pincus pronounced the word with pleasure. "I haven't seen a *cholent* in such a long time."

"I'm Rachel from Suite 42. May I come in?"

He hesitated for a moment, then said, "Why not? We're neighbors."

"Do you have a kitchen?" she asked.

He pointed to the hot plate on the table.

Using her red oven mitts, which looked like boxing gloves, she put the pot down. "Have a smell," she said, lifting the lid.

The steam escaped in a billowing puff of onions, garlic, beef, and kidney beans. Pincus inhaled the scent, his nostril hairs curling in delight.

"I don't make it often," she told him. "But yesterday, I don't know, I suddenly felt in the mood."

"Ach!" Pincus exhaled ecstatically. "You know what the German poet Heine said about *cholent?* 'The heavenly food that our dear Lord God himself once taught Moses to cook at Mount Sinai.'"

Rachel laughed, first noticing the huge painting of a young woman with watchful green eyes. Pincus saw her looking.

"That's Sylvie," he introduced her. "My wife."

"Nice to meet you," Rachel hailed her. "So should we sit down and eat a little? Before it gets cold." She looked around the room. "Do you have another chair?"

"I'm not prepared for company," Pincus said, shrugging. "I have nothing here except books."

"From the building?" Rachel asked as she dragged over a turquoise leatherette armchair, with one arm missing.

"It used to be in the lobby," he said. "Saul gave it to me."

"I figured. It matches the couch downstairs."

Rachel sat down and crossed her legs. Her short dress rode up her thighs, revealing lovely legs in black silk stockings.

Pincus looked away modestly.

"Speaking of which, Saul told me something about the hotel being bought by someone."

"What?"

"I didn't get the whole story, but Saul said we should keep our ears open."

Pincus shook his head. "I don't like the sound of it."

"I'll see what I can find out from my contacts in real estate. You know that's what I do? Sell real estate."

As she recrossed her legs, her dress slid farther up her thighs. She pulled it down.

"Did Faye send you?" Pincus asked, sitting down across from her. "So I won't go hungry."

"No, of course not."

"All these years I've lived by myself since Sylvie died, and Faye worries about my eating." He smiled indulgently.

"Actually, it was my idea," Rachel said softly, leaning toward him. "I just thought, why not? You're alone tonight. I'm alone. It's Shabbes. I thought it might be nice to get to know each other. And we're neighbors too."

"Yes," Pincus said, not looking up, his passion in his plate. "Cholent," he said rapturously. "I haven't tasted it in such a long time. Such soft potatoes."

For a guy who was skin and bones, he ate with gusto. "You're probably healthier not eating cholent too often."

"*Danks Got,*" he said. "For an old man, I feel okay."

Rachel looked at him frankly. "I don't think you're an old man."

"I'm sixty-eight."

She leaned farther over to him. He could see her cleavage. "You don't seem that old," she said, running her tongue over her teeth.

He shrugged, continuing to eat. "But I am."

"Where are your glasses?" she asked, interrupting his reverie.

"My reading glasses?"

"No, silly! To drink." She giggled wickedly. "I brought something."

He pointed to the cabinet.

She took out two jelly jars. From her small pocketbook, she removed a bottle, a salt shaker, and a lemon.

"What's this?" he asked.

"Something delicious," she answered. "Have you ever had tequila?"

He shook his head.

"It's a Mexican drink," she said as she poured the clear liquid into the glasses, humming. "Da, da, da, da, da, da, da—" Then suddenly, she sang out, "Tequila!"

"I don't drink except a little red wine on Shabbes, of course."

Rachel sliced the lemon. "Never mind that. Here's how you do it." She poured a little salt on Pincus' hand. "Lick the salt on your hand, drink the tequila, and then take a bite of the lemon," she instructed. "Watch me."

Rachel licked the salt on her hand, gulped the tequila down, and bit into the lemon. "Go on," she urged.

"Okey-dokey," he assented helplessly. His pink tongue lapped the salt, then he took a sip of the tequila, swallowed, and began to cough.

"Oy!" he said gasping. "My mouth's on fire!"

"Bite on the lemon!" Rachel urged.

He licked the salt again, tried a smaller sip, and bit into the lemon. Then he smacked his lips. "Not bad when you get used to it." He tittered. "First, *cholent*, then tequila." He took another sip and toasted Rachel. "*L'chaim*. To the Last Hotel, where such nice people live in the building like you."

"Yes," she beamed. "How long have you lived here?"

"Seven years," he said. "And you?"

"Since Harvey died. Five years ago."

He nodded, continuing to sip.

"You like?" Rachel asked.

"Very delicious," he affirmed, licking his lips.

"Another?"

"Why not?"

Rachel poured tequila into two glasses. As Pincus was about to drink, she stopped him. "We have to lick the salt first," she said.

She poured a small mound on Pincus' hand. As he bent down to lick the salt, she reached over and held his hand. Then she licked the salt from his hand as well, looking into his eyes meaningfully.

He dropped his eyes.

"Prost!" Rachel clinked his glass.

When he hesitated, she encouraged. "Down the hatch!"

Pincus gulped his tequila.

"Here." She fed him the lemon slice, then bit the other side.

They both giggled.

"Oy! The vorld is turning a little," he said.

"Are you all right?" Rachel asked, reaching over to stroke his arm.

"I think so." He shook his head back and forth. "If I keep this up, I'll become a *shikker*. A drunk."

"As long as you don't become a *shiksa*," Rachel joked.

They both laughed. "You're a funny voman," Pincus said.

Rachel smiled, licking her scarlet lips.

Suddenly, Pincus felt something under the table. Was a hand slipping over his leg? Moving over his fly? Rachel was stroking him! Before Pincus knew what was happening, he popped up.

"Like a young boy," Rachel purred in his ear, beginning to unzip his fly. Her eyes closed, her lips on his. "Such a big boy!"

He couldn't help smiling to himself. Just when he thought that his days on this planet were numbered, he'd become a ladies man. Oh Sylvie! Are you playing tricks on me? Can the dead perform magic?

"No, no," he cried out. "I can't. It's not right—"

"Ssssh," she whispered. "We're the only ones who will ever know."

To be a Lothario at this age? A Don Juan? He didn't even know how it happened. One minute, they were eating *cholent*, the next thing he knew, she was unzipping his pants. Pincus was in shock!

Vixen! Bathsheba! Pincus separated himself from Rachel. "Your *cholent* is…uh…very…delicious," he said, pushing her hand away from him.

She smiled. "My grandmother Sadie's recipe."

"Thank you very much," he said.

She leaned toward him again. "We could get to know each other better." She took his hand, pulling it under her dress, up her leg.

"*Veys mir!*" he cried out when he felt the hair between her legs.

"Shhhh," she tried to still him.

He pushed his chair away from the table. "Vot do you think? I'm a gigolo? Your friend is my…" He didn't know what to call what they were. Not his girlfriend. She was over fifty. But not just his lover. "You know."

"Faye's not my friend."

"Why not?"

"She lies." Rachel was inspired.

"What?" he demanded.

"You really think she has a daughter in Baltimore?"

"Of course," he answered. "Why would she lie?"

"I'm sure she has her reasons." She reached out for Pincus again. "None of it matters. We have each other tonight," she purred.

This time he removed her hand firmly. "You must go now." He hesitated, seeing a blush spread across her face and neck. "I'm sorry, but this I can't do."

"You don't know what you're missing," Rachel said, sitting up.

"Have you no shame?"

"Heaven on earth."

Pincus stood up. "Don't worry. I won't say anything to Faye."

"What's to say?" Rachel stood up, straightening her dress. "You liked my *cholent*, right?"

"Yes," he admitted. "I did."

Rachel took her bottle of tequila and the salt shaker, dropping them into her pocketbook. "Keep the lemon," she said.

After grabbing her red oven mitts, she picked up her iron *cholent* pot. Without a backward glance, she stepped out, shutting the door behind her. Instead of the elevator, she took the back exit door and walked up two flights. The neighbors didn't have to know.

"Damn," she muttered. "That bitch Faye has a good man!"

Penthouse

Leah let herself out the metal door. The frigid winter air hit her face. She took a deep breath. Ah, she sighed. Breathing was a good thing. Often she forgot for whole days.

As she stepped onto the gray tar, she thought of the roof on 1657 Grand Concourse, where she'd grown up. Summers she, Maya, Vivian, and Debra slathered themselves in baby oil with a couple drops of iodine, for color, then placed towels on tar beach. Lying on their backs, they held their homemade reflectors: manila school folders wrapped in aluminum foil.

Now she stared up at the huge-looking water tower, whose top came to a triangular point with a steel fence around it. Grass seemed to grow in patches on its surface. She bent over the opaque glass pentagon of the skylight, which had metal wire, and tried to peer through it. She couldn't see anything.

"Up on the roof..." she chanted in a whisper. It was such a New York City phenomenon. Water towers like urban castles. "I climb way up to the top of the stairs and all my cares just drift right into space..."

The roof was what made living in her father's hotel bearable. No one else in the building seemed to know. And she wasn't talking. She was sure if her father found out, he'd have a cow. It's not like she came up here to jump. Though the thought had occurred to her more than once. "I'll just kill myself," was her default mantra. But not seriously. And she wasn't going to trip and fall off the roof.

As she lit her pipe, she turned toward the lights of Broadway. People were going to Lincoln Center to see dance, classical music, opera. She could see them walking, tiny, brightly colored filaments on the distant street. Inhaling deeply, she imagined the smoke flowing throughout her body, then rising back up, encircling her head.

Leah, the less favored of Jacob's wives. The less beautiful one, who is full of fruit, and blossoms with offspring while her husband labors in the fields to possess her sister Rachel. She believed it was her story, though she had no sister. She had a rival who had taken over, and once again, she was less favored. Luba...

Yes, she knew that Luba's family had protected her father, until they couldn't. Still, it had been so fast. And Leah missed her mother so intensely, more than she'd ever thought possible. Why was she thinking about this? Sometimes weed did that. Made you go places that you had no inkling were even worth thinking about.

She knew her father had a good heart. Saul had loved her and her impossible mother. But it was something insane, absolutely wrong that he married Luba after only a few months. Okay, he waited the year. Exactly. They were wed at City Hall. He actually wanted her to come to the ceremony. No way, she said. Sorry, Dad.

After that, she got an unlisted number, moved in with Angela. They hadn't spoken for months, and then she needed a place. She had nowhere else to go. And he gave her the penthouse dump. But it was somewhere to live.

I'll go downstairs later, she decided. See if he's around. It was time. She would go look for him soon.

"Maybe I'm not that unhappy," she said softly. "Maybe I just think I am. I think too much. Maybe I need an education in happiness. How to feel it. How to know when it's happening."

That's when she found herself thinking of her neighbor with the bad skin. Just like that. It came into her head. He had left her more things. A book of New York hikes and bike paths. A not-bad-looking black lace scarf with silk fringes. An unopened jar of strawberry preserves. Maybe he liked her. She ought to tell him about the roof.

Once she had been into men—until the last asshole fucked her over. And then she met Angela, the devil cunt. She discovered that women could screw with you just like men. So where did that leave her?

"On the roof, it's peaceful as can be, and there the world can't bother me..." she crooned softly.

Maybe she would show Fred the door to the roof. That was a gift. The freedom, the space to just be. Probably he didn't even know about it. You had to go up to the penthouse, then up a flight of stairs. He'd get a kick out of it.

Maybe he even got high.

She sat down on a step by the roof door. Did she really want to share this? No. But he was kind to her. Having him as a friend wouldn't be so bad. But she'd have to talk to him about his personal hygiene. Not that she was prissy. The guy didn't wash. His skin was horrible, his hair an uncontrolled gray Jewfro that grew out of his ears. And when did he last launder his blue jeans?

The sun had dropped into the Jersey skyline like an egg yolk. From the roof, she could see the mighty Hudson River. Technicolor pinks, oranges, and periwinkle. Even if it was air pollution. What a show. She took another hit.

Suite 52

As she entered the hotel lobby, Amber nodded to Saul. She was pooped from a long day of lingerie. God, her feet hurt. As she hobbled in her Fiorucci heels to the elevator, Saul approached her.

"You know that place I told you, where Duc works?"

"Studio 54?"

"He came in a few minutes ago. He's not working tonight."

"Saul—"

"Look, he's a single guy and, you know, why not?"

"You old matchmaker!" she teased.

"The hotel's going to hell," he grumbled. "Might as well live while you can."

Did Saul know? Amber mused once again as she rode up the elevator. She assumed he did, but maybe he didn't. He was Old World. Men were men, women were women. Many people had no idea. She didn't tell. Why should she? Certainly no one at work. She had confided in Hana, who lived next door.

"All women are transvestites," Hana responded. "Wearing war paint on their faces and pantyhose." She guessed that's why she refused to wear a bra, even the Vanity Fair nude she gave her.

As Amber walked past Suite 55, she could hear Hana's typing. The girl pounded on that typewriter like it was a war machine.

Amber unlocked her door. She threw her coat on the brass-post bed, then threw herself on the pink satin pillow, flung her heels across the room, wiggled her legs in the air. "Free at last," she cried aloud. Standing around in heels for seven hours could take the living spirit out of you. "28A to 52 DD," she said with a sigh.

Crossing the room, she turned on her stereo. Inserted a cassette. The one she treasured most in the world. Now she fast-forwarded it. Pressed PLAY.

The insidious driving guitar began, repeating the same lick over and over and over. It was said he tuned all his guitar strings to the same note.

Lou Reed and the Velvet Underground. Amber had listened so many times, the cassettes melted. Twice. As a boy, lying between the speakers in Andrew's room while his parents watched *Dynasty* downstairs. Mesmerized by Lou Reed's nasty, churlish voice. Waiting for the time when he could leave behind, like a chrysalis, a life that wasn't his.

New York City is the place where they take a walk on the wild side.

The saxophone solo played over the fadeout was performed by Ronnie Ross, who taught a young David Bowie to play the saxophone.

She never lost her head even when she was giving head...

How he worshipped them all. The only way he could stand his life was the knowledge that he would grow up and leave Andrew behind. There was a there there. And that's where he was. He was a she in New York City.

And the colored girls go DOO DOO-DOO, DOO-DOO DOO.

Amber hadn't had a boyfriend in a long time. Her girlfriends thought only of their elaborate costumes, trawling after-hour clubs, lip-synching to Barbra, Aretha, and Chaka Kahn. But Amber was a romantic. And in her own way, shy.

One evening when she was heading uptown, she told the taxi driver, "Please stop for a moment."

She saw Duc standing in front of Studio 54, almost a half foot taller than everyone around him. Dozens of people clamored at the door. Definite B and T. Bridge and tunnel. Clearly they didn't make the cut. When the place opened in '77, Rubell had told the doormen, "Cast a play mixing beautiful nobodies and glamorous celebrities."

Amber studied his mocha-colored skin, the long black braid down his back. A white silk scarf was tied around his neck, and he held a clipboard. He pointed to a white woman wearing an enormous Afro wig and a Rasta guy, unhooked the velvet rope, waving them through the pearly gates.

She could have approached Duc then.

"Hi, neighbor." She flashed her flashiest, pearliest smile.

"I've seen you on the elevator," he said, giving her a warm welcome. "Come in, come in." He unhooked the velvet rope.

"What time are you finished here?"

"Way past your bedtime."

"What do you know about my bedtime?"

She had continued uptown in her taxi. Now she paced her room. Faye's story with Pincus had inspired her, but it wasn't like she could cook a brisket. What could she offer? What would he like? She didn't know him, except from seeing him in the elevator, but he looked so strong, so masculine. She imagined he could make even a big girl like her feel petite. That beautiful skin. The glossy, straight hair. He looked like a Samoan prince.

Yes! She embraced her pink satin pillow. Of course she loved men. Adored them, especially the masculine ones. Did that mean she was gay? No. She was a red-blooded passionate woman, and soon all her parts would match.

Just then, Amber's eye caught a pile of videocassettes stacked on her bookcase. She studied the titles. *Eyes of Laura Mars. The Thomas Crown Affair. Bonnie and Clyde. Network.* God, she loved Faye Dunaway. People said she looked like her. *Some Like It Hot.* Yes, that was it! He probably never saw the film. What a total hoot! Some like it hoot, she joked to herself. Sometimes she found herself so witty. She reached for the VCR case, studying the photograph of Marilyn Monroe, Tony Curtis, and Jack Lemmon.

What else? Fritos? English muffins with peanut butter and banana? Cream cheese with A1 Steak Sauce? S'mores? Her cuisine was still from hunger bachelorhood. She could make Rice Krispies Marshmallow Treats. Macaroni and cheese. No. Something else. Yes! Eureka!

From the top drawer of her dresser, she took out a plastic baggie. Yes, there was still a little stash of marijuana. She wasn't really a smoker but liked to keep it for emergencies. Like now.

She went to her fridge. Yes! She always kept a roll of chocolate chip cookie dough in her freezer. Just in case.

Placing the roll on a metal sheet, she began to slice it. Four cookies should do it with a generous sprinkling of weed on the top of each cookie. Turning on her toaster oven, she let it heat up. She worked the marijuana, which was ground into a fine powder, into the dough. Then she placed the sheet inside the oven. The timer was set for five minutes.

She turned on the hot water in the shower. While she waited for it to scald, she stripped. Shampooed her hair, which was hers, not a wig, like some of the other girls. Conditioned her gorgeous tresses. Washed her voluptuous breasts with French perfumed soap—she'd told the plastic surgeon: "Make 'em big and bouncy."

Hair wrapped in a mauve towel, she inspected her face in the magnified mirror. Selma, her electrolysis lady, usually did a good job. But you couldn't be too careful. With a stern Gestapo gaze, she searched for errant hairs. When she was finished, she applied a Swiss mud mask, which was turquoise, and sat on the closed toilet to blow-dry her hair. She checked out her legs, which she'd just had waxed.

She checked her old friend, Andrew. Like an old sock, it sat in its cup, under her tight bikini panties. Never mind that. Go to sleep, Andy. She slipped on sheer black panty hose.

What if Duc wanted a run-of-the-mill female? One without, well, baggage. Could she go through with it? It was only one floor up. What did she have to lose? No risk, no life. Dr. Tannenbaum had told her he admired her courage. After she rinsed her face, she splashed grapefruit toner, then a vitamin E moisturizer.

What to wear? She flung open her closet door. What might Duc like? Her Samoan prince. Amber decided on a low-cut black dress, a little like Marilyn's. She brushed her hair, put on gold gypsy earrings. A spritz of Joy. Red lipstick. The timer went off.

Whew! The room was scented with baked marijuana and a little chocolate. Amber inhaled deeply. Mmmmm. He'd like that. God, she hoped the smell didn't escape into the hallway. She wrapped the cookies in silver foil. Grabbed the *Some Like It Hot* video. Looking in both directions in the hallway, she snuck out.

"And the colored girls go DOO DOO-DOO, DOO-DOO DOO," she sang as she walked to the stairwell. Only one floor up. Take a walk on the wild side.

Suite 45

Monica picked up the black phone receiver, then hung up. She wouldn't do it. She wouldn't be naughty. She wouldn't act on impulse. She would control herself. That's what her group taught her. Instant gratification led to instant destruction. She must let the men she dated…breathe. Not suffocate them with her needs, her hunger, her well of depression.

His phone number haunted her. She tried to forget it. She should wait for him to call her. Eight-seven-three, nineteen forty-seven. Like a diabolic tune, it repeated in her head. Eight-seven-three, nineteen forty-seven. She knew he was there. She'd seen him in the elevator. She picked up the phone again and began to dial the number. "No!" she cried out. "I won't do it!"

The addict's cry. It was useless. The fix was right there, in her hand. She needed to talk to him. If she heard his voice, everything would be all right. Who could pass that up? She dialed the number, then took a deep breath. Hung up before the ring. Jesus! I'm mad! She dialed again.

It was ringing! The phone was ringing. Each ring gripped her heart with ecstasy and terror. Ring. Ring. Ring. Until his voice came on. "You've reached the office of Dr. Tannenbaum. Please leave your name and any message. You can speak as long as you wish. You will not be cut off…" *Click.*

Oh yeah, Dr. T.? He cut her off when she tried to tell him how she felt. He was hateful. She knew it. Despicable. An insect. A toad. He would never accept her anyway. She was the forbidden *shiksa* who Jewish men lusted after, then dumped for some large-hipped Jewish girl like her upstairs neighbor Hana.

She longed for him beyond reason. His dark curls falling across his forehead as he fucked her. Was it purely physical? Chemical? He was her heart's desire. It was a sickness of sorts. She knew it. Sex was her substance of choice. Her abuse. Her self-abuse. Never mind that.

For the last few months, she had lived for his phone calls, their weekly rendezvous, usually Friday evening, when he didn't have a group. Shabbat. It probably turned him on to be with his goya and eat pork loin with mint jelly, and shack up at the Times Square Inn.

He said they could no longer meet at the Last Hotel. He had to separate his work life. His patients might see him. When they went out, she met him at the hotel's bar. Monica always wore something brilliant, memorable, fascinating. Last night, it was under her clothes: a black lace camisole with an industrial zipper! (Bought at Lord & Taylor's from that witch Amber, who could enchant her into spending a bundle.)

It had been hotter between them than ever before. He had been insane with lust. Now she just wanted to say hello. Hi, how are you? How great it was. Was it good for you too? Special? They hadn't used anything. She wanted to tell him that she could feel his sperm piercing her egg. Yes, she was fertile! How she was still so excited by him that she had masturbated after he left. How she wished he didn't have to leave, but, of course, he did.

Had it been the ludes last night that made him so wild? Monica liked ludes a lot. Lewd lady! She dialed his phone number again, waiting, fear in her chest, clutching the receiver, ring after ring. She just wanted to hear his voice. Was that too much to ask? This time, she hung up before the message began.

What would Emerald do? Monica had played Emerald Lee for many years. Emerald was a cunning nymphomaniac who did things like sleep with Gabriel St. John, a powerful businessman, stealing him from his wife of many years and his children. Then she had an affair with her teenage stepson and seduced her mother's new husband. Now Emerald attended a sexaholics group that met weekly in a church where she had designs on Pastor O'Malley.

Emerald was imperious. She cut through the world like a sharp, shiny blade. Emerald would just go downstairs to Ronald's suite. She would press the bell until he opened the door.

"Emerald, why are you here?" he would demand. "We can't, you know very well…"

"We have to talk." Emerald mouthed the words in the mirror.

"Not now… I can't right now…"

"I have to talk to you *now*." She stared into his eyes. The camera focused on her eyes, smoldering suggestively. He could not resist their lure. He would take her into his strong arms, kissing her furiously.

"The cab is downstairs," she would whisper.

Monica knew she was a drama queen. That's why she made lots of money, the six-figure kind. Yet she lived in the hotel. Friends told her to move to the East Side. To an elegant building with a doorman. She preferred "La Vie Boheme."

Monica looked down at her watch. 9:30 p.m. Where the hell could he be? She had seen him in the elevator earlier. It had taken all her willpower not to say something. Now she just wanted to hear his voice. *Was last night special for you too? Darling, I was ovulating. Did we make a baby?* No, she couldn't say that. It was part of the deal. She felt so alone. "Bogie!" she called for her furry loveball.

Just then, Monica heard something. Could it be? The downstairs doorbell was buzzing. Or did she just imagine it? It buzzed again.

She ran to the bell and pressed the TALK button. "Who's there?" she called.

The response was garbled, as always. Why couldn't someone invent an intercom that you could actually hear? She tried again. "Who is it?" The voice downstairs sounded familiar. No. Couldn't be. The sheer energy of her desire had been heard. He'd come back to her. "Ronald!" she called out his name. He just wanted to give her a warning. He did care about her.

She rang him in, then stood up straight, closed her eyes, took a deep breath. She threw her head forward, letting that mane of hers cascade over her face. Then she threw her head back, running her fingers through her hair. She opened her satin kimono. Her cleavage poured out like a Renoir. She checked in the gold leaf mirror. A perfect pose. She spritzed a little Obsession.

Now she listened keenly for the sound of the elevator. Nothing. Maybe he couldn't wait. He was walking up the stairs. The doorbell rang.

Slowly, she floated to the door, enjoying every delicious moment of anticipation. She took her time, adjusting her décolletage. "Just a moment," she nearly sang with joy.

When she opened the door, Monica blinked in disbelief. She pulled her kimono shut. "Who the hell are you?" she demanded.

"Szechuan Balace?" the small, dark-haired man pronounced hopefully, a greasy brown bag in his hands.

"Huh?" Monica stood frozen, clutching the robe to her chest.

"Szechuan Balace?" The man looked confused, slightly panicked, pulled out a yellow bill. "Number 45?" he asked. "Cold sesame noodles?"

Monica stirred as from a dizzying merry-go-round. "Oh…Yes…I called before. I'm sorry. I forgot…Just a minute," she said. "I'll get my wallet."

She gave him a five-dollar tip.

Monica stood at the green Formica counter in her kitchenette and opened the white container. She didn't bother finding a bowl, even sitting down.

Chopsticks in hand, she dove into the noodles, slurping them, peanut sauce sluicing into her mouth, on her lips. Licking her lips. Oh, it was good! Chopsticks made it so easy. Just dig in and chow down. More, more, more. An orgy of taste and texture! So very delicious. She was overcome, lapping the long noodles into her mouth, twisting them with her tongue.

When she came out of her trance, she discovered an empty container. She had wolfed down every last peanut butter–drenched noodle.

"What a bad girl I've been," she said to her mirror self.

She rushed into the bathroom, shut the door behind her, and locked it. She stared into the mirror lit by five Hollywood lights. Her interrogators. Yes, she was fat. She was old. No one would ever love her. How could they?

She knew she shouldn't, but she must. The gluttonous monster who lived inside of her had just pigged out on a trough of carbs, oil, peanut butter, fat. Five thousand calories, at least. She could lose her role! Become impoverished, homeless. Starve to death. She had no other choice. Her reflection was her only witness.

Bending over the bowl, she did the two-finger exercise, plunging her second and third fingers down her throat until she gagged.

Foods of different colors and consistencies poured out of her painted mouth, everything Monica had eaten that day, cascading into the bowl.

Afterward, Monica sat limply on the edge of the tub. A hot washcloth over her face, where she left it for a few moments. Then she doused her face with cold water.

In the kitchenette, she poured herself a glass of seltzer and lit a clove cigarette. The sweet smoke gently enfolded her. She'd try Ronald again in a few minutes.

Suite 55

Hana changed out of her gray sweats into black jeans, knowing they fit well, and an embroidered velour shirt. She wore a white silk camisole underneath. Amber had given it to her for her birthday.

"What can happen?" Hana asked aloud.

The hotel was where she lived, these were her neighbors, just a few feet away. And then there was Saul. He had probably left already. But she could always call Henry.

She looked down at the stack of pages hot off her Selectric. How she longed to show someone her new poetry. It was so different from her prose. She wanted to hear her own words aloud with a witness. On impulse, she threw the pages into her Channel 13 canvas bag.

After locking the door, she snuck into the stairwell, which felt vaguely illegal. There was a filthy skylight covered with black chicken wire. A bulb had burnt out. The stairwell was dim. She grabbed the railing. As she walked down the stairs, twelve steps between each landing, she noticed gray metal fuse boxes, huge black pipes wrapped with a thick fire hose. The walls shone of grease caked with ancient dirt, old fingerprints, paint spots. She came to the second floor and opened the door.

This journey into the netherworld of the Last Hotel suited her nefarious descent. Several days earlier, they had shared an elevator ride. Dr. T. had smiled at her before he got off.

"I don't know your name," he said to her. She'd felt her cheeks burn. She'd seen him do his number with Monica, who lived right below her. And then he had called her.

Now she stood in front of Suite 21, staring at a white plaque with black letters: *DR. RONALD TANNENBAUM, Ph.D.* She knocked on the door, waited a few seconds. A buzzer sounded, and the door unlocked into his suite. He stood in the doorway.

"Hi," she said, noticing his white loose-fitting Indian gauze shirt, drawstring pants. Was he wearing underwear?

A warm smile spread across his face.

"I'd given up hope," he said. "I thought you might be in the midst of a creative spurt."

"Actually, I had a good writing day. But it's nice to see another human being that I don't have to create."

"That's very curious."

"Said like a true shrink."

"We don't actually like that term."

"Well, I'm not that keen on the profession."

"Come in," he said.

She looked around. The living room was his office—framed diplomas (Long Island University, Adelphi), two chairs, a couch or rather the couch, with requisite box of tissues. The more she looked, the more the place gave her the creeps.

He showed her the bedroom: an enormous waterbed with black satin sheets, reflected like double vision, on the mirrored ceiling.

She backed out. "I see…"

He grinned. "It works for me."

"Well, speaking of work, I'm trying to finish a manuscript to submit to the Yale Younger Poets contest." She sat down in the smaller, designated patient's seat and opened her bag. "If you win, they publish your book. My poetry teacher, Helen Youngman, was a Yale Younger poet."

"Shall we have some wine first?"

He brought out a bottle of Chateau Sainte Colombe Cotes de Castillon. "I visited this vineyard, near Nice. A beautiful villa with grapevines overhanging the balcony. They served it with the most amazing brie." With much ceremony, he uncorked the bottle.

He raised the cork to his right nostril and sniffed with discrimination. Then he passed it to Hana. "Take in the scent," he said.

She did.

He poured wine into two cut crystal glasses, placed on the wooden table.

"Cheers!" he said. "I'm glad you came."

"*L'chaim.*"

"A nice Jewish girl," he teased.

"You're stereotyping me," she said.

"Only kidding. How do you like the wine?"

"Love the oaky body, the bouquet…"

He nodded contentedly, sipping his wine. "Tell me about yourself."

"I'm a writer," she declared.

"You have a job though?"

She nodded. "I work in publishing."

"Do you like it?"

She shrugged. "Considering that I'm an underpaid serf? But it allows me to write."

"I see."

"Would you like to hear something I've been working on?"

"Sure," he said unsurely.

Hana pulled out a black portfolio overflowing with typed pages.

"My poems will tell you a lot more about me."

"Well, all right." He settled into his leather Eames chair.

"You can give me feedback, if you like. But I'd prefer if you didn't tear my work apart."

At that moment, the phone rang. Dr. T. stared at it. "I'll let the answering service pick up. Go on," he said. Stretching his legs on the matching ottoman, he took a long, ecstatic sip of wine. "Entertain me."

Hana stood up. She closed her eyes as if to garner inner strength. After a few seconds, she opened her eyes. Hana began slowly, her voice soft and artfully modulated. "The first poem is titled 'Poetess.'

Her poetry's not dipped in pink
Dappled purple, menstrual
Though her hips are ample.

Near-sighted she's not
Nor her hair nested in a knot
Like a strangled peacock.

She wears rouge and means it
Gadding about in glass slippers
Rubber-soled so as not to slip

Wantonly, wanting to spill
In a great white belly flop
With the grace of a seal.

To live she steals poems
One ear pressed to hear the click
As her fingers turn the wheel."

"Oh! I like that one, except I don't know about the menstrual blood."

"There's an internal slant rhyme. Purple. Menstrual. And the coloration, of course."

"Oh, I see."

Hana continued. "Kamikaze. The Japanese word translates to mean divine wind. 'Kamikaze.'"

Crazy, in love with the dive
The steel-hearted knife of it
Rising-sun flags on her sleeve.

The white scarf is tied
Around her white throat
As it was done during the war.

This time it is real.
She hears the roll of dice.
It is her teeth.

She cuts the plane's engine
Saying it: Tenno Heika Banzai
Long live the Emperor.

In divine wind
There is no water
Not even a prayer."

"Is it about suicide?" Dr. T. asked.

"That's the literal meaning. But I see it as my artist manifesto," Hana said. "No holds barred. Go after your own personal truth."

"I don't know poetry."

Hana rolled her eyes. "People think they have to be taught poetry. It's basic, like music. Just close your eyes and listen."

He looked down at his watch.

"I'd like to read you another poem. It's short," she said, starting to read. "'Fire Dancer.'

At ten I saw magic: a paper snake
Lit by matches danced as if charmed
Burning in phosphorescent milk
Dance only in fire! it hissed.

My feet are dipped in asbestos
The scarab on my wrist is luck
In the trill of a lunatic flutist
I dance and the paper dolls burn."

"Very good, Hana," he said as soon as she was finished. Working himself out of his chair, he stood up. "Thanks. I really enjoyed it. Would you like a little more wine?"

"I'll just read you the opening of 'Legacy.'

I have read the coffee grinds in my cup
They say no father ever loved his daughter.
He always feared her yellow hair, her lips
Violet as her mother's vulva..."

Dr. T. interrupted her. "I think I've had enough, Hana."

"But I'm not finished."

"Why are you reading this to me?"

"Because I consider you an intelligent reader."

"Look, I spend many hours everyday listening to people scream, cry, and talk, right here, right in that chair you're occupying. It's not what I do with my free time."

"Are you saying that I'm like one of your patients?"

"Clients."

"I don't care what you call them." She collected her pages, which had fanned on the floor.

"Would you like some more wine?" he repeated.

He poured a half glass for her. As she raised it, the telephone rang again. Dr. T. shook his head.

"A client?" Hana asked.

The phone kept ringing. "The service will pick up in a moment."

The ringing stopped, then started again.

"I really don't know who…" he said. "Just ignore it."

"So tell me. What do you think of my poems?"

"I'm no expert on poetry. I liked the one about the poetess. Then it got kind of heavy."

"Is there something wrong with that?"

He shrugged. "As for the last one, it seemed rather crude."

"What did you like about the poems?"

"Strong images. Good use of language. You have a great sense of rhythm."

"Thanks," she said, smiling with pleasure.

"Can I say something else?"

She nodded.

"How old are you, Hana?"

"Twenty-eight," she answered.

"As I said, I don't know anything about poetry. But I'd think if you want to have a career and make a living as a writer, you should write prose. There's no audience for poetry. Try writing a novel."

"I have a prose work in progress. "

Hana leaned forward in her chair as if she might attack. "But I've read my poetry to hundreds of people in cafes and churches. Did you ever hear of the

Poetry Project at St. Mark's Church in the Bowery?"

He shook his head.

"Allen Ginsberg read there, Gregory Corso, all the famous poets."

"I didn't get that last poem about the vulva," he said.

"You seemed upset by it."

"No, that's not—"

"It's Oedipal, isn't it? And you're the shrink. Isn't that how you reduce everything that is original, a little twisted, peculiarly individual—into unresolved issues and neurosis?"

"Why are you so angry?" he asked.

She stood up. "Because you're all full of shit. You guys are always trying to manipulate."

"Have you ever been in treatment?"

She nodded reluctantly. "Oh, yes. Your colleagues have taken thousands of my dollars. And you know what I got for it?"

"I hesitate to ask."

"S.O.S.—same old shit. Meeting men like you who seduce women on waterbeds with mirrored ceilings." She paused, then spat the words. "And I happen to know you've been shtupping my downstairs neighbor Monica."

"Oh?"

"These rooms are not soundproof."

"You were listening?"

"I don't even know why you invited me."

He stood up. "Anyway, uh…"

"Hana," she reminded him.

"Of course." He laughed lightly. "I have a couple things I need to do. It was nice of you to stop by for a visit."

"All right," she said, holding the sheaf of poems against her chest, then straightening the stack. She stuck them into her Channel 13 bag, then looked up at him.

"This has been great," she said. "I already have some ideas for revisions."

"Glad I could be of service."

The phone rang again. He closed the door behind her.

Hana didn't notice. She was thinking that she had to find a word other than *vulva*. It was crude.

Lobby

Saul walked past Pete, who looked up from the turquoise vinyl couch. "How ya doin', Saul?"

"Don't you have any place to go?" he demanded.

"Wha's happening..." Pete began, "with the hotel?"

"If I were you, I'd start looking for another room. That's all I'll say. Now go."

Pete stood up unsteadily. "We know where I'm not wanted." He rang the elevator bell. A moment later, the door opened. Leah stood there. Pete wavered into the elevator past her.

"It's good to see you're still alive," Saul grumbled as Leah strutted out.

She dropped her voice. "Let's not talk here. Can we go for a walk?"

"So we'll go for a walk, daughter of mine."

Saul opened the door for her. Leah walked several feet in front of him. As if she didn't want anyone to know.

"I'm parked on 73rd and Amsterdam. We can talk in the car."

This one was a 1979 Chevrolet Caprice with matching blue velour seats. Saul liked new cars. He unlocked the passenger door. Leah slipped inside her father's car, as she had done since she was little.

A long time ago, she dreaded sitting in his cars as he drove her to places he didn't want to go. He only wanted to rest when he wasn't working at the factory in New Jersey, but her mother forced him to drive the child here, *schlepp* the child there. She never joined them, preferred to use the precious time for one of her projects. Ruth's hands were never idle. She was always *potchkying*. An embroidered table cloth, mosaic tiled table, sewing her fashion fantasies into her and her daughter's often dreaded reality. "I want store-bought clothes!" Leah shrieked.

As he drove her to some friend's house or to buy art supplies, Saul clutched the wheel like he wanted to choke it. "Damn it!" Screaming at red lights, at pedestrians, cars passing him, honking his horn furiously. He couldn't stand to wait. Sometimes she feared he would get violent. But it was just his voice that bellowed inside the confines of the car.

She looked at her father now, who looked older since the last time she saw him. He gave her a resigned smile.

"So," he said.

"So," she answered.

"How you doing?"

Leah shrugged, pulling her black trench collar up. "Everything's okay."

"You have enough money?"

She shrugged again. "I'm working overtime at the magazine."

"Here." He took out his gold money clip and gave her two twenties.

"Thanks," she mumbled.

"You know, Leah, things are changing at the hotel."

"What do you mean?"

"There are some people...Do you remember Viktor Last, my partner?"

"We went to his son's bar mitzvah."

"Ha! That's exactly what I said. Well, Viktor passed his share on to Jonah. That's his name."

"And?"

"And he, this Jonah Last, and his lawyer came to see me. I didn't even know. They bought out the other partners' shares."

Leah gasped. "No!"

He nodded.

"What about you?"

"What about me? They've got a lot of money. Somebody or some company is bankrolling them. I'll do what I can, but I'm a little fish here with these sharks—I don't know."

"You mean Jonah Last is going to sell the hotel?"

"Well, he can't yet because I haven't agreed to hand over my fifteen percent. But they're putting pressure on me," he said. "The bastards."

"Can't you go to court?"

"I've been and I will, Leah."

"Does that mean everyone will be evicted?"

"They say they won't do anything. That it's a non-eviction conversion."
His head dropped into his hands. "What can I do? I'll keep working because
they say they'll keep me on. That's a joke. It's all a joke, a not good joke."

"Will you tell the residents?"

"Most of them already know. How come you don't know? You don't talk
to nobody? I don't understand you. I never did. And you still haven't come
out to visit us."

She shrugged.

"If you could just make a little effort. I'm not asking you to give me the
moon."

"Dad, I told you. I'm not ready to meet her. Subject closed."

He shook his head. "You're so much like your mother."

"But I look like you," she said. "At least that's what people used to say."

"Leah, they got me," he said, bending over. "I have my family, my health,
thanks God, and they take away my hotel. I thought I could work here at least
another ten years."

Leah turned to her father. "What will you do, Dad?"

"We have some savings, thanks God, and our health. We'll be okay. You
know I play the stock market for years?"

She nodded.

"I've done well," he told her. "Now listen to me, Leah. I've done very
well, at least on paper, unless the market crashes. And since you are my only
one, you will one day inherit a good amount of money."

"God, Dad. I'm so broke. Couldn't you give some of it to me now?"

"Why are you broke? You work for a living."

"I have debts, Dad."

"Debts? I never had debts in my life."

"Credit card debts."

"You pay those thieves 18 percent? Oh no! Why didn't you come to me?"

"You think you would've just given it to me?" she argued.

"You never asked me."

"Trust me, you wouldn't have approved."

She turned away from him, staring out the window.

"What's going on, Leah?"

"I can't talk about it." She looked into her lap.

"I know you go with women," he said flatly. "Of course, I'd rather you got married and had a baby, but if that's your nature—"

"How do you know?"

"In the hotel, you see lots of things."

"You've known all the time, Dad?" She began to cry.

"It's all right," he said, stroking her head for the first time in thirty years.

She had a memory of being with her father and mother at the Bronx Zoo. Saul had stood in front of the caged orangutan, beating his chest. Yes, he was handsome, almost movie star–like, when he was younger.

Leah hated to admit it, but it seemed her father had found some kind of peace with Luba. Calm compared to what he was like. He'd had a temper, and when he started to scream, it was hard for him to stop. Now he was no longer the raging, hurt animal that he had been when she was growing up.

"What will happen to the hotel?"

"I'm trying to get a postponement hearing," he said. "Who knows?"

"You know, the attic I live in—"

Saul raised his voice. "I told you I didn't want you to live there. But you insisted. I would never rent it!"

"Hold on, Dad." She grabbed his arm. "It's a great place. The Last Hotel. Living here has been a trip. You know Fred?"

"From the sixth floor?"

She nodded. "He leaves things for me at my door. Like books and CDs. He left me a pair of gloves he washed."

Saul broke into a broad smile. "Oh, yeah. Fred. That lunatic. Suite 62. Always on his bicycle, looking for junk on the street. He got me a TV for Henry after his junkie son stole his."

"Thanks, Dad," she said. "I mean it." She opened her door. "I have to go now."

"What's your rush?"

"I've got to do something."

"Don't be a stranger."

She waved to him as she walked up 73rd Street. Maybe she'd cop from Kofi later.

Suite 64

Duc sat against the headboard of his double bed, a white nubby spread at his feet. A dark-skinned hairy giant, his long legs, big feet extending beyond the mattress. He was reading the leaflet an earnest Bahamian woman had handed him in Grand Central Station.

AM I GOING TO HEAVEN?
Check all the things you think are required.

Obeying God's law and commandments
Offering gifts of charity
Doing your best
Living a good life
Doing Good Work
Following the Golden Rule
Tithing or giving money to the church
Maintaining church membership
Attending church regularly
Saying your prayers
Fasting
Having a water Baptism
Taking Holy Communion
Being born of Christian parents
Completing Confirmation
Taking the sacrament of Penance
Giving Extreme Unction

FIND THE ANSWERS INSIDE

In her neatly ironed white shirt, floral print skirt, and shiny patent pumps, she had reminded him of women from his church. Even of his own mother, who prayed to Jesus daily.

Duc tried to be a good Christian. He'd been raised by good Christians in Savai'i. Even his family name was Christian. Though he loved Jesus and had been an altar boy, he sinned. He repented, and then he sinned. "*Inter faeces et urinam.*" That's what he remembered from the Jesuit school. We are born between feces and urine.

Since he'd come to New York City five years ago, it was getting more and more difficult. There were so many temptations. In the club, women threw themselves at him, offered him money. So did men. Oh, the traps. Everywhere. If you weren't careful where you stepped. It was like dog shit on the street. Cockroaches. He only had few, thank God.

Duc looked around. Though he had been in this small furnished hotel room for three months, he had added little to its basic set up except the wall hanging above his bed. He turned to look at it. It was a traditional Samoan weaving. Sometimes he could stare himself into its intense blue sky, summoning the scent of teuila, the flaming red birds of paradise.

He'd had a lover for several months, Florentine, who was a bartender at the club. But Duc couldn't get over the shame. If his mother could see him. That was part of the problem. Florentine was a good man but was involved in some things he shouldn't be. A joint was fine, but hard drugs only brought down their users.

Duc turned on the TV. That's how he learned his American English. He went through the stations, then stopped. That soap opera actress from the fourth floor. *Forgive Us Our Passions*. He watched for a few minutes. God, she could play a corpse. He picked up the other leaflet the woman in Grand Central had handed him, which had three illustrations with accompanying captions.

"HOW DO YOU VIEW JESUS?"
As a newborn baby?
A dying man?
Or an exalted king?

"Jesus!" Duc said aloud. He turned on the faucet in his small sink. Soaked a facecloth in hot water. Placed it on his face. That's when he heard a knock on his door.

Who could that be? No one ever knocked on his door. He looked at his watch. Could it be Henry the super? Why would he come up? Saul had probably already left. He replaced the cloth on his face. Maybe they'll go away.

Another knock. Sighing, he stood up. When he opened the door, he discovered Amber standing in his doorway holding a videotape and a plate of wrapped cookies.

"Hi," she said smiling.

"Hi," Duc answered hesitantly.

"I'm Amber. I live in Suite 52. One floor down."

"Sure. I've seen you in the elevator."

"I've always wondered what the rooms are like up here. Who else lives on the sixth floor?"

"Do you know Fred? The one with the bicycle?"

"Who brings in all the junk?"

He nodded.

"He must be some neighbor."

"No one has ever seen the inside of his place, but it doesn't smell great."

"Who else?"

"You know Pete Mahoney?"

"The guy always sitting in the lobby, sipping something?"

"That's him."

"And you all share the toilet and shower, right?"

He nodded.

"I don't even want to imagine that." She paused. "This may sound a bit forward, but I was sitting in my little room, about to watch my favorite movie." She showed him the cover. "Have you ever seen this?"

He shook his head as she handed him the video. *Some Like It Hot*," he read aloud.

"An American classic directed by Billy Wilder with Marilyn Monroe, Tony Curtis, and Jack Lemmon. You've heard of Marilyn Monroe in Somalia, right?"

"Samoa," he corrected her.

"I knew that," she said, shaking her head. "I'm losing it."

"Of course. And Tony Curtis too. We love American movies."

"But you haven't seen *Some Like It Hot?*"

"Actually, I haven't."

"It's an amazing Hollywood film."

"I've heard that."

"Are you doing anything right now?"

He looked around. "Not really, but—"

Do you have a VCR?"

"Sure."

"Why don't we give it a try?" she suggested. "May I? I'm just being a good neighbor."

Duc considered it. He liked Amber's spirit, how she put herself out in the world like that. Also he had a suspicion. Maybe an intuition. There was something about her.

She entered his apartment, looking around. "Oh, this isn't bad."

"It's only thirty dollars a week."

"What a bargain!" Her eye caught the woven wall hanging above his bed. "Gosh, that's beautiful."

"It's from my country."

"It looks handmade."

"My mother gave this to me when I was leaving. She made it herself."

"What an amazing gift."

"She told me, 'So you won't forget where you come from.'"

"Really, it's very special." She was still holding the plate. "I brought you something else."

She handed it to him.

"Do you know what it is?"

He shook his head. "I have no idea."

"A treat."

"What kind of treat?"

"You'll see." Amber approached the edge of the bed. "Why don't you let me make this up a little," she said, shaking the bedspread. "Would you put the tape in the VCR?"

"Sure," he said unsurely.

As he bent down to insert the video in his Sony player, Amber appreciated his lovely Samoan ass. He was very fine indeed.

"It's booted up," Duc said.

"These are special cookies," she said.

"Oh?"

"I made them myself, or rather, I doctored them myself. They are garnished with mari-ju-ana."

"No!" he exclaimed.

"Yes." She lowered her voice. "Would you like to try one?"

"All I can offer is water."

"Do you have tea?"

"Oh yes," he said, walking toward his tiny kitchen unit. "We're very English and drink tea."

She handed him a cookie.

He hesitated. "What kind of stuff is it?"

"I don't remember. Mexican sativa?" She took a bite into a cookie. "Go on," she encouraged.

He took one bite, then another. "Not bad. I like chocolate chip."

Amber sat down on the edge of the bed, in front of the TV. Duc brought two cups of tea, placing them on the night table. As the film credits rolled, Amber was still munching on her cookie. He sat down next to her.

"Do you feel anything?" Duc asked.

"It takes awhile to get into your system, but it lasts longer." She leaned back on his bed.

For several minutes, they watched as Tony Curtis and Jack Lemmon witness George Raft murder someone. He and his goons spot them. They run away, carrying their musical instruments, pursued by his men. When Curtis and Lemmon discover an all-female band, they decide to dress up as women and join them.

"I think I feel something," Amber said, giggling. "My nose is itching."

"That sounds like fun."

"And dry mouth."

"Me too." He passed her a cup, then sipped from his own. As they continued watching, Duc moved a little closer to Amber.

"This is fun!" she said.

"Totally unexpected."

"Saul's been pushing me to talk to you," she confided. "He told me you were off tonight."

"I never thought he cared," Duc said.

"The man has a tender heart. And for some reason, he likes to talk to me, tells me his problems."

"Sad about the hotel, though I've only been here a few months."

"Awful! I never thought I'd stay here this long—three years—but it's been great." Amber looked at the screen. "Oh, here comes a good part."

Jack Lemmon is getting dressed up for his date with Joe E. Brown on his yacht. He puts on a hideous wig, an awful dress, and hobbles away in his high heels.

"You know, I hate to say it. Hollywood got it wrong," Amber remarked. "They don't look like women."

"What would you know about that?"

"A little," she said.

"Just a little?" he asked slyly.

Marilyn Monroe began to sing as she strummed her ukulele.

> *Running wild, lost control.*
> *Running wild, mighty bold.*
> *Feeling gay, reckless too…*

Duc reached for her. She melted into his arms. They shared a long, luscious kiss. And then another. Wonderful deep, deep, endless kisses. Submerged. Submarine-race watching, as Murray the K called it.

"How's the dry mouth?" he asked.

"Wet," she answered. "And you?"

Duc reached for her breasts. She let him nuzzle there. Andrew stirred. His hands began to move down her body.

She held him back. "Hey, let's get to know each other a little."

"I know what I want to know."

"What's that?" she asked.

"That I like you."

"Wait," Amber cried. "I love the final scene!"

"In the first place, I'm not a natural blond," Jack Lemmon told his ardent admirer. "I smoke all the time. I can never have children." Finally, he removed his wig and shouted to his admirer. "I'm a man!"

Joe E. Brown smiled haplessly. "Well, nobody's perfect."

"You're what I've been looking for," Duc declared.

"You mean it?"

"I wouldn't say it if I didn't."

"You know I'm a little different."

"Yes." He continued to kiss her breasts.

"I am different," she repeated breathlessly.

He continued to kiss her.

"I'm pre-op," she tried to explain.

"It's okay."

"Do you know what that means?"

Bending over Amber, Duc crooned. "Yoo, hoo…You can come out now."

"You know!" she cried.

He nodded.

"Don't hate me."

"You have no idea how perfect you are," he said, thinking he could introduce Amber to his mother.

Sofa Club

Pete Mahoney, ensconced in the turquoise vinyl couch, was enjoying his beverage in a brown paper bag, sipping through a straw. Lenny walked into the lobby, carrying a rolled up racing form under his arm.

"Did Saul leave already?" he asked.

"Yeah, said he had to go to the bank, then was going home."

"So wha'd you do at the office?"

"I lost on Tricky Dick."

"We all lost with Tricky Dick. Now we've got that actor who will probably be the next president."

"What, you prefer that idiot Mondale?"

"Pete, have you heard anything else?"

He shook his head. "Saul says they can't do nothing unless he sells his share."

"What does he have?"

"I heard 15 percent."

"He's not gonna give up this place. Just like that. Without a fight."

"He doesn't have the dough to fight these vultures."

"What we need is a money person."

"You know anyone who has some extra moolah, like a couple hundred thou?"

Lenny shook his head. "Not in my line of work. I mean, I could always win big."

"That big?"

At that moment, Pincus walked in, carrying his overfull leather briefcase. "Good evening, gentlemen," he said.

"What's good about it?" Pete asked.

"No gentlemen here."

"Now you sound like Saul."

"Shit," Pete said. "This is home. I'm comfortable here. I have my friends. I even like Saul."

"What do you mean?" Lenny said. "He's the main attraction."

"Saul looks tired," Pincus observed.

"All this is wearing him out."

"Did you talk to your brother-in-law?" Pincus asked.

"He's looking into it, but it's a long shot if they sell the building. We don't have any legal rights as statutory tenants. We don't even have leases. We never signed anything..." His voice trailed off. "Fred went downtown to the tenant board. They gave him some numbers to call."

The three men sat lost in their thoughts for several minutes.

"It's over," Lenny said flatly. "Maybe not tomorrow, but it's happening all over the city. They call it 'gentrification.' The rich throw out the working man."

Pincus shook his head. "Sometimes it's time. Faye and I, maybe we'll live together. In sin," he giggled softly. "But she wants to move downtown to Greenwich Village. She's kind of Bohemian."

"Bohemian." Pete belched loudly.

Pincus ignored him. "I like it uptown. I wouldn't mind living in Riverdale."

"I bet nothing's going to change yet. But when it does, I'm selling my taxi and medallion. I can get big bucks. Esther and me gonna buy a Winnebago. I like to drive. We can go to Atlantic City, Las Vegas, Reno..."

"Bon voyage." Pete belched again.

"What's the matter with you, Pete?"

"Both of you guys sound hitched," he said. "I never thought I'd hear it. Not in a hundred years. Especially from you, Lenny. You called them all wallet sniffers."

"Not this one. Estie lets me sniff hers."

"Urrrgh!" Pete made a sound like he was about to puke.

"You're just jealous," he said.

"It's pathetic." Pete made a face. "You know the score. They're sweet till they're not, then they take you to the cleaners."

"Maybe not."

Pincus smiled wistfully. "We all met here in the Last Hotel."

"You want a plaque?"

"Where you gonna go, Pete?" Lenny asked.

"When it's time, there's another hotel on Eighty-Second Street and Columbus. The Endicott. Like here, except a rougher clientele."

"I'll miss this," Pincus said. "Sitting on the sofa. Talking every night a little."

Pete took a long sip as he slowly slid down the couch. "I thought it would be my Last Hotel."

"Come on, old man," Lenny said, propping him up.

"You don't know shit from Shinola," he muttered.

At that moment, Hana entered the lobby, hoisting her Channel 13 canvas bag over her shoulder, filled with folders and blue cardboard boxes.

"So you've heard what's going on?" Lenny asked her.

"I'm not sure what you mean," she answered.

"It looks like the hotel might get sold, and then we'll probably all have to leave."

"What about Saul?"

"Who knows?"

She shook her head as she pressed the button. The elevator arrived. Reardon walked out. He bowed his head as he stepped past Hana.

"Hey, Reardon," Lenny said. "What do you think?"

"I think it's damn rotten. I've been in the hotel for over ten years. And that doesn't mean anything?"

"The tenant board will give us a pro bono lawyer."

"Look, there are two separate issues here. Our apartments. And Saul. What's going to happen to him?"

"He said they want to keep him on, but it's just a matter of time. He knows it too," Lenny said.

At that moment, the elevator opened. Gittel came out, carrying her thermos. "Halo everybody! Halo!" she said. "I have hot tea with lemon."

Suite 62

Fred discovered Leah's note as he opened his door. The ruled sheet looked ripped out of a notebook. "Maybe I'll find something for you," he read aloud. What did she mean by that?

Fred began to sweat. He could feel his heart pounding. Suppose she got the wrong idea? He didn't mean any boyfriend/girlfriend kissypoo. He wasn't looking for anyone.

Usually he sold his stuff, but not always. Besides, she could use Italian leather gloves and a scarf. He thought the hike book might be good for her, get her outside. But more than that, forget it. And yet. He looked at the note again. What did she mean about finding something for him?

Leah was hot, in her way. He could feel it. Hot and depressed, the sexiest combo around. Made you feel like you were in an existentialist novel. Sartre or Camus' *The Stranger*, which he'd just found on 73rd Street. She was definitely strange. Possibly gay. Yes, that must be it. He always fell for dykes. Their very unavailability made for great fantasy. That's the role women played in his life—objects of fantasy, like luxurious vacations on yachts around the world. Around the world. That would be fun.

He turned on the TV. Ronald Reagan's smiling face.

"All I can say to all of you is thank you, and thank you for more than just George Bush and myself, thank you, because if the trend continues, we may very well control one house of the Congress for the first time in a quarter of a century. We have already picked up some governorships and—"

Fred turned the TV off. "Fascist pig," he mumbled. His eyes fixated on the wooden box in his bookcase, filled with red sticks of dynamite.

He leaned back into his green La-Z-Boy and began to undress his upstairs neighbor, taking off her black trench, the fedora she wore over her face, her eyes just barely visible. He removed it, met her dark eyes. "Take off your clothes," he demanded. She stripped for him, flinging her black lace brassiere at his face.

Just then, the doorbell rang. "Wha'?" he called out. "Who is it?"

"Your neighbor," the voice answered inaudibly.

He shook himself awake, already regretting leaving behind the fantasy. He tucked his shirt into his pants, then opened door.

Leah stood in the doorway. "Have you ever been up on the roof?"

"Wha'?"

"The roof. Upstairs. There's a door, then a stairway to the roof."

"Why would you go to the roof?"

"Haven't you ever been on a building roof?" she asked, amazed.

"I grew up in the suburbs," he admitted. "There were no high roofs."

"No tar beach," she said. "You were deprived."

"We went to Rockaway."

"Well, should I show it to you?"

"Now?"

"I don't think anyone knows about it."

"Sure. Let me just get my keys."

The sun was sinking like an orange beach ball as they opened the roof door. Both stood silently for several moments and stared.

"Pretty amazing, huh?" Leah said. "To find this is in the middle of the city."

"Did you hear the Reagan speech?"

"I can't stand him."

Wisps of pink and purple cotton candy clouds floated over their heads.

"This will all be over soon. They're taking the hotel away from Saul."

"I know," she said. "He told me."

"He did?"

She nodded. "He's my father."

"Saul is your father?"

Leah looked down.

"I can't believe it."

"When I needed somewhere to crash, he gave me the space."

"I still can't get my brain around you being Saul's daughter."

"Well, I am. Okay?"

"Okay. So I went down to the tenants board a few days ago. There's something called a non-eviction conversion, but why would they do that? We don't have leases."

"I know," she said.

"It makes me furious. Everyone in this city is so fucking greedy. All they ever think about is money. Decent people live here."

She nodded.

"I've lived at the hotel for seven years. Do you know how much stuff I have? They're not gonna get me out of my room." He stamped his foot. "That's all there is to it."

"What are you going to do?"

"I won't go quietly," he said. "I can't say any more."

"Like what?"

"Let's enjoy this while we have it." He indicated the sky, which had turned indigo. "I wish I'd known about this place before."

"I know. It's so special," she said.

"Look, you can see Lincoln Center."

"Yeah, and there's that weird replica of the Statue of Liberty."

"Mike O'Neal erected it over the Liberty Café."

"Hey, do you want to share a doobie?" Leah asked.

"A fellow smoker!" he exclaimed. "Light it up."

She took a joint out of her back pocket. Lighting it, she drew in the smoke, then passed it to Fred, who looked happy.

"I have to tell you something, Fred. You know, between us. I'm gay," she said, backing off. "At least I think so. My last relationship was with a major cunt, Angela."

"That's cool."

"But let's hang. Okay?"

"Why not?"

Fred exhaled through his large yellow teeth.

Suite 32

Faye opened her door.

"You ready?" Pincus asked.

Faye locked her door, then took Pincus' arm. They entered the elevator together.

As they walked past the Sofa Club, Pincus asked, "How's everything?"

Pete shrugged.

Lenny looked up from his racing form, unlit cigar in mouth. "Not bad. Where ya going?"

Faye smiled. "For a walk in the park."

"Jeez," Pete said to Lenny.

"What?" Lenny turned to Pete. "Ya know, it's not the worst thing in the world."

"You're giving in too. Gonna let some woman ruin your life."

"Find yourself some lady. You're getting weird, Pete." He picked up the racing form. "So what do you think the chances are for Gorgeous Ugly George?"

Faye winked at him as they stepped out the lobby door.

Pincus and Faye walked past the Dakota, peering inside the immense courtyard. A uniformed guard stood next to a metal shelter.

Crossing Central Park West, they made a striking older couple. Faye in tight black pants, a well-fitting sweater the color of her hair, and walking shoes. Pincus in a pair of new-looking blue jeans, probably his first, that Faye had bought him, of course, and his plaid jacket and muffler.

They entered the park at 72nd Street. Gittel was bent over, feeding bread crumbs to the pigeons. They surrounded her, noisily pecking the grass as she talked to them in Hungarian.

"Come, Faigeleh." Pincus led her to an empty bench.

"So what's the news with the hotel?"

"According to Lenny's brother-in-law-yer," Pincus said with a smile. "That's a play on words."

"Go on."

"We tenants don't have a foot to stand on. We're statutory tenants without leases."

Faye sighed. "I wish we had some time."

"I think we do," Pincus said. "Saul is going to court to get a temporary restraining order."

"But we'll have to move out eventually," she said sadly.

"We can get a huge place uptown with a view of the Hudson River," he said.

"I always wanted to live in the Village. Go to the Lion's Head bar and hang out with writers and journalists like Pete Hamill." She'd done that a few times, looked at the author's framed book jackets. "The Village reminds me of Paris. The little streets, small buildings, book shops, bakeries."

"I like to be uptown, near Fort Tryon Park, the Cloisters, the old streets. The George Washington Bridge..."

"We'll see," Faye said.

"There's something I have to tell you. I've wanted to tell you about it, but I'm very ashamed," Pincus began, looking down.

"What could be so bad?" she asked.

"It's bad. I didn't want to tell you, but I can't keep it from you any longer. I have a guilty conscience." He looked away.

"Okay, Pink. Out with it."

"You know your friend Rachel?"

"Yes..."

"She came to my apartment when you were away."

"Did she bring her lethal *cholent*?" Faye asked.

He nodded. "How did you know?"

"That Rachel never stops."

"What do you mean?"

"She's a nymphomaniac. What do you expect?"

"It was a good *cholent*." Pincus laughed. "So you're not angry?"

"Next time I see her, I'll pour cyanide into her martini." She smiled. "I'm not going to say anything. I've found you. You're a diamond. She's just catting around, hoping to get lucky again. She tested you. You've got character, unlike my ex, putzface." She hugged him. "You can be trusted, Pincus."

"Promise you'll stay with me," he said. "I don't want to be by myself no more."

"Is that why you want to be with me?"

"No, no. Faigeleh, just be my Faigeleh."

"I'm sure I'll never be anyone else's Faigeleh." She turned to him. "I have something to tell you too."

"Okay," Pincus said nervously.

"Do you believe in unnatural occurrences? Supernatural things like ghosts?"

"I believe that the world is full of spirits, visible and invisible."

"I never told you about the ghost who visited me." She laughed in embarrassment. "It was too weird to talk about."

"Faigeleh, I tell you my *bubbe-meises*, you can tell me yours."

"Remember when I came to your apartment with the brisket that first time?"

He nodded. "Of course."

"That day as I was preparing it, something came through my fire escape. I know it sounds totally…"

"What?"

"At first I thought it was a man in a hooded cape. But then I saw a ruby ring and realized it was a woman. She told me to add garlic to the brisket and suggested that you and I get together."

"No!"

"Yes. And this is the weirdest part of it. She told me she was Sylvie. That's before I even knew your wife's name."

Pincus took a breath. "Sylvie had a ruby ring. I gave it to her when we were engaged." He paused. "She was buried with it."

Both sat silently for a few moments.

"I don't believe in that kind of thing," Faye said.

"I know…" His voice trailed off. "These things, they make you wonder."

"Well, I should give thanks to her. She told me that there was more to you than meets the eye."

He giggled boyishly. "I wonder if she's happy now. She kept telling me I should find a woman. She was right, but I didn't know it."

"Afterward, when I tried the window, it was painted shut. And that night, I lit Shabbes candles, something I don't usually do."

Pincus kissed her. "Shall we go to the Famous Dairy Restaurant for the Early Bird Special?"

"Yes, Pinkeleh."

"I love their stuffed cabbage."

"I want a potato knish," she said.

He laughed. "You know what *knish* means in Yiddish."

"You always tell me."

"A vagina," he said giggling. "I love your knish, Faigeleh."

Suite 27

"Jeezus!" Reardon grumbled, stubbing his knee against a metal chair. He shoved it like a sparring partner. The chair tipped over. He lifted it and placed it by the table. Then he picked up the Marlboro pack and shook it. A cigarette rolled out. Lighting up, he inhaled deeply.

Two in the afternoon and Reardon had just awoken after a long night. Usually, he kept his intake down, sipping wine or a few beers, and a lot of black coffee. But at midnight, the Dublin crew rolled in for a nightcap, and some hours later, a second bottle of Johnnie Walker Red, which he had a few fingers' worth.

Now his head was pounding. His stomach turned. He took a long draw on his smoke. Began to cough. "Holy Mother of Christ!"

It had been a good night at the bar. Lots of people, lots of drink. The jukebox played Frank Sinatra and Frank Zappa. Some youngsters wanted disco, but he had standards. No disco at his bar. Counting the till. Five thousand dollars. But now he was goddamn paying for it.

He had stumbled into the Last Hotel at 4 a.m. No one around, thank God. He entered the elevator and pressed 2.

In the early hours, pathetic, sodden, fallen soul that he was, Reardon had stood in front of his door, checking that it was his door, Suite 27, but his fucking key wouldn't fit into the fucking lock. He was to about to go back to the elevator, down to the basement to ask Henry, when, finally: *click, spin*. He was in. He didn't remember getting out of his clothes, into bed.

Reardon had been a bar man most of his life, after he'd given up acting. He'd had a few film roles, a brief appearance in *Amarcord*. But there was too much bullshit. Too many assholes to lick.

Sure, he wasn't a movie star, which he'd been groomed for. Universal Studios had brought him out to audition for a TV series, which he didn't get, and put him up with three other actors in a bungalow on Sunset Boulevard. Too much coke was sniffed off the surface of their glass coffee table.

Reardon had lived at the hotel since 1970, when Patty left him. He was fine with that, but she'd taken his one and only Collie, their daughter, to San Francisco. The Last Hotel, four blocks away from the bar, was as much commitment as he could handle. He still thought about moving to be closer to her.

He'd worked at the Shamrock for the last twelve years. And he prided himself on it. It was his bar, though there were other bartenders, and he didn't own it, of course. But he felt like it was his place. People came to see him, to talk to him, though he kept his own counsel most of the time. Except the occasional joke. "The past, the present, and the future walk into a bar. It was tense."

Reardon walked the bar plank, which added several inches to his six feet, with rooster pride. A bartender wasn't someone who just poured drinks. You had to know the bar, of course. He flipped the colored bottles, cascading liquor into multishaped glasses in an instant. Moreover, you had to know people. How to keep things light, when some of New York's heaviest creatures crawled in, and keep things jovial, watch for the troubled ones, the ones who'd had too much to drink, keep things bright, the patrons thirsty. It required a certain gift. "Did you hear about the dyslexic who walked into a bra?"

Red-eyed, barefoot, cigarette dangling from his lips, Reardon lumbered into his kitchen, about the size of an NYC parking space. He raised the sleeves of his ancient white terrycloth bathrobe, then poured water into his expresso maker, and filled the metal cup with Italian. Then, from the mini fridge Saul had given him, he took out tomato juice, a lemon, an ice cube tray, and a bottle of Stoli from the freezer.

"The hair of the dog that bit you," he pronounced aloud. Or at least he thought he did. What dog? Booze was the dog, he supposed. What breed? He'd read that a hangover was the body's response to alcohol withdrawal. Something about dilation of the blood vessels. Better to withdraw gradually.

He poured a quarter glass of Stoli and filled the rest with tomato juice. A squirt of lemon. He added Worcestershire, Tabasco, a little white horseradish. Down the hatch. He sipped his espresso. With his straight silver hair, shaggy though it was, he looked like a commercial for coffee.

He turned on the tube. Nothing but soap operas. He stopped going through the channels when he saw his neighbor, Monica Powers. She was a looker. Right now, she was emoting about something or other. A terrible actress though. Like all the other bad actresses he'd seen emote on stage, and off, especially at the bar. He searched for basketball scores, politics, but nothing at this hour. He switched the TV off and downed the rest of his Bloody Mary in several sips. Oooh! His whole body shook like a wet dog. "Jeezus."

There was the time that the five of them traveled to Ireland together. Maddy O'Brien, Christopher McCarthy known as Cart, Patrick Devan, Ciarnan Joyce and Yours Truly Reardon. They crawled Dublin's pubs on their knees, on their bellies, bellowing Irish doggerel, Maddy crooning "Danny Boy" in his famous tenor. Ciarnan was from the fair city. He took them to Oliver St. John Gogarty, the Brazen Head, the Stag's Head, where he heard the curse of Mary Malone.

Last night, at the bar, he recited it from memory. That's how loaded he was. "May the curse of Mary Malone and her nine blind illegitimate children chase you so far over the hills of damnation that the Lord himself can't find you with a telescope."

A couple people applauded.

One thing that Reardon knew was booze, and he could hold it. Like a bull. He'd been accused of a hollow leg, an unholy tolerance. But not this night. He'd given in. Surrendered to the devil. He loved the hell out of those mates! It had been great for everyone to be together again. "What's the difference between an Irish wedding and an Irish wake? One less drunk." Just like old times before marriages, deaths, AA. But there was a price, which the rigmarole rolling in his head kept reminding him.

Now he felt as if he could puke. He went into the bathroom, but could only manage a few dry heaves. A smoke. He needed a smoke. He shook the red and white pack. Nothing came out. Impossible. It was totally unfucking unacceptable—he had run out of cigarettes. "No, Jeezus! No! Not now!"

This was the limit. He jumped into the shower. The hot water pelting his back, his head, awoke him from his stupor. "Oh, Benediction!" he sang out.

Oh, the years of nuns in Catholic school in their black robes, which made them mysterious, even, on occasion, enticing. He had an image of Sister Ruth. He'd once caught a glimpse of her legs when she sat down. The height of his adolescent erotic fantasy!

He threw his white terrycloth bathrobe over his wet body, tying its belt around his waist. He stared at himself in the steamed mirror that he cleared with his hand. He grabbed his razor. A rotten racket, that Hollywood business.

In the early afternoon light, Reardon's face looked like a mask of a very handsome man: the angular bone structure with its steel beam cheek bones, deep-set coal eyes, the intense black brows, and slightly pugnacious Irish nose. His hair had turned silver in his twenties, and he wore a ruler-straight side part. Because of the way he looked, some people expected him to be a certain way. That wasn't his problem.

He slipped into last night's jeans with clean knickers, pulling out a black turtleneck from the top shelf in his closet. He had five black jerseys, which he rotated. Grabbing his wallet, sunglasses, and a black leather jacket from the hook, he was out the door. Something to eat wouldn't be bad. Coat the belly. But first, a carton of smokes.

Slamming the door behind him, he walked to the elevator. It was just two floors, but he couldn't handle even that. He pressed the elevator button. It was on the fourth floor.

As Reardon stepped in, he noticed the pretty older woman from the fourth floor. He had seen her before. Dark hair and flashing eyes, her name was Rachel, he thought. He nodded to her as he walked to the back. She wore a short black dress and high heels.

The elevator started again. That's when they both felt a jolt. "Jeezus!" Reardon muttered. The car came to a complete stop, throwing Rachel against Reardon. Startled, they looked at each other, then moved away to opposite sides of the elevator.

"Oh, excuse me."

"I'm so sorry."

Then the lights went out.

"What the hell is going on?"

"Saul! Henry! Help!" Rachel called.

No answer.

"Are you all right?" Reardon asked.

"I think so," the feminine voice answered. "How about you?"

"It looks like the elevator's stuck," he grumbled.

"Oh no."

"I know."

"I hope it won't be long."

"I'd kill for a smoke," he said.

"You don't have to kill anybody," she said. "I have Virginia Slims."

"God bless you!" he cried out. "Mother Mary…"

She hunted through her large bag in the dark. "I can't see anything."

A light flashed from downstairs and the door opened. "Who's up there?" Saul called.

"It's me, Reardon from Suite 27, and…"

"Rachel," she called out. "Suite 42."

"Okay, listen carefully. We have a problem. I called already. Someone is coming. The cable's stuck and the electric short-circuited. You're fine as long as you stay where you are. I'll leave the door open a crack. Reardon, tell her some jokes," he joshed. "I'll stop by in a few minutes."

The light became a thin crack.

"Let's have that smoke," Reardon said gruffly.

"Do you think we should? There's a limited amount of oxygen in here."

"Well, he did open the door."

"Not much," she said.

"I gotta have a cigarette," he implored.

"I understand," she said.

"I'll just take a few puffs."

"Is there something we could do to distract you? Something that will keep your mind on other things?" she whispered.

"Like what?

"Like this."

She reached out in the darkness, kissed him on his neck, giving him a light vampire nibble.

"Oh!" He gasped.

She ran her lips up his neck, and whispered in his ear, "Have you ever wanted to do something naughty?"

"Huh?"

"Something totally forbidden?"

"Like what?"

"You know."

He stared at her, just making out her form in the darkness.

"You're a very handsome man, but I'm sure you know that." She held him, and kissed him on the lips. "It's kind of sexy, isn't it?"

"I'd say so. This is a great way to stop smoking."

She kissed him again.

"Nice." He sighed.

"Yes." She leaned back into his embrace. "I don't mind being stuck a little."

"Neither do I."

They slowly lowered themselves to the floor of the elevator. He rolled on top of her. "Might as well get comfortable," he said with a chuckle.

"Hmmmm…" Rachel sighed.

After a few minutes, the elevator jolted again and the lights came on. The elevator began its slow descent, coming to a stop at the first floor. Reardon leaped to his feet. Then he took Rachel's hand and helped her up.

He coughed, clearing his voice, then looked at Rachel and grinned sheepishly. Her lips were a vivid red. So were his. She smiled at him.

Saul opened the door. He studied them both. "Everything okay?"

"Here's your smoke," Rachel said, placing a cigarette between his lips.

Suite 21

Dr. Tannenbaum peeked out from the door of Suite 21, looked both ways, locked up, and took the stairs.

He found Saul sitting at his table with the *New York Times* stock pages spread out before him. He was writing figures in a notebook.

"Can I talk to you about something?"

Saul looked up. "Nu?"

"I'm moving out."

"When?"

"I have the movers coming on Thursday."

"What time?"

"Five a.m."

"Isn't that a little early?"

"Less traffic," he said.

Saul pondered this for several moments. "You sound like you're in a hurry."

He nodded. "I am."

Saul examined him. "You're a psychiatrist, right?"

"Actually I'm a clinical psychologist."

"Whatever you say, sir."

"Actually we're very different. A psychiatrist is an MD."

"Look you're all the same in my book. People come to you because they have problems."

"I suppose."

"I'd never come to a stranger, sit in an office, talk about my problems. I was in Auschwitz. This is my number." He raised his sleeve and showed his tattoo.

"Be that as it may, Saul, I'm moving out. As you know, I've invested quite a bit of money in my suite, particularly in the bedroom. I have a state-of-the-art king-size waterbed and…" He paused. "A mirrored ceiling."

"Yes, I remember when you hired the workers."

"I'd like to get something for leaving the furnishings behind."

"What were you thinking of?"

"Just the bed cost five hundred dollars."

"I see."

"Look, it's a great room. Do you want to see it?"

"We all saw it when the waterbed leaked last year."

"Oh, yes," he said. "What do you think I can get for my stuff? It makes the place more valuable, of course."

"You're absolutely right." Saul's face brightened. "I know just the person you should talk to. He's the new man. Here, I'll write down his name. Jonah Last. This is his home phone number. No, he doesn't mind if you call him at home. He's got funds. Say hello for me."

"Thanks."

As he turned to leave, Saul stopped him. "There's something I've been wanting to ask you."

"Yes?"

"How much do you charge for a session?"

"I have a sliding scale."

"What are the numbers?"

"Usually between sixty and a hundred dollars."

"Whew!" Saul whistled. "I should be a head shrinker."

Dr. Tannenbaum smiled indulgently.

"Any forwarding address?" Saul asked.

He shook his head.

Saul looked him in the eye. "So let me ask you something? Is it that actress in Suite 55?"

He recoiled momentarily, then shrugged. "She keeps calling me."

"Someone said she's pregnant."

"I don't believe it." He shook his head. "And if she is, it's her own damn fault. There's just too much craziness for me right now," he said. "And then Hana the writer on the fifth floor assaults me with her poetry."

"Assaults you with her poetry," Saul repeated, nodding thoughtfully.

"Yeah, she just came to my place and took over."

"I see," Saul said slowly.

"She writes poetry about her vagina and you don't want to know."

"Okay, that's enough." He stood up, towering over Ronald. "Well, I listened to you. How much do you owe me?"

Suite 22

As Lenny opened the door to his suite, Esther closed her eyes, taking a deep breath. Usually they met in her suite. The last time she came over, she had been unprepared.

"That's me," he had told her. "That's who I am. 'I yam what I yam,'" he had mocked himself.

"I can live with that," she had responded. "I suppose."

She liked Lenny a lot, but there could be all kinds of germs and insects here. She took another deep breath and opened her eyes. Much to her surprise, Lenny had actually cleaned up.

"Your place looks, uh, better, Leonard," she said.

He had thrown out his collection of pizza boxes, partly eaten Chinese food cartons, cans of Rheingold...Swept up, made the bed, not to mention the dirty socks and even emptied the ashtrays from last week's poker night.

"I could tell that you thought this place was a dump. And you didn't say anything. That's a nice thing about you. Never mind that." Lenny cried out as they walked into the room, "We're rich, kiddo!"

"Are we?"

"Look at this!"

He opened a large navy blue bowling bag with red letters that spelled *BROOKLYN BOMBERS*. Turning it over, dollar bills of all denominations flowed out of the bag, floating onto the bed like greenish butterflies.

That morning, Lenny and Esther left the Last Hotel, took the A train to Aqueduct at Rockaway Boulevard. "The Big A," Lenny called it as they entered the race hall. They'd each bet one hundred dollars on a trifecta Lenny had suggested after studying the racing form.

"You're fun," she said, as they took seats in the grandstand. "I never did anything this crazy before!"

"Ya only live once," he had said.

"It's just money."

"Yeah."

"I'm glad I have my own income, and I'm not interested in yours."

"That's why I like you. You're not a wallet sniffer."

She turned to him. "Huh?"

"Most of the women I meet," he had said, looking into her eyes, "or the, you know, women I met before you."

And now they were staring at several thousand dollars on Lenny's bed.

"We did the impossible," he was saying. "A trifecta of three losers—who all got the call this morning and ran for their lives."

"It was a miracle."

"Just like you, babe." He rubbed up behind her. "That's quite a rump you have on you Madame Big Bucks."

"Yes, I suppose it is."

"Can we?"

"What?"

"You know."

He grabbed a handful of dollars and sprinkled it over her.

She took a pile and threw it back at him. Soon they were having a fight, flinging dollars at each other.

They both fell backward on the bed in a fit of laughter.

"Do you have any idea what this means to a working stiff like me? Oh, I'm not complaining. I make a good wage since I own the cab and the medallion. But this, this…"

She smiled at him.

"You got a pretty smile. How about I ravage you on a bed full of dough re mi?"

Esther helped Lenny unbutton her denim shirt, undo her four-hook brassiere, out of which flopped her huge bosom, nipples like succulent mushrooms.

She lay back on the bed. Lenny sprinkled dollars over her ample body, which felt feminine and desirable.

"Ravish me, my Brooklyn prince," she crooned.

Afterward, they sat up. Several dollar bills still clung to their wet, naked bodies.

"What should we do with all this dough?" Lenny asked.

"God, I don't know," Esther said breathlessly.

"I want to go to a game at Yankee Stadium with seats behind home plate. I used to be a Dodger fan, but they blew off New York for L.A. So far the Yankees have been loyal, and ya gotta love those Mets."

"How much does that cost?"

"Who cares? And a new Zenith thirty-seven-inch color TV. What's your fantasy?"

She closed her eyes. "I'm sitting on a balcony overlooking a turquoise sea, sipping a rum drink with a paper parasol." She sighed contentedly. "I want to be where the weather is an angel who kisses you head to toe with a golden tan and warm water to swim in."

"Well put, Estie," he said. "Let's book it!"

"Yes!"

"Mad money!"

"Oooh!" Esther wrapped her fleshy legs around Lenny's.

"You're my good luck charm," he said, kissing her neck.

"And you're mine."

As she lay in the bed, she thought about a new set of sheets. A print. New pillows too. Maroon curtains would be nice. And a vacuum cleaner.

Esther turned on her side, rising on her elbow. "What's going to happen to the hotel?"

"Nothing good," he said. "I heard Saul's going to court to get a temporary restraining order. But it's just a matter of time."

"I feel bad for him."

He nodded. "We all do, but there's really nothing to do. We're sitting ducks, waiting for the ax to fall."

"What's going to happen to us?"

"You mean—Us—with a capital U?"

"Well, I actually meant the greater, more general us, but since you mention…"

"*We're,*" he declared, "going to have to find other places to live."

"What are you thinking?"

"Getting a house on wheels."

"You mean a hippie van?"

"No way, Estie. All the comforts of home, and then some. A disgusting, hoggish Winnebago with a shower. A great stereo. TV, of course." He looked at her. "And you at my side, kiddo. You do have a driver's license?"

"Of course."

"Lots of New Yorkers don't."

"I used to live in the suburbs." Esther was a little in shock. "Really, Lenny? We haven't talked about—"

"I know. It just hit me. I could sell my cab. We could go on the road. You and me, babe. If you want that." He looked into her eyes. "Do you?"

"You never said anything. I can't just..." she began.

"What?"

"I have all my stuff..."

"That's what storage is for. Estie, I've had this vision of driving west on Route 66. The mountains, the deserts. Truck stops. Have you ever been to the Grand Canyon? Do you remember the TV program with Martin Milner and George Maharis?"

"Of course." She hummed the theme.

"We could travel across the whole country," he said. "On Route 66. See the purple fields of majesty..."

Forget the vacuum, Esther told herself. She'd buy a black leather jacket.

"Vroom, vroom..." Lenny sighed dreamily as he snuggled asleep in her arms.

Lobby

Saul locked his tiny office, picked up his coat, and left the hotel at ten. He took the IRT local at 72nd Street. As the subway sped through the ventricles of the city, he opened his *New York Times* to the stock listings. Citibank was up to 74. He bought it at 57. P&G was 35. Okay. He bought two hundred shares at 27. Not bad. He got off at the City Hall station.

Climbing the steps, he entered a massive government building with stone columns, mosaic tiled floors, a huge brass chandelier, none of which he noticed.

When he entered, he had to fill out several forms in triplicate. Yes, he was a naturalized American citizen. 1962. They had tested him on the Pledge of Allegiance.

As he entered Room 112, Saul saw the long line at the Clerk's Office window. He just needed an index number to start the lawsuit. It would go to the Supreme Court. It sounded so important. The lawyer Fred got from the rent board told him he could sue for a violation of partnership agreement.

They hadn't moved in ten minutes. *Boge*. God. He could be here all day.

He tried to calm down. Be patient. To just read his newspaper, but sweat began to pour out of his skin, drenching his armpits as he waited on line.

He looked down at his watch. Already fifteen minutes had passed as he stood on a long unhappy line with only one window open, the other three shut, only God knew why. A dim-looking woman with large gold earrings sat at the open window.

Usually Saul went to small claims court. That putz Spiros still hadn't paid the seven hundred fifty he owed. Not one penny. So the partners insisted. That he had to take Spiros to court was a sad thing. He liked the man.

Most of the claimants were *kvetches*, complainers, whose dry cleaners ruined their best suit, whose crowns cracked on a chicken bone, who fell in a pothole. Or a brick from a building dropped on their head. Physical therapists, contractors, architects, trying to collect outstanding bills. Last time he was at small claims court, a guy sued a garage for scratching up his Jaguar.

A room full of *shnorrers*, he had thought. Maybe he'd get his few hundred bucks. Over time. Spiros would send him a check for ten dollars every month. More like water torture than payments. He looked down at his watch again.

Time never stopped moving. Not even for a second. The minute and hour hands stuck in place. Then when you weren't looking, the minute hand leaped forward.

Every morning at four thirty, he'd had to line up to be called and counted. The German soldiers shouted, "APPELL! APPELL!" If someone was missing, they could stand the whole day and night too. Though he wrapped his feet in trash, his toes were frostbitten from standing in the snow. "APPELL!" He must not think of this now.

Saul's claims were always small. Not like those millionaires in municipal court, suing for hundreds of thousands. And they got it too. A crack in the sidewalk, an exploding Coke bottle.

He should have been a lawyer! Last time, it was for that Episcopalian priest who slashed the mattress. Was he fighting the devil in his room? Then he had the *chutzpah* to demand his deposit back.

Gelt. Money. So much like the English word *guilt.* He and Ruth had not felt a pinch of guilt when they finally started receiving their checks from the German government. It was a pittance compared to all they'd lost.

The German checks allowed Saul to join Viktor's forty percent. Bolek, Janusz, he, and Heniek had pooled their savings. Together, they bought a thirty-year lease for the hotel in 1968. Saul's share was small, but he would manage the place.

And now Viktor had passed it down to his son, who was destroying the business.

Saul looked ahead of himself. There were five people in front of him on the line. He checked his watch. Twenty minutes. This was how he spent the hours and minutes of his life. It was pathetic. It was shameful.

His claims were always small. He felt grateful to be alive, to have found Luba, his beloved bride, after all these years. His true love. Yes, he'd spent thirty-five years with Ruth.

They'd met in Germany after the war. Ruth had been in Belsen with her sister, Juliana, but lost her at the end. She had lost everything, as had Saul. They got together like two sticks, rubbing against each other, trying to build a fire that might warm their frozen bones. Saul married Ruth in the DP camp and then three years later, she gave birth to their daughter Leah.

He'd been a good husband to Ruth. There was always food on the table, shelter over their heads. It was a tragedy that she died. But she was not meant for happiness. Her heart was dark and bitter; she was a *farbissiner*.

Two years ago, he had decided to attend a gathering of Holocaust survivors in Jerusalem. After nearly a lifetime as a husband and a father, he had found his Luba. The last time he'd seen her was when she was a child.

In 1940, when the Aktion began, when Jews had to leave their homes and were forced into the ghettos, Saul stole away. Luba's family, who were neighbors, had built an apartment in the upstairs crawl space. Saul had joined his father and three other men, who were hidden there. He was thirteen years old.

Later, the Gestapo came to the house and pointed a rifle at Luba's throat. "Where is your father?" they demanded.

"I have no father," she answered as she was taught by her German mother, Elke. "He's dead."

When the soldiers discovered Jewish men hidden upstairs in their house, she was sent in a transport with her mother. They were separated in Auschwitz. Luba never saw her mother again.

A year later, Saul found Luba, half-starved, her beautiful blonde hair lopped off. In the soup kitchen at Auschwitz, he saved scraps of meat for her, loving her enough to live through the war to find her afterward.

But he didn't find her after the war. Saul checked the HIAS listings, asked people, described her. Luba's father had died in Treblinka, and the Jewish agencies didn't know the whereabouts of Luba's mother since she was German. How could Saul have known that Luba would end up in Uzbekistan after the war, where she married another survivor, Wolf. She had no children.

My Luba! She was his world now, his everything. It shamed him to admit that he was as crazy in love with her as the day he saw the ten-year-old girl. He wanted so to give her things, to protect her. But he couldn't protect her from his own daughter.

Was it Saul's fault that she hated him? That she hated Luba? He had gone through plenty with Ruth. And it broke Luba's heart that Saul's daughter wouldn't open her mouth to her. He was a simple man. He didn't know what to do.

He thought if he gave Leah a place at the hotel, he'd see her. But he never did. Didn't she ever leave her room? How could she stay upstairs in that rat hole and never come out? What did she do up there?

He took his wallet out of his pocket. The new one. He pulled out a snapshot of Leah dressed in an identical dress as Ruth, standing against a cherry blossom tree in Brooklyn Botanic Garden. Then he looked at another photograph, of his beautiful Luba, with the white blonde hair that shone in the sunlight like wheat.

He still called the wallet new because he'd had another wallet, a leather one, from his early months in America. He had kept it for years. It was already falling apart when he managed the Harlem Arms uptown on 122nd Street.

One afternoon, a teenage boy in a blue knit cap walked into the lobby. He looked around but saw no one. He flashed a gun. Saul wasn't stupid. In an instant, he opened the cash register. "Here." He had handed him the contents of the hotel cash register, knowing not to look into the eyes of the hooligan. Just like with the Germans.

"Your wallet," the boy added gruffly.

Saul took out his worn leather wallet. As he gave it to him, he said, "Listen, you can take all the money, but would you give me back, please, the picture in the wallet."

The hooligan had punched Saul in the stomach so hard, he fell to the floor. Then he started to run.

Though he wasn't young, Saul was tough. He moved every new mattress and box spring in the hotel. Whenever a tenant had a problem, Saul ran up the stairs, not waiting for the elevator. He turned off leaky faucets, raised windows painted shut, pulled out air conditioners in the winter.

Summoning superhuman strength, Saul stood up and chased the crook down the block to Broadway, calling, "Police! Police!"

Saul kept running down Broadway, looking for a cop, but the crook escaped with his wallet. It contained the only photograph he had of his father. Afterward, bulletproof glass was installed at the Harlem Arms.

Was there justice in this world? To even ask the question was childish. He had seen it all and then some. Yet a man had to act as if there was justice.

America *gonef.* You thief, you stealer of dreams, of desires, of livelihood. He'd had work—honest, good, clean work. He managed a hotel with nearly forty residents. And it was being taken away from him. Like a plate of food, snatched from his hands. America *gonef.*

The Last Hotel would be gutted like the brownstones on the West Side. The walls would come down. It would be renovated, remodeled with recessed lighting. All that would remain would be a shell of the hotel.

He looked ahead of himself to discover a young Puerto Rican woman with teased black hair standing in front of him. She hadn't been there before. He was sure of that. He'd been on this line for almost an hour, and she thought she could just sneak ahead of him? This is not allowed!

"Excuse me, miss," Saul said quietly, trying to control his temper, "But I didn't see you on the line before."

"I been here," she answered curtly, not turning around.

"Miss, you have to stand on line like the rest of us." When she seemed unimpressed, he added, "We all have been standing here a long time."

She turned to face him, her thickly painted eyes glaring. "Who do you think you're talking to, mister?"

"You snuck in front of me on the line!" he said quietly.

"What did you say?" she demanded. "I been standing on this here line, and suddenly this man just starts talking at me!"

"No, you haven't!" Saul insisted, imploring the people behind him. "You weren't here five minutes ago. I know. I saw with my very own eyes. Go to the back of the line, where you belong."

The other people seemed not to notice.

"You can't talk to me like that," she said.

"Lady, please." He felt a stab of pain in his side.

"If you don't leave me alone, I'll call the police!"

Suddenly, he felt short of breath, woozy in the head.

"Next," the clerk called out from the window. "Who's next?"

The Puerto Rican woman walked up to the window and handed over her forms.

His knees wavered. His complexion turned ashen. Saul took a deep breath, closing his eyes.

When he opened them, he saw that everyone was staring at him. That's when Saul realized that he was at the front of the line. "Mister, do you hear me?" The clerk's dark eyes pierced him.

Saul stumbled to the window. He held on to the window ledge as he tried to pass her the first form. "Here," he whispered.

"Do you speak English?" she asked, leaning away from him like he was contagious.

He handed her the other forms, trying to stand up straight. "I...eh...am not well," he said, swaying back and forth, trying to hold on to the window ledge.

"Do you have a Social Security number?" she asked slowly, enunciating each word.

As his legs buckled underneath him, he said, "What do you mean? I am the manager of the Last Hotel, 53 West 72nd Street." He lost his balance and collapsed on the floor.

Lobby

At age sixty-four, Luba Ehrlich had taken a new name, her second husband's. She had been sad to lose Wolf. Her first husband had been a good man, a stolid man, who made her feel safe. She didn't know what to do with herself after he died. So she took a job in a D.C. hospital, where she had a second cousin.

That's when she received the letter that changed everything. It was on official stationery from the Lodz Survivors Society. Lodz. The city where she had been raised. Her eyes raced through the letter. They wanted to honor her? For the heroic feats performed by her family in saving Jewish lives during World War II. They called her a "Righteous Gentile." Finally, they invited her to a survivors gathering in Jerusalem.

After the ceremony to honor her and other Righteous Gentiles, she had seen Saul standing in the corner by himself.

He looked different, of course. In Auschwitz, he was a tall skeleton. He was still unusually tall with a huge shock of dark hair. She had taken a deep breath and approached him.

He had recognized her immediately. "Lubcha!" he cried out.

"Salek," she said softly.

As they embraced, he had whispered in her ear: "Finally I found you."

"No, I found you."

Poor Saul. How he hated being stuck in the house. Normally, he woke up at six, got to the hotel by eight, but Dr. Farber told him that he had to take it easy. He couldn't go back to work yet. "You have to build up your strength, Saul."

Now that he was back home, Luba and he fought. He had never been around the house so much. She wouldn't let him budge. But it was Friday. Checks must be collected. Saul started to get dressed.

"One heart attack isn't enough?" Using all her strength as a nurse, which was considerable, she took him back to his bed. "You'll stay at home until the doctor says you can go back to work."

"And what are we going to live on? Air?"

"I'll collect the checks for you. It's just for a few weeks, Saul. I don't want to lose you—again," she said gently, wrapping him in her large arms. "Come on, you stubborn *choleria*!"

He was getting stronger every day. But you didn't just get up from something like this and dance. He had to be patient and not get so nervous. *Nervosa*.

"You don't know anything."

"Then tell me, husband," she murmured. "I'm your wife."

"Yes." He nodded. "My Lubcha."

He often called her by her childhood Polish name. It moved her terribly. So strange that they should be together. To have such luck so late in life.

"Business is not so good, Lubcha."

"I know, darling. But you'll be stronger soon."

"No, something else."

"What?"

"The hotel is finished."

"What about the lawsuit?"

He shook his head. "I can't do nothing. Especially now. They can have my share. Let's take the money."

"But I thought Abramovitz said—"

"He told me it's a lost cause unless I have a rich uncle. We have nobody. I can't do nothing," he repeated sadly. "It almost killed me."

"Do you still want me to collect the rent?"

"Of course."

"Do the tenants know?"

"Most of them."

"What about Leah?" she asked.

He shrugged.

"Does she know her father had a heart attack and almost died on the table?"

"I tried to call her. Her machine doesn't even pick up. But I told her about the hotel the last time I saw her."

"Did you talk?"

He nodded. "We sat in the car. She's so lost, Luba."

"She's a stone on your heart," she said. "That's what she is."

"I know. But I have other problems. Like the Endicott Consortium—that's what they call themselves. But I'm still the manager, and you are Madame Manager."

Saul then explained how the safe is located inside the last drawer in the file cabinet, which is on the floor. He gave her a slip of paper with the combination. Various keys in a plastic bag. A current tenant list with little notes in his impatient scrawl next to the names.

Luba never liked the Last Hotel. For one thing, the neighborhood frightened her. During the short walk from the 72nd Street subway station, bums accosted her, filthy palms open. Drug addicts hanging outside buildings, passing a cigarette back and forth, women dressed like men, garbage everywhere. Ugh, the smell of it! But what could she do? Saul was the manager and she was Madame Manager.

Which was why she was standing in a crummy office the size of a water closet, with a metal desk, a wall of small cubbyholes, a cabinet that opened to a wooden board with hooks and keys hanging from them.

Luba had worn her good clothes so she'd look professional. A suit, pearls, earrings. A silk scarf. Very European. And her black Lady Marlene long-line support. The edge of the desk had already torn her stockings.

As she reached for Saul's tenant list, a wire from the nonfunctional intercom scratched her arm. "Leonard Katz," she said.

"Lenny," he said, removing his unlit cigar. "How's Saul?"

She put a mark next to his name as he paid his rent.

"He's stronger, but he still has to rest. He wanted to come back to work today, but I said no."

"And he listens to you?"

"You must be a bachelor."

"Not as much as I used to be."

Suddenly, she felt uncomfortable talking to this stranger about her private business.

"Such a shame about the hotel," he said. "I'm thinking six months max."

"Less than that," she said.

"We like this place. We like Saul." Lenny grinned. "Well, tell him Lenny says hi."

"Sure."

Around noon, the telephone rang. She picked up the receiver, noticing a crack across the mouthpiece.

"So far a few people gave me checks," she reported. " A very glamorous lady with red hair. Amber—let's see. No! It's impossible. I don't believe you." She laughed. "And this little Yiddish man, carrying a thick folder of papers…" Her voice trailed off. "Pincus….No, no. Don't you dare. No pizza! It's not good for you. I'll pick up a chicken at the deli. You have to be on your diet, *bondit!*"

Hana stopped by the desk. "Are you Saul's wife?"

She nodded. "Luba."

"Hana Wolf."

"Oh, you're the writer," she said. "Saul told me about you."

"How is he?"

"To tell you the truth, Saul has seen better times. But he's getting stronger all the time. You know he had a heart attack."

"I didn't know exactly."

"The medics got to him on time. He collapsed in the court building."

"But he's going to come back, right?"

"Sure," she said tentatively.

"He isn't?"

"You know a consortium, whatever monster that is, plans to buy the building."

"How can they?" Hana demanded, outraged. "The Last Hotel is an institution. A historic relic."

"Saul tried his best, but he can't do anything. And then his attack. He just can't fight no more."

"We got a letter. But they said nothing's going to change."

She looked at Hana like she was a moron. "And you believe them?"

"I guess I do, or I did..."

"You better look for an apartment," Luba counseled.

"This really feels like home, or the kind of home I imagined I could have in the city where I could write," Hana said, entering the elevator.

Luba watched the elevator door shut. On the lonely streets of Manhattan, the residents had found a little hamlet—population several dozen—where they could park themselves until the next opportunity, relationship, catastrophe.

Several moments later, Luba looked up to see a woman darting past her in a pulled down fedora and trench. She walked out of the cubicle.

"Leah?" she called.

The younger woman looked up blankly, then turned away.

"Excuse me, but don't you know who I am?"

Leah turned to her. "Luba? What are you doing here?" she asked. "Where's my father?"

"Saul had a serious heart attack."

"What?" She gasped. "I didn't know."

"Didn't you wonder why he wasn't here all week?"

"I rarely see him." She hesitated. "Is he all right?"

"He collapsed on Monday in the court building. They took him to Emergency at Bellevue. It was a real nightmare."

"Why didn't anyone tell me?"

"You don't answer your phone."

"I'm sorry," she said, choking up, tears welling in her eyes. "Is he all right?"

"He's recovering. And you know how hard it is for him to sit still. I had to force him not to come to work today. The man is a nervous wreck. He'll get another attack."

Leah shook her head. "I thought he was indestructible."

"We're all indestructible, until we're not. He needs time to recover. I don't know if I can keep him home long enough. He doesn't know how to relax."

As she spoke, Leah had the fantasy of passing a joint to him. Getting her father high. That would zone him out a little. Or maybe she could teach him to meditate, to breathe deeply, visualize a peaceful place...

"Why don't you come and see him?" Luba asked.

Leah looked at her father's new wife. He had someone to help him, to do his bidding. She was alone. Not really. This Righteous Gentile lady with Lodz beige hair offered her hand.

Basement

Saul coasted down the Grand Central Parkway in his midnight blue 1979 Chevrolet Caprice. As he drove, he stroked the velour seat. He liked his car. It only had thirty-four thousand miles. He turned on the radio.

"TEN-TEN WINS, TEN-TEN WINS, TEN-TEN WINS NEW YORK, THE LATEST NEWS IS..." He turned up the volume. He opened the window. Ah!

To be out of the house at last. He was not meant to rest. To sit around and watch television. He hadn't thought about it before, but he hated the house. Ruth had used a decorator, and he'd never changed a single satin pillow. Same old avocado carpet, white and avocado brocade couch he never liked, the cut glass punchbowl on the crystal base. His bride deserved better.

As he shifted into the right lane, he tried to imagine living in Florida. Palm trees. Sunshine. He could put a down payment on a condo. They wouldn't even have to sell their house. No. He shook his head as he slowed down. Not him. That was living death. Palm trees and all.

He turned off the expressway, approaching the Queensboro Bridge. He looked to the left—clear—and drove on the ramp to the upper level, where he could see the New York City skyline.

How many times had he made the identical trip to the hotel? Every morning for nineteen years minus weekends and returned back the same way, every evening, five times a week. Fifty-two weeks. Four thousand nine hundred and forty times. Minus vacations, days off: four thousand eight hundred. And this time was the last time. He exited at 60th Street and turned up Third Avenue.

Yes, he'd sold out. Joined the other partners in the abandonment of the

Last Hotel, which had always made money. But not enough for Jonah Last and his ilk. He'd given in, but at least he forced them to pay. Yes, pay. He wouldn't go cheap. For his outstanding fifteen percent, he made them write a check for one hundred thousand dollars. The partners would die if they knew. But he wasn't talking. The bastards. Besides, Saul knew it was chicken feed. They'd turn the property over for a million or two, flipping it like a golden pancake.

The Last Hotel would be gutted. The framed walls torn down, replaced by cardboard ones that halved the rooms. They'd be renovated with remodeled kitchens, repainted sheet-rocked smooth walls. All that would be left was the shell of a place where they all lived. His residents were mostly respectable, professional people of a respectable age, many well over sixty. Soon they'd be homeless. It was a vanishing world. Just like after the war. When nothing was the same. Their home in Lodz, demolished, even the street.

But this was reality, he reminded himself. Realty. Real estate. Saul was taking the money for his measly fifteen percent and getting out for good. He was a not a young man. He was not a strong man anymore. He had a weak heart. And there was his Luba. Though it was difficult for him to think of it, this time was for him, for them. To have some pleasure in this life.

It had come to him last week. Just as he was getting ready to fight the partners again. He had argued to continue managing the hotel. That's when the sky rumbled outside their house. A streak of lightning shot across the sky. He heard a voice. "Shmuck, you're going to work your whole life?"

"What else is there?" he answered humbly. "A man works."

There was more thunder. "Live a little, *shmegegge*. Enjoy yourself."

Enjoyment. What was that? What had he ever done for the pure enjoyment of it? Nothing. A man eats, sleeps, works, puts food on the table. He was a Holocaust survivor, lucky to be alive at all. The rest was a bonus.

Saul thought about his daughter. Leah had come to see him at the house. He was lying on the couch when she entered.

"Dad!" She approached him fearfully. "How do you feel?"

"I've been better."

"But your heart."

"The doctor said if I control myself and not get so nervous, I could live to a hundred. But I can't help myself. I can't even sleep," he fretted.

Leah, who was dressed in her usual mourning black, took a chair and sat down next to him. "I'd like to try something. But you have to trust me. Do you trust me?"

"What are you talking? You're my daughter."

"I've been studying a relaxation technique. Maybe it could help you. Close your eyes," she said. "Softly. Don't press your eyes shut. Just let your lids slowly drop down. Yes. That's very good."

Speaking in a soft, gentle voice, she began. "I want you to take a deep breath through your nose. Hold it. Then exhale through your mouth. Let me hear you. Breathe in, slowly, slowly, now breathe out... I want you to imagine a white staircase. Beginning at a hundred, I want you to go slowly down the stairs, breathing in, breathing out. Each breath allows you to relax more deeply. The breaths getting deeper with every count. Ninety-five, going down each step...ninety..."

Before she knew it, she could hear her father's soft snoring. Leah felt she had never loved her father as much as she did during that hour of his sleep.

"Dad," she had said to him afterward. "I'm so glad you're ..." She hesitated.

"It'll take more than a little heart trouble to kill me."

"Did you like that exercise?"

"I don't know," he said. "I fell asleep. But I tell you, Leah, I feel relaxed. Yes." He smiled. "You're a good girl."

She kissed his hand suddenly.

But when she offered him the marijuana cigarette, that was too much. He'd asked her if she smoked this stuff. She shook her head, said she had bought it for him.

That's when he decided he would use some of the money to help her get an apartment. He'd put down a deposit and the first month's rent so she had something in this life. She was a good girl. *Meshugenah.* Yes. "We all are," he said aloud.

The truth of it struck deep in his gut, in his chest and throat. Yes, he'd help her. She needed it. Bessie had told him about the gifts she received. Saul had figured out it was that junk collector, Fred, in Suite 62. Leah smiled when he asked her. Maybe they'd get together. Two *meshugenahs.*

He was walking away from the whole thing. No more fighting. No more going to court and standing on lines like an idiot. Their house in Queens was paid off. Both of them received German checks monthly. He'd have unemployment insurance. And he could invest the money.

It was a hard thing to learn when you've worked since you were a child. When you were a slave and a prisoner. But not impossible. He'd take his Luba to…Aruba. "Luba to Aruba," he said aloud as he drove. He didn't even know where Aruba was. Where could they go?

Israel. Yes! Of course. The choice so obvious that it startled him. They could live in *Eretz Yisrael*.

"At my age?" he said aloud. He could hardly read Hebrew anymore. He, who had been a *cheder* boy in Poland, knew nothing now. But he could study with Luba. She could convert. Go to the mikvah. She'd be his Jewess. Yes. They could use his energy or what was left of it. He drove up Broadway, turning at 72nd Street.

The search for a parking space began. When he came early, he could find one easily. But midday was a pain. For several minutes, he drove around the block, turned on Central Park West, to 73rd Street, continued, one more go around. Then he saw it from a distance, approached what looked like an honest spot. No hydrant, no weird signs. He held his breath like a hunter stalking prey. Yes, yes, it was a space! His space.

He moved forward several feet, about to back into the spot. At that moment, a car slipped into the space from the back. Saul couldn't even imagine how he did it.

"What the—!" He darted out of his car and approached the other car window.

A young man wearing very dark glasses looked at him. "Sorry, old man."

"Don't sorry me, you hooligan. That was my spot. Move your car!"

The man turned the wheel, switched his car off. He then stepped out. "We got there at the same time," he said, walking away from Saul.

"That's bullshit, and you know it!"

In the past, even though he was probably thirty years younger, he might have chased after the man, arguing. Now Saul began to sweat. His breathing, labored. He sat down in his car and remembered what Leah had shown him. He inhaled through his nose, filled his chest, then extended his belly. Slowly,

he exhaled. Breathe in, breathe out. Again. one…two…three…inhale…
one…two…three…exhale. Again. Breathe in, breathe out. "Close your eyes,"
she had told him. "One…two…three…inhale…one…two…three…exhale.
Imagine a white staircase…" He sat like this for a few minutes.

When he opened his eyes, he felt calmer. Then he started up the car, moved
forward, stopped at the red light. He did feel better. He would have to tell
Leah. That breathing lesson really helped him. Maybe even saved his life. He
inhaled deeply, exhaled, continued driving until he found a space on Riverside
Drive. Turned the ignition off. Then he lifted a large black bar, locking his
steering wheel. He began the long, chilly walk uphill to Columbus Avenue.

The wind off the Hudson River battered him. It made him feel like an old
man. He looked shrunken when he reached the hotel. He entered the lobby.

Pete sat on the turquoise vinyl couch.

"Still no work?" Saul asked.

"Hey!" He jumped to his feet. "It's good to see you, old man?"

"So where are you moving to?"

"The Endicott Hotel."

"Oh, I know the owner. It's like this place. A little bigger. How much is
the room?"

"Fifty dollars a week. Just a studio. My unemployment should cover that."

"I'm going down to see Henry," he said, pressing the elevator button.
"Good luck to you."

"It's good to see you, Saul!" he said, sitting back down on the couch.

"Don't you have anyplace to go to?" Saul barked, grinning broadly.

He took the elevator to the basement. It was once his basement. His
fiefdom. He rang the bell.

Bessie came to the door. "Hello there, Mr. E.!" She reached over and gave
him a hug.

He pulled back, surprised.

"We worried about you," she said, fussing over him.

"Okay, okay."

"We didn't know if we'd ever see you."

"I'm all right. But I came to say good-bye to both of you. I couldn't fight
them no longer."

"I don't blame you," Bessie said. "Enough is enough."

"So where's my man?"

"You're asking me? Check the blackboard."

"Does he write on it?"

"Yeah, just like you used to do it."

Saul looked at the blackboard. He looked at his watch. Nothing written in the slot.

"Well, I'll look for him," he said.

"If I hear from him, I'll let him know you're here," she said.

Just then, the elevator door opened. "Hey, Mr. E.!" Henry cried out, an enormous smile spreading across his face. "Pete told me you were here. Hey, you're lookin' good."

"I know I look terrible. But I wanted to come back. How are things in the hotel?"

The two men grasped hands.

"What do you think?"

"Don't ask." Saul shook his head.

"The residents are looking for other places."

"Good."

"They want me to stay since I know how everything works. Say they'll keep me on. I can stay in my apartment."

"Until they don't need you," Saul said.

"It's rotten what happened, Mr. E."

He shrugged. "Don't worry. I made 'em pay."

"Didn't you want to keep working?"

To make things simple, he answered, "Luba won't let me." He pointed to his heart. "Bad ticker."

"Sorry about that."

"If I don't strain myself, I can live a long time. You're not a young man, Henry. You should take it easy too."

"I hear you." He looked at his boss of so many years. "Mr. E.," he began, his voice faltering. "You're a fine boss."

"You seemed like a good man when you first came to see me at the hotel."

"That was over eighteen years ago."

"And I was right."

Saul reached into his pocket. "Here," he said, handing him a ring of keys with a flashlight.

Henry tried out the flashlight. It worked. He flashed his enormous smile. "This is cool. Thanks."

Saul choked up. "Don't be a stranger," he said.

He got back into the elevator.

When he stepped into the lobby, he discovered a large cardboard box on his table. He figured it was a tenant's mail-order package. He was about to shove it over but looked at it first. *SAUL EHRLICH* was written in large block letters.

He sat down. He felt nervous as he opened the box. Could it be the hotel's tax documents? Bills? Lying on top were several issues of the *Jewish Daily Forward*, English Edition. He examined them. "Must be from Pincus." Next, he picked up a thick book: *Critical Essays by French Feminist Writers*, edited by Faye Meyer, Ph.D. What was this? A white satin garter with a note on Rachel's pink stationary: *You're still the sexiest guy around.* Saul's face was beginning to burn.

There was an autographed headshot of Monica in a frame. Reardon must have contributed a shot glass with the words *SHAMROCK INN*. Hana offered a manuscript of poems. Esther and Lenny, a pair of lottery tickets. Amber gave him a lock of strawberry-blonde hair tied with a red satin bow.

A white envelope. He ripped it open. A picture of Roy Rogers, lasso in hand, galloping on a horse.

HAPPY TRAILS TO YOU!
The Residents of the Last Hotel

The card was signed by all of them.

He placed each item back into the box. That they would do something like this for him…Then he carefully closed the box. Who organized this? They gave him such wonderful things. He choked up again, but not in a scary way. A heart-feeling, heavy-hearted way. Like his chest was full. He took a deep breath, then another one. No one had ever given him a present like this. It moved him more than he could admit. He wanted to knock on each of their doors. His stomach started to groan.

That's when Saul realized he was hungry. Health be damned. He walked down 72nd Street, carrying his box, to Gray's Papaya. He ordered the special: two hot dogs with sauerkraut and mustard and a papaya drink for 99 cents.

Maybe he'd come back to the hotel later. Maybe he'd wait to see the Sofa Club. To thank them and the other people. All of them. He'd really grown fond of so many of them. The Americans. *"Dayenu,"* he said to himself. Enough. It was enough. Very enough.

Suite 49

Lenny put plastic cups and paper plates on the coffee table. China was stupid, he said. It breaks.

"We'd have to wash it."

"Okay," Esther conceded. "You're the man. Come on, boss me around."

He grinned happily.

They had invited the usual and then some. Henry and Bess said they'd stop by. Faye had phoned Saul. Luba had politely taken the information, but they didn't expect to come. Monica, the soap actress, and the young writer from the fifth floor, Hana, were invited. So was Amber. Even Pete and Gittel. They had tried to reach Dr. T. And Rachel, of course.

The doorbell rang. Pincus and Faye made their entrance. Pincus in a dark suit, white shirt, and red silk tie. Faye wore a bare-shouldered taffeta gown in the exact hue of her hair, more fire engine than usual, fake emerald baubles.

Esther, who wore a dark silk pantsuit, looked at her old friend curiously. "Is there a bar mitzvah I don't know about?"

"Don't you get it?"

"What are you talking about?"

"This is the last time we'll all be here. In the Last Hotel," Faye said. "It's an occasion."

"*Excusez moi*," Esther said.

Faye handed her a bottle of Chateau Sainte Colombe Cotes de Castillon.

"From the good doctor's stash?" Esther asked.

Faye nodded. "Seems he departed in such a rush that he left behind a few things."

"How'd you get into his room?"

"Henry came in with me."

"And?"

She grinned. "Never mind, you. Believe me, there wasn't much. He took most of his stuff."

"Does anyone know where he went?"

Lenny shrugged. "He's a *shyster*."

"He abandoned a king-size waterbed, not to mention the mirrored ceiling."

"Really?" Lenny's face lit up with interest.

"Darling," Esther said. "Those things don't travel on vans."

"Not on our van," he answered. "We could just check it out."

"I can ask Henry," she demurred.

"What's this about a van?" Pincus asked.

"We're going to get ourselves a motor home," Lenny said. "One of those Winnebago type trailers that hog the highway."

"What? A hippy van?" Faye asked.

"No, of course not. It'll have all the conveniences of home."

"Really?" Pincus looked amazed.

"So Estie, now you want to live in a trailer park?"

"We'll travel all over the country. We'll stop. Sometimes we'll stay in motels. I can't wait actually!" Esther declared.

"What are you going to do with your furniture?"

"That's why storage was invented. I'm going to rent a unit. Store everything." She paused, then said, "Possessions be damned!"

Faye sat down. "That's radical."

Esther sat down next to her. "What are you going to do?"

"I always wanted to live in the Village. Pincus likes it uptown. We'll probably get two places with visiting rights. Two domiciles. Makes it more romantic," she whispered.

The doorbell rang.

"Who else is coming?" Pincus asked.

Esther opened the door. Henry and Bessie stood in the doorway. Both were dressed nicely. Bessie wore a red satin hat, placed at a rakish angle. She smiled.

"Happy New Year," he said.

"Not yet," Faye warned. "Though I'll welcome it. Things can't get worse than this year."

"What are you talking about?" Bessie asked.

"Well, there's our new president for one thing."

"Don't get political now," Esther said. "It's great to see you! Come in, come in."

They handed her a bottle, which she laid down on the table. "Thanks. What would you like to drink? We have wine. Rum and eggnog."

"The eggnog sounds delicious," Bessie said. "Can I help?"

"Lenny, could you…"

"Right this way."

"How ya doing, Henry?" Esther asked.

He dropped his voice. "Lenny doesn't have his pistol?"

"No."

"That's a good thing," he said.

As they approached the kitchenette, the doorbell rang again.

Rachel, in mink and a black sheath, hobbled in very high heels. "Reardon said he'd try to get someone to take over for him." She handed Esther a bottle of champagne.

"Hi, Henry," she said. "Don't you look handsome? Hello, Bessie."

The doorbell rang again. Pete and Gittel walked in at the same time. "I brought some hot tea," Gittel said, holding out her thermos.

Pete carried his paper bag of booze. "I'm set," he said. "How's everybody doing?"

"Welcome, welcome."

"Did you invite Saul and Luba?"

"Sure, but they wouldn't come."

"Remember how we snuck around last year?"

"And the rat?"

"And the gun?"

"I was thinking about Saul too," Pincus said quietly.

"Me too."

"He's better off," Pincus said. "He doesn't need the headaches from the hotel."

"Still."

"Time for a toast," Esther said. "Our first one anyway." She paused. "To Saul Ehrlich."

"Yes," Lenny said. "A very good man. An honest man."

"Who had seen worse than any of us can know, but still got up every morning and came here."

"He gave all of us courage," Esther said.

"He could be such a pain," Pete said, "but I liked the guy."

"Remember how he'd inspect our checks every week?"

"Honestly, I miss him screaming at me," Henry said.

"Mr. E. was a very decent man," Bessie added.

"Yeah."

"A helluva guy."

"*L'chaim.*"

"To Saul."

"May he live forever."

They all clinked plastic glasses.

"Did you hear he's moving to Israel?"

"No!"

"Yes. He's making *aliyah.*"

"What's that?"

"When you immigrate to Israel to live."

"That makes sense in a way," Pincus said.

"Him and his Luba."

"They're both the last vestiges."

"What a story that is."

"Of a nearly extinct world."

"Just like us."

"Well, he got a pretty penny for his share, I heard."

"Anybody know?"

"I heard a hundred thou."

"*Mazel tov,*" Pincus said.

Faye turned to Esther. "So tell me, what did they offer you for this palatial suite?"

"One thousand two hundred and fifty dollars," she said softly. "And you?"

"A thousand. My place is smaller."

"Sweetheart deals," Lenny said, joining them. "What a *misnamer* that is. Anyway, I got eight hundred. So did you, Pincus. Right?"

He nodded. "Rachel's the big winner."

"Wha'd you get?"

"I shouldn't say." She dropped her voice. "Fifteen hundred. Hey, I'm in the business."

"I'm getting shit since I'm on the top floor, bathroom in the hallway," Pete said wistfully.

"To the Last Hotel, where we all met," said Rachel. "Well, you and I knew each other," she said, looking at Faye. "And you knew Esther."

"To the very last days of the Last Hotel," Faye said, toasting.

"Yeah," Lenny added.

The bell rang again. Enter Monica, whose suite was several doors down on the same floor. She wore a sexy stretch burgundy Danskin, but looked piqued. At that moment, Hana stepped out of the elevator. She followed Monica in.

"Hi ladies!" Lenny called out. "Get yourselves something to drink."

Monica turned around and first noticed Hana, who wore an embroidered Indian top and velour pants.

"Oh," said Monica, meeting her glance. Then she turned away.

Hana poured herself red wine. Chateau Sainte Colombe Cotes de Castillon. "This looks familiar," she said.

"Doesn't it?" Monica said.

"He's a piece of work," Hana declared.

"You don't know."

"Oh, I could tell. A manipulator," she said. "These shrinks are expert. And what about that room with the waterbed?"

"And he wasn't even a real psychologist," Monica declared triumphantly. "He got a Ph.D. in French literature, then took a few psychology courses."

Hana dropped her voice. "Are you really pregnant?"

"Of course not. I just wanted to—how do you say it—fuck with him."

"Good for you, girl. I just wonder where he'll surface next."

"He was talking about a workshop in Psychic/Karmic Release at Esalen."

Esther turned on the television. The crystal ball glowed on the top of 1 Times Square. Twenty more minutes. She switched the channel. A clip of Ronald and Nancy Reagan standing in front of their Christmas tree. Close-up: the warm smile and twinkling blue movie-star eyes.

"What are you going to do, Rachel?" Esther asked.

"I'm looking into an apartment at Lincoln Towers."

"That sounds nice."

"They have a long waiting list, but I know someone."

"You know someone everywhere."

"Aren't I lucky?" Rachel grinned. "I hope Reardon can make it tonight. He was waiting for a replacement to come in."

"What about you?" Esther asked Hana.

"I'm going to get a room at the Chelsea Hotel," she said.

"A perfect place for a writer," Esther said.

"I know."

"And you?" she asked Monica.

"I'm keeping my options open," she answered.

That's when the first explosion shook the apartment.

"What was that?"

"It sounded like something blew up!"

"Holy shit!"

Henry leaped to his feet and ran out of the suite. "I'm going upstairs to see what's what."

"Okay, everyone," Lenny called. "Out, out, out." He chased them. "Go down the stairs."

Esther was followed by Rachel, who grabbed her champagne bottle. Faye, Pincus, Gittel, Pete. Hana rushed out of the apartment, with Monica right behind. They tried to avoid each other as they rushed down the stairs.

Bessie called into the stairway: "Henry, where are you?"

"What's happened?" Esther asked.

"Don't talk," Lenny said. "Just get out of the building. The whole thing could blow up with us in it."

All ran outside. Faye tried to call 911 from the phone booth on the corner, but it was broken. Lenny ran into the Greek diner. As they stood looking up at the flames on the sixth floor, it started to snow. But the flakes were gray. Strips of paper floated down over them. They ran around picking up the pieces of paper.

"'*And then the selfsame well from which your laughter rises was oftentimes filled with your tears…*'" Hana read aloud. "What is this?"

"Mine says," Esther read, "'*Increased knowledge of the unconscious brings a deeper experience of life and…'"*

"'*After her father's death, Yentl had no reason to remain in Yanev,*'" read Lenny. "What is this?"

"They're from books!" Faye exclaimed. "That's Isaac Bashevis Singer."

"Look at this," Rachel said. "'*There are the so-called inert gases in the air we breathe. They bear curious names of erudite derivation which…*'"

"It's all so literary!" Hana exulted.

"Pretty weird if you ask me," Lenny said.

Just then, Henry ran out of the building, followed by Fred, whose wild hair was gray with smoke. He carried a duffel bag. Leah, knapsack strapped onto her back, was behind him. They joined the others.

"What happened?" Lenny said.

Henry shook his head. "Don't ask."

Fred looked around. "I won't give the capitalist pigs the satisfaction. They can't have my room!"

He turned to his neighbors. "Look, I hope no one's stuff got messed up. But they can't just throw us out like we're garbage." His voice dropped to a conspiratorial whisper. "If anyone wants to know, you didn't see me. Okay?"

"Me too," Leah said breathlessly.

He grabbed her hand, and both darted down the street, running across Columbus Avenue through a red traffic light. A yellow taxi honked at them.

Two fire trucks arrived. Noisy, red, eel-like as they twisted around the corner. Several firemen ran into the building.

Lights flashed, sirens blared around them. At that moment, Amber, wrapped in a white fox coat, arrived on the arm of Duc, the Samoan bouncer from Studio 54. They looked besotted with each other.

"What's happened?" she inquired.

"Why is everyone outside?" Duc asked.

Hana pointed upstairs, where it was smoking from the sixth-floor window.

A few moments later, two firemen approached them. The older one wore a hat that said *CHIEF.*

"It's all right," said the chief. "Just a little conflagration, mostly burned itself out. A lot of smoke though. What a mess." He shook his head. "Who lives in Suite 62?"

No one answered.

"We found these." He held out two blackened sticks of dynamite. "Someone put these between pages of books."

Pincus gasped. "Oh no!"

"Does anyone know who lives up there?" he repeated.

The residents looked at each other. "We don't know who lives where," Amber said, shrugging. Her fur coat fell open, revealing her considerable cleavage.

The chief was staring for a moment, then confronted them. "I can look it up in the register."

Duc stepped up. "I live on the sixth floor, but I wasn't here."

"Anyone else?"

"Actually," Monica, who had stood silently until then, piped up. "We had this crazy shrink living in the hotel. He split. That was his room."

"What was his name?"

"Doctor Ronald Tannenbaum." She paused, then spelled it out. "That's T-A-N-N-E-N—"

Hana looked at her.

"Where is he?" asked the chief.

"That's what we'd like to know. He's gone like the wind."

"Aren't you famous or something?" the chief asked.

"*Forgive Us Our Passions*," she declared with pride. "Emerald Lee."

He grinned. "Would you mind autographing this? My wife would really get a kick."

Monica took his pen and signed the back of his report.

"You can return to your apartments. There doesn't seem to have been any damage except for Suite 62. What a mess!" he repeated. "Whoever lived there had a lot of junk."

He paused. "We'll have to investigate this, of course. Everyone, let's go!"

The firemen returned to their vehicles.

"What time is it?" Esther gasped, looking at her watch. "Three minutes!" she shrieked. "Where's that champagne?"

Lenny grabbed the bottle. For a few moments, he wrestled with the cork. Finally, a geyser of champagne rose up and gushed out. Lenny opened his mouth and chugged it down.

"Sorry. No fluted glasses."

He passed the bottle to Esther, who took a delicate sip. "Delish," she said.

"Here," she said, passing the bottle to Rachel.

"Oooooh," she said, rolling it on her tongue, then gave it to Faye, who took a sip and passed it to Pincus.

"To 1981, God help us!" he said, taking a sip. "May it be better than 1980."

"An evil year," Faye said.

"The sale of the Last Hotel," Pete said.

"John Lennon murdered..." Hana said, "just down the block."

"Yes."

At that moment, Reardon appeared. "What's going on here?"

"Happy New Year," Rachel said, pulling him to her. She passed him the bottle of champagne. "I saved you a sip."

"Fred in Suite 62 didn't want to move, so he blew up his suite," Lenny explained. "He put dynamite between the pages of books,"

"No." Reardon whistled in disbelief. "Did anything happen to the other suites?"

"The firemen didn't think so."

"We should go inside and see."

"It's kind of heroic when you think about it," Hana said, "in a demented sort of way. How he didn't want to give in."

"Fred just didn't know what to do with all his junk," Lenny said.

Reardon bent over and picked up a slip of paper from the street. He began to read, "'*Ask your body what it feels like having...*' What the hell is this?"

"From Fred's books."

"And Saul's daughter went off with him," Rachel said.

"He has a daughter?" Reardon asked.

"You know that woman with the hat and coat who looks like a spy?"

"In the penthouse?"

"I think her name is Leah."

"Weird."

"I keep thinking about John Lennon," Hana said. "It happened right down the block from where we're standing. December 8th. Three weeks ago."

"That was such a tragedy," Esther said.

"Horrible."

"I ran down the street as soon as I heard the announcer on the radio.

'John Lennon's been shot as he was entering the Dakota,'" Hana continued. "There were already hundreds of people gathered in front of the gates, holding candles, playing guitars, singing." She began singing softly, *"Imagine there's no heaven; It's easy if you try..."*

"John, we're thinking about you tonight," Amber said.

"I'm thinking of Yoko upstairs on the top floor of the Dakota."

"And their sons, Julian and Sean." Hana continued.

Esther checked her watch. "Okay, everyone! NOW! All together: TEN... NINE...EIGHT...SEVEN...SIX...FIVE...FOUR...THREE...TWO...

"HAPPY NEW YEAR!"

They screamed, they cheered, they hugged each other. Even Hana and Monica.

"It's nice for us to spend New Year's together again" Esther said.

"Soon we'll be an extinct species," Faye said.

Rachel raised the empty bottle of champagne. "To the Last Hotel."

They all gazed at the awning with its missing chrome letter.

"Lust Hotel!" Rachel grinned, squeezing Reardon.

"Thank God, you didn't burn down," Esther cried.

"We're history." Lenny draped his arm over her shoulder.

"Imagine how Saul would have reacted!"

"Can you see it?"

"Saul's no more," Pincus said sadly. "Not here anyway."

"At least he made some money."

"And he's going to Israel," said Hana dreamily. "A Holocaust survivor makes *aliyah*. It's poetic justice."

"It's fucked up, if you ask me," Pete said.

"It's all over," Rachel said, holding on to Reardon's arm.

"Let's go back inside," Esther suggested. "I'm freezing!"

"I want to remember it," Faye said, staring up at the hotel.

The residents slowly filed back into the building.

Faye stood still.

"Come, Faigeleh." Pincus took her arm.

"They never fixed the sign." She held back.

"It's cold out here."

"Our Lost Hotel."

Yiddish Glossary

aliyah emigrate to Israel

alte kocker old-timer

beshert fate

bissel a little

bondit bandit

brosts breasts

bubbe-meises grandma's tales

chai Hebrew word for life

chazzer pig

cheder Jewish school

cholent stew

choleria a Yiddish curse, "a plague upon you"

dybbuk spirit from a wandering soul

farbissiner sour puss

farshtinkener rotten

gelt money

gevalt exclamation

gonef thief

gornisht nothing

gutte nacht good night

krechts moans and grunts

kugel noodle pudding

kvetch complain

l'chaim to life

malmaloshen Yiddish language

meshuggeh crazy

meshugenah crazy person

mikvah ritual bath

mitzvah good deed

nebech useless person, loser

neshomeh good soul/spirit

pisher a nobody

potchky play around

Shabbes weekly day of rest, Sabbath

schmaltz chicken fat

Shehechiyanu blessing

shikker a drunk

shiksa non Jewish woman

shivah ritual of mourning

shlemazel unlucky person

shlemiel chump

shmegegge whiner

shmendrick pipsqueak

shnorrer freeloader/beggar

shtetl small village

shtup fornicate

shvartzehs black people

shyster crook

tuches buttocks

tzatzkeleh a babe

tzedakah charity

veys mir oh no

yahrzeit memorial candle

yekkers German and Austrian Jews

yetz, the evil inclination

zeyde grandpa

zhlub crude person

ziskeit sweetness

zoftik succulent

Acknowledgements

My father, Benjamin Pilcer, managed the Endicott Apartments Hotel between 1968 and 1992. This novel is an homage to that exhilarating time in New York City. The hotel became a co-op long ago.

I want to thank my friends and students, who listened—as well as Jacob Makler, my son, and husband, Morton Makler.

My mother, Lusia Pilcer, and her "Knitters and Kibbitzers" at the Sterling Aventura helped with the Yiddish words.

My intrepid agent, Gareth Esersky of Carol Mann Associates.

Judy Tipton, designer extraordinaire.

Special thanks to Lisl Cade.

The Virginia Center of Creative Arts gave me a place to germinate the original idea.

And Naomi Rosenblatt, of Heliotrope Books, for so many things.

Thanks, all.

The Author

Sonia Pilcer is the author of six novels including *The Holocaust Kid*. Recently *Teen Angel*, and I-Land have been reissued by Intoprint Publishing. She was born in Augsburg, Germany, and grew up in New York City, where she still lives on the Upper West Side with her husband and son.

CPSIA information can be obtained at www.ICGtesting.com
Printed in the USA
LVOW04s1950080115

422040LV00024B/711/P